D0097898

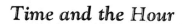

Time and the Hour

BOOKS BY FAITH BALDWIN

Girl on the Make
Broadway Interlude
Garden Oats
Laurel of Stony Stream
Magic and Mary Rose
Mavis of Green Hill
Three Women
Those Difficult Years
Departing Wings
Thresholds
Alimony
The Office-Wife
The Incredible Year
Make-Believe
Today's Virtue
Skyscraper
Week-End Marriage
District Nurse
Self-Made Woman
Beauty
White-Collar Girl
Love's A Puzzle
Innocent Bystander
Wife Versus Secretary
Within A Year
Honor Bound
The Puritan Strain
The Moon's Our Home
Private Duty
The Girls of Divine Corners
Men Are Such Fools!
That Man Is Mine
The Heart Has Wings
Twenty-Four Hours A Day
Manhattan Nights
Enchanted Oasis
Rich Girl, Poor Girl
Hotel Hostess
The High Road
Career By Proxy
White Magic
Station Wagon Set
Rehearsal For Love
"Something Special"
Letty and the Law
Medical Center
And New Stars Burn
Temporary Address: Reno
The Heart Remembers

Blue Horizons
Breath of Life
Five Women in Three Novels
The Rest of My Life With You
Washington, U.S.A.
You Can't Escape
He Married A Doctor
Change of Heart
Arizona Star
A Job For Jenny
No Private Heaven
Woman on Her Way
Sleeping Beauty
Give Love the Air
Marry For Money
They Who Love
The Golden Shoestring
Look Out For Liza
The Whole Armor
The Juniper Tree
Face Toward the Spring
Three Faces of Love
Many Windows
Blaze of Sunlight
Testament of Trust
The West Wind
Harvest of Hope
The Lonely Man
Living By Faith
There Is A Season
Evening Star
The Velvet Hammer
Any Village
Take What You Want
American Family
No Bed of Roses
Time and the Hour

Poetry
Sign Posts
Widow's Walk

Juveniles
Babs: A Story of Divine Corners
Mary Lou: A Story of
    Divine Corners
Myra: A Story of Divine
    Corners
Judy: A Story of Divine
    Corners

Time and the Hour

Faith Baldwin

Holt, Rinehart and Winston
New York   Chicago   San Francisco

228

Copyright © 1974 by Faith Baldwin Cuthrell
All rights reserved, including the right to reproduce this book or portions thereof in any form.
Published simultaneously in Canada by Holt, Rinehart and Winston of Canada, Limited.
Library of Congress Cataloging in Publication Data
Cuthrell, Faith (Baldwin) 1893–
Time and the hour.
I. Title.
PZ3.C973Ti [PS3505.U97]   813'.5'2   73–12856
ISBN 0–03–012231–7
First Edition
Printed in the United States of America

Come what may,
Time and the hour runs through the
roughest day.
Macbeth, *Act I, Scene 3*

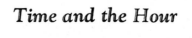

Time and the Hour

❦ 1 ❧

It is possible that prior to the interference of the serpent Eden had the perfect climate, that Paradise is similarly and eternally blest and that there are even those whose votes are cast for the lost continent of Atlantis. However, the world as we know it suffers from climatic flaws. These the residents of Little Oxford resented, as it destroyed the image to be confronted with too much, or too little, rain; with drought, floods, blizzards, ice storms and even occasional hurricanes—and, of course, as a rule, a few days, or weeks, of rising temperatures and soggy humidity in leafy summer.

On one such day, Vanessa Steele sat in a rocking chair in her kitchen, which was cooled by an electric fan and a desultory, halfhearted breeze at the windows. Vanessa moved a large palm-leaf fan before her face and talked to her cat, Shadow.

"I suggest we call," she said. "She's been there about ten days now; must be settled. Don't panic. I haven't seen a dog on the premises, but that's not to say she won't get one. Women, presumably living alone, generally have to have something alive around—a dog"—Shadow growled —"a cat"—Shadow smiled—"even a bird"—Shadow licked his furry chops. "Maybe she's a cat person; we'll have to find out."

Shadow sitting on the top of the refrigerator, twitched his shoulders. He remarked loftily that people who weren't cat people were to be scorned as well as pitied and would Vanessa please not dwell upon canines. Not that he couldn't, if necessary, hold his own.

He could indeed and had often proven it. He was a very large, heavy, but exceedingly light-pawed, swiftly moving feline, intensely black except for a small white star between brilliant emerald eyes.

"Her name's Stacy Armitage," Vanessa informed him, "Mrs. maybe—that's Ms. nowadays. She's been divorced recently. People have been going in and out of the studio. Marcia Boyd, for one, that nice little Katie Palmer— Marcia rented through her—and Amy Irvington. Seems Amy knew Mrs. Armitage some years ago, and that's how come she's here." Vanessa looked at the kitchen clock and added aloud, as Shadow was still present, "I'll reconnoiter from the back porch."

Shadow jumped down from the refrigerator and followed her. Vanessa was aware that he disapproved; he always distrusted sudden impulses in two-legged animals. She was often glad that, unlike Tobermory, Shadow couldn't talk back; well, not exactly.

On the small roofed back porch trellises supported crawling vines. There were two battered basket chairs, a matching wicker table, and a larger one, bearing a small vase of flowers, three books and a pair of binoculars— good ones; she'd bought them in Japan.

Standing on the back steps she lifted the glasses to her eyes and directed her attention across her side yard and a considerable meadow, and then focused on the studio cottage which had recently been leased from Lee Osborne and his widowed sister, Marcia Boyd. Nothing stirred there, and in a neat circular driveway, protected by hedges, only the new tenant's small car sat, broiling in the sun.

Shadow reclined, relaxed on the porch railing, his tail curled about him, and permitted his eyes to follow, indifferently, the regard of his slave.

Vanessa came up the steps, put the binoculars down, and addressed her familiar. "You'll have to be leashed," she said, "just in case——"

Shadow protested in a loud, compelling voice.

"No good complaining," she told him. "We'll walk first to the Barkers'. Hush. I know you don't like their dog and he despises you, but I don't want any quarrel with the Barkers; they're good neighbors. I'll take a basket and we'll get a few tomatoes and cucumbers, a dozen fresh eggs, maybe a posy. Then we'll call on Mrs. Armitage. She's an artist. I don't know what kind. Brace yourself for someone who puts a slab of wood on the floor, sticks her feet in a bucket of paint and then dances. Come here at once."

Shadow approached, reluctant but curious. Vanessa snapped the leash on his red collar, picked up a basket and together they walked sedately to the Barker Farm, the tall splinter-thin woman with the brown, lined face and the big black cat, conversing more or less amiably on the way.

That afternoon Stacy Ware Armitage was working in her rented studio. She was aware of the outside heat and the quiet, but the room with its cathedral ceiling was cool. She wondered how cool in winter? But Mrs. Boyd had assured her that the furnace was almost new, the fireplace drew well and there was plenty of wood in the shed. The quiet was unusual; the road which turned the corner at Lessing Lane and then went past the studio and the big Osborne house had been almost free of traffic since early morning.

Stacy liked being alone if she could be occupied and not do a great deal of remembering, asking, wondering. She also liked people and she had seen a few during the past ten days while getting settled. Amy Irvington, of course, whom she had asked earlier that summer, over a telephone wire, if there might be an available studio in Little Oxford. Amy had promptly asked Stacy to come and stay with her for a weekend; she'd done so, three times, before Katie Palmer, the young real estate agent, had found this house. They had both been very kind. In fact, no one had ever been kinder to Stacy than Amy, whom, some years ago, she'd feared, wept over and for a time hotly disliked. As for Katie, on the day Stacy, her car and other belongings had arrived in Little Oxford, Katie was inside the studio, arranging flowers, putting fruit and vegetables in the refrigerator, and also a casserole, to be heated for supper.

Katie had said, "Don't think for a moment that I made it. I can't cook. You know that, having been to Baker Street for dinner. Jeremy's practically a Cordon Bleu. When I have this baby, Jeremy will have to make the formulas."

The doorbell rang, and Stacy, in shorts, sandaled feet and smock, went to answer it. She hadn't heard a car drive up.

She opened the door to complete astonishment. Standing on the flagstone entrance was a woman who could have been any age from fifty to ninety. Though she appeared to be hipless, she wore faded cut-off hip huggers, blindingly colored shirt and, tied about her head, an equally colorful, if clashing, scarf. Beside her, on a leash, was the biggest blackest cat Stacy had ever seen. He held her startled gaze almost hypnotically, and beside him was a basket of vegetables, flowers and what looked like an egg box.

She started to say, "Thank you, but I don't need——"
when Vanessa spoke.

"Not selling anything," said the visitor. "I'm Mrs.
Steele—Vanessa Slade Steele—a neighbor, from around
the corner. You Mrs. Armitage?"

"Yes," admitted Stacy, stunned.

"This is Shadow," said Vanessa, indicating the cat, who
inclined his massive head. "We thought we'd come call,
being neighbors. If you're busy say so, we'll come another
time. Brought you something from the Barker Farm. You
must have seen their vegetable stand? Nice folks, horrible
dog. Are you allergic to, or scared of cats?"

"No, I like them. Please come in," Stacy said, smiling,
and Vanessa thought: Interesting little thing; not exactly
pretty; looks as if she had temperament. Wow, she
thought further, recalling something her grandson had
said as he watched one of the Barker girls walk past
Vanessa's house: "Maybe she won't make the centerfold
but, wow, is she ever stacked!"

"Would you pick up the basket? Sometimes I creak in
weather like this," Vanessa said. "Old bones."

She and Shadow followed Stacy into the big room and
Vanessa stooped stiffly to remove Shadow's leash. He
stretched and yawned and Stacy said softly, "He's beautiful. I'd like to paint him." She put out her hand, but
Vanessa warned sharply, "Don't try to pet him. When he
wants you to, he'll demand it."

Stacy, indicating the basket, said, "I'm very grateful,
Mrs. Steele. All Little Oxford people have been wonderful."

"They're sizing you up, same as I am," Vanessa explained carelessly. She looked around her. "I like what
you've done in here," she said.

"The studio was well furnished," Stacy said. "I brought
only a few personal things." She thought: Damned few to

show for the years. "Please sit down, both of you. "You'll find the love seats comfortable, I think. I'll put the basket in the kitchen."

"Eggs in the icebox," advised Vanessa.

Shadow leaped to the mantel above the fireplace, settled himself in a big, old Chinese bowl, curled his tail about it and closed his eyes. Stacy took a deep breath and Vanessa, from one of the love seats, said, "Don't fret. He never breaks anything in our house unless he's mad at me—and I've found a way to forestall that. He never breaks anything in any one else's either, unless he's mad at them. . . . That bowl yours?"

"Why . . . yes."

"Good period," said Vanessa. "I bought a couple of smaller ones in Hong Kong."

Stacy excused herself and went into the one-story wing which contained her bedroom, bath, and nearest to the living room, the kitchen. When she came back, Shadow was obviously asleep and Vanessa had not moved. As Stacy settled herself opposite, her guest asked, "Mind if I smoke?"

"Of course not. There's an ashtray on the table beside you."

Vanessa thrust two long thin fingers into a shirt pocket and extracted a short thin cigar, almost the color of her tanned skin, and a kitchen match, which she struck on the sole of her serviceable walking shoe.

"You'll like it here," said Vanessa, looking about the room which was full of light from the great windows and skylight. "This place has good vibrations. . . . You know Marcia Boyd and Lee Osborne well?"

"No. I met Mrs. Boyd through Mrs. Palmer—and I met Mrs. Palmer through an old friend, Amy Irvington."

"Yes, I know," said Vanessa. She took the scarf from her

head—revealing the whitest, wildest, short hair imagina-
ble—and smiled, showing teeth that were white, uneven
and certainly her own. As she flicked an ash into the
Spode saucer she said, "Marcia's an agreeable woman. Do
you know her brother?"

"No. He's abroad, I believe. Mrs. Boyd signed the lease.
I've never met him."

"He's a charmer," Vanessa said, "and a bachelor. But it
won't pay to get notional as he's completely undomes-
ticated, which is why Shadow likes and envies him. No
leash. Marcia works her head off inviting unattached
young women to dinners and picnics, but she gets no-
where. Not that Lee's antiwomen."

Stacy said, "I've been exposed to charmers." She
thought: What a fantastic woman. She talks like a part-
time Old Mother Hubbard and I wonder if she went to
college and, if so, where?

Vanessa leaned back, half closing her eyes. They were
enormous and of an indefinite color—gray-green, green-
gray, with sudden lights in them like those in a smoky
opal.

"Let me make you some tea, Mrs. Steele," Stacy offered.

"No thanks. Another time perhaps. I just came, as my
grandson might say, to case the joint. Not that I haven't
been here before. Lee Osborne's father built this studio
for him, and his grandfather built that Victorian edifice
which Marcia and Lee own, fifty-fifty. The last people
who rented this place were average. He was supposed to
be a writer. I don't know what she was supposed to be, but
you didn't have to be clairvoyant to figure out what she
was." She shrugged. "You're a great improvement. Mind
if I call you Stacy?"

"Why, no," said Stacy, who did.

"Family name or does it stand for something?"

"Both. It's Anastasia."

"Greek," said Vanessa, "or Russian? Suits you."

"Well, Greek," said Stacy. "My father's grandmother was Greek and was also Anastasia."

"Everyone calls me Van," said her visitor, "from the grocery boy to the clergy, the president of Rotary to the garbage collector."

"You were born here?" asked Stacy, interested.

"No. But I came a long time ago and bought a house just to have something to come back to."

"Come back from where?"

"Anywhere. Europe, Asia, down under and various often overrated islands. I've been most places. I knew one day I'd get tired of traveling and use the house not just as a stopover but to stay in—until I'm taken out, feet first. Before I turned sixty, a lot of fun had gone out of what's erroneously called the open road. I'm seventy-five," she added and ground out the cigar, "and now I have all outdoors and inside, a fireplace, a cat, a bed which fits my bones. Books, of course; radio, music when I want it. No TV. No phone. I also have good food. That's the last vice, and a fine one if you've a reliable digestion. I thank God for mine. . . . I hear you're divorced, Stacy."

Stacy stiffened (the watching remarkable gray-green eyes missed nothing), but after a moment she said, "That's right, Mrs. Steele."

"When you get over me being nosey," Vanessa told her, "you'll call me Van. I'm divorced too; have been for over forty years. It wasn't as usual then or as respectable, at least not among the people I was unfortunate enough to know. You remember that line in the White Knight's song? I assume you're acquainted with prissy little Alice?"

"Oh, yes," Stacy answered, and felt the desolation of a moment ago seep from her mind. "Quite recently we became reacquainted, when I illustrated new editions of the Alice books."

"So that's what you do? I was afraid of soap-pail collages, abstractions, metal sculptures, soup cans and what I call dart-board painting."

Stacy laughed. This ruthlessly rude old woman could infuriate and then calm you; she was a sharp winter wind, or a cool summer breeze, or a stinging stimulating shot in the arm.

"I'm afraid I do none of that," she said. "If I could, I'd be more in demand. I do illustrations for children's books, dust jackets for them and for adult novels. I also work on my own, but I haven't had an exhibit for some time."

"I remember now. You and Amy Irvington, before she was married, worked at Lovemay's, the publishers. You knew that Remsen Lovemay's still alive and lives, now, in Little Oxford?"

"Yes, I met him at Amy's earlier this summer. Tell me, how do you know so much about me? I've been here just ten days."

"I ask. It's the only way, really."

Stacy laughed again. She had, for a small woman a robust, uninhibited laugh. She said, "You're incredible. . . . But tell me—I've forgotten—what the White Knight said."

"It's in his song. I've always thought it a very accurate description of a good many marriages; it's, 'or madly squeeze a right-hand foot into a left-hand shoe.' "

She rose abruptly and Shadow hurtled from mantel to floor and went over to his leash, lying on a love seat. Vanessa snapped it on, straightened with an effort, and spoke in her almost baritone voice: "I came out of curiosity—I'm addicted to prying—but not to bore you— that's the unforgivable sin. I won't ask to see your work.

When you want me to see it, you'll show it to me. And I'd like you to come to supper. I'm a tremendous cook. Even Jeremy Palmer says so. If you know Katie, you must have met Jeremy? . . . Any allergies?"

"Spinach," said Stacy faintly.

"Lucky I didn't bring you any; I'd have to take it back; I don't like waste. With Adam, my grandson, it's eggs. You'll meet him sometime. He's nineteen. He drops by now and then when he can escape from college. He's also allergic to studying. He's amusing, and he'll probably fall in love with you."

"Why would he?" Stacy inquired. "At nineteen?"

"Sex," said Vanessa promptly. "You're loaded. . . . Let's see, today's Thursday. I haven't a phone as I told you."

"I haven't yet. If I must telephone, I go to Mrs. Boyd."

"How about Monday night?" asked Vanessa. "You go out, turn right, walk around the corner and you'll see the house. Kids around here have thought for years that it's haunted. The old witch and her cat. Even when I just came between planes, trains, boats, horses and camels. Make it six o'clock. . . . Do you have a bicycle?"

"No."

"I have. I hate cars unless they cost over ten thousand dollars and are chauffeur-driven. Besides I never learned to drive. I advise you to invest in a bicycle. If anything happens to your car, you'll go for broke. At the rates the Little Oxford Taxi company charges, it would take all your alimony—if you were foolish enough not to get a settlement instead. Unless of course," she added briskly, "Mr. Armitage is poor, however honest."

Shadow muttered, and Vanessa said, "Oh, be quiet! Haven't years of living with a doddering old woman taught you patience? Say *au 'voir* to Stacy, and come along."

Stacy went to the door with them and Vanessa said, "I like you; how much I won't know for a while. See you Monday. If you can't come, send a carrier pigeon, or one of the neighbor's kids. Up beyond the Osborne house there's a swarm of them; name's Collins. They come in all sexes, all shapes, ages and sizes. If I'm stricken with leprosy, I'll send Shadow. He'll get in through a window if the doors are shut, and if he screams—I've always suspected there was a Siamese in his ancestral tree—then come a-running, for I'll need help."

As they went out the door, Shadow looked up at Stacy. His features were composed, his tail did not twitch, he made no sound, but Stacy could have sworn he was laughing.

She closed the door and went back through the studio to the kitchen to make herself a cup of tea. Sitting at the counter, she thought: If there were tea leaves, I'd ask her to read them. Unlike Shadow, she found herself laughing aloud . . . and for the first time deplored that she must wait for her own telephone. This would be such a good moment to call Amy or Katie or both.

When Vanessa had knocked on the door, Stacy thought, I should have asked, "Friend or enemy?"

She could be either, Stacy reflected, like most people. But Vanessa Steele wasn't most people. Probably a deliberate eccentric, Stacy concluded, or perhaps not deliberate?

I'd rather have her for a friend. But the last thing I should do is try to ingratiate myself. She'd see through me, Stacy decided and, mindful of things she must do, she left the kitchen, looking forward to Monday.

❧ 2 ❧

In her mailbox on Friday Stacy found a stack of letters and bills forwarded from the small hotel for women in which she had lived for nearly a year before coming to Little Oxford. There she'd had a good-sized living room in which she could work and also see friends. She could walk to Lovemay's—greatly enlarged since her time there —and to other publishing houses; she could take a bus to theaters, concerts, museums and galleries. But the city had depressed her: dirt, pollution, perilous streets and noise. Picking up dropped threads had depressed her more. Of the men she'd known casually, for instance, one or two were much as they had been—in a word, impossible. The girls with whom she worked, or met outside of Lovemay's, were married, the majority with small children and naturally concerned with their own lives. Most of them were sorry for her, and asked her to dinner, or to have lunch. Some of them, curious about Bob Armitage, said, "But I thought it was such a marvelous marriage," with a question mark at the end of the sentence.

Stacy sorted the mail on the kitchen counter. One letter had come direct, from her mother in California. Stacy could have predicted the contents: the martyred whining over weather, the yard man, the inefficiency of her housekeeper; the plaintive "I hope you'll be happy among strangers. I'll never understand why you wouldn't come out to live with me; after all we have only each other," and the usual reference to her gastric problems—"I don't much like my new doctor. He's young and, of course, very modern, but so unsympathetic"—and finally, "Please call me as soon as your telephone is installed."

Other than that there was only the calendar of Mrs. Ware's recent activities which seemed to be neighbors, church, garden club and social events. But there was a P.S. —"I thought you might be interested in the enclosed."

It was a newspaper clipping and Stacy opened it idly. Mrs. Ware frequently sent her daughter items from the local paper, published in the suburb in which she lived; this was a picture from a Los Angeles paper and beneath it was the caption, "Mr. and Mrs. Robert Armitage on their arrival from Hawaii."

Stacy did not read the rest. She looked at the picture. It wasn't bad of Bob. He was smiling; he had his arm around his wife's shoulders. She was smiling too—a pretty woman, even in the newspaper picture. Stacy's mother had sent the clipping without comment. She strongly disapproved of divorce. She'd been, as Stacy had known since she was a child, extremely unhappy in her voluble "sacrificial" way with Stacy's father, if not as unhappy as he'd been with her. He'd tried, after Stacy was grown and about to leave for the East, to persuade Pauline Ware to divorce him . . . and Stacy thought, now, looking blindly at the clipping: Bob had more guts than Dad . . . or Mother more than I.

She tore up the clipping. She'd learned painfully during her recent months in the city not to lie awake nights and pray that the second Mrs. Armitage be struck dead. The fact that she hadn't been proved that no one had listened.

Yet the divorce hadn't been her successor's fault. Stacy had come to that conclusion months ago; probably it wasn't Bob's either. Sometimes she rather envied her mother, now a happy, or at least contented, widow who had been relieved of her burden. "A husband who drank too much and ran after women" was how she characterized him, sighing, to her numerous friends. A burden who had died in an accident—the fast car spinning around the narrow corner had been an accident—and left her, as the phrase goes, "well provided for."

Stacy opened the other letters and found one from a woman she'd known for six weeks in Nevada; she, too, lived in California and had sent the same clipping with the comment: "Frame this, look at it every day and promise yourself never to make the same mistake again. That's what I do with the picture I showed you. He hasn't married again. He can't afford it unless some gal with a bank account falls for his blue eyes. I'm having a ball. How about you? We're lucky, Stacy, no kids."

She tore up that clipping also. She had wanted a child; Bob had not.

She looked at the letters and bills and reached for her checkbook, recalling Vanessa's remark about "a settlement." Bob had insisted on that. He was making money now as his brother's partner; he had also married it. Stacy had wanted desperately to refuse his terms. Her lawyer had thought them fair and remarked that there were states in which she could be divorced by her husband on grounds of insanity. So she'd said she didn't want Bob's money, reflecting that it probably wouldn't be his money, and her lawyer had then asked, "So, what will you live on?"

She had her father's insurance, which had come to her at the time of his death, shortly after her marriage, in the form of an annuity. She had, as well, her talent.

"My dear girl," said her lawyer, "artists are a dime a dozen. You don't want this divorce; your husband does. So it's only fair that he pay for it."

She'd been fortunate. When she and Bob were living in Chicago, she had taken excellent courses in art. And, as he was often away, she'd converted a little den into a work room and painted there. She'd always painted well. The art editor at Lovemay's had greatly liked her designs, her work in general, and, as he'd asked, she'd kept in touch with him . . . a very nice man, Jim Swift, twenty years her senior. She was unaware that he'd been a little in love with her. He was married, he had three children, and Stacy had been in love with a young man in the accounting department from the moment she saw him and was miserable with it, for Bob Armitage had other interests than the small dark girl from California.

She had seen Jim shortly after her return to the East; he'd put on weight; he was as kind as ever, looking at the little she was able to show him of her work, painted there in the high-rise apartment house overlooking the lake.

He'd said, "You can draw, Stacy, as well as paint. I've always known that. You have a delicacy, imagination. Suppose I give you a manuscript to read, one that just came down to the art department. It's a book for kids, pure delightful fantasy."

So that was how she started; she had introductions to other art editors; orders came in. When she did her first dust jacket for Lovemay's, Jim whistled. He said, "I felt you had a taste for the Gothic . . . I'll remember." And later, taking her to lunch, he'd said, "Did you ever know I was almost in love with you, Stacy?"

She'd answered, startled, "No . . . you couldn't have been!"

"Oh, but I was. Not that I was tired of or misunderstood by my wife. You do remember Harriet? She's a darling. But there's something about marriage in Suburbia and working in the city that weaves dreams, even without the second martini. Some men try to realize that. I didn't." He touched her hand. "Good luck," he said. "I'll help, all I can."

Thinking of this, she said to herself, "So go to work this minute, even if it's hot and you hate letters from California and newspaper clippings."

On Saturday night she was going to a buffet supper which Amy Irvington was giving for her. "You simply must meet the others in our little zoo," Amy had said, "and as our house is too small—I'd have to put Benjy in the washing machine—my adorable in-laws have lent me theirs. Remember when you met Ben's grandfather, you promised you'd show him some of your work. Even though he retired from Lovemay's years ago he still owns stock in it and takes a great personal interest in the books they produce."

She'd take Mr. Lovemay the sketches of the current dust jacket, another Gothic. Since his wife's death he'd lived in the guest house belonging to the older Irvingtons, and tried, his grandson had told her, to accommodate to New England after all the years in France.

He was a beautiful old man, Stacy thought. In fact, the Irvingtons, young and old, were wonderful people. She thought: I must ask them about Vanessa Steele. . . .

Stacy was working that afternoon when she heard brisk footsteps on the flagstone and someone called through the screen door.

"Stacy? It's Marcia."

Little Oxford was a first-name place. Stacy went to the door, and said, smiling, "Please come in. Unless you're collecting the rent."

Marcia Boyd was an attractive, slightly overweight woman in her late thirties; she had a round, tanned face and fine blue eyes and her most astonishing feature was a great deal of short, platinum-gray hair.

"You're working," she said, "I'll never learn. Lee used to throw me out of here."

"I was just about to stop. How about a long cold drink, or is it too early?"

Marcia came in and sank into one of the love seats. Her bare legs and her round firm arms were brown. She wore the Little Oxford summer uniform—shorts and a shirt. "Can't stay. . . . Curious how in such a short time and with a minimum of effort and belongings you've stamped this place with your personality."

"What is my personality?" Stacy inquired, sitting across from her.

"Oh . . . half gypsy, half Puritan," Marcia answered. "I majored in psychology and drove all my friends nuts. I intended to get my Master's and perhaps a Ph.D and teach, but then I met Douglas and we were married."

Stacy nodded. She knew about Douglas Boyd. Considerably Marcia's elder, tremendously successful, he had been killed in a car accident some eight years ago.

"Are you comfortable here?" Marcia asked. "I'll worry about you until they get the telephone connected. They swore it would be by the middle of next week."

"I'm fine," Stacy assured her, and added, "Will you be going to the Lovemays' tomorrow night? Amy said she was asking you."

"My dear, that's what I came to tell you. I'm driving to New York tomorrow to meet Lee at Kennedy. We're staying over; there's a man he wants to see on business. Also two old friends will be there over the weekend. You'll meet them eventually. They usually come by for a visit during the summer. I wanted to tell you that if you'd like to use the telephone or need any help, I've briefed Cora —you know—my housekeeper? So just run over anytime. She makes bad coffee, usually, but has a light hand with cake."

"Thanks," Stacy said. "Are you staying away long?"

"Till Monday sometime. . . . What are you looking at?"

"Your hair," said Stacy, "with the sun on it. It's lovely."

"Oh, this." Marcia ran her hands through it. "Not a patch on Jessica Banks', and wait till you see Lee. He has the hereditary premature gray crop, but his is whiter than mine and curly. I have only a reluctant wave. I tried tints and rinses and dyes. . . . Lee used to scream; Douglas would shake me till my teeth rattled; and they both made the same unflattering pronouncement that with the ordinary brown hair some of the ancestors had, including my mother, I'd look like a plain healthy female citizen, but that being gray made me distinguished and that, as I grew older, I'd look younger. Fat chance. . . . I wish I hadn't said that; I've gained six pounds recently."

She sighed and Stacy, to change the subject, said, "Mrs. Steele called on me yesterday."

"Van? I would have said she'd turn up before. She's possessed of an insatiable curiosity, but it isn't unfriendly. What do you think of her?"

"I don't know. I think I could like her."

"We do. In fact, she's one of Lee's favorite people. I can't go quite that far because sometimes she scares me— or maybe it's her cat."

"I've met him too. I like cats."

"I don't especially. I suppose she told you she's been divorced for donkey's years?"

"Yes, and has a grandson."

"This isn't really gossip," said Marcia, "because everyone knows it, since Van obliges by telling. Her husband divorced her, and he was given the custody of their child, a son, Warren, who was then about three years old. He didn't see his mother until he was twenty-one. He comes here occasionally with his wife. The grandson, Adam, has always had access to her."

"What happened to her husband, if that isn't asking too much?"

"Heavens, no! She'd be glad to tell you. He died some years ago. More or less a recluse, according to Adam who is as outspoken as his grandmother. He was very difficult, also filthy rich. Van was given the income from a trust fund—as a bribe, I suppose, so she wouldn't fight the divorce. I doubt that she would have; she would have lost anyway, and knew it, but perhaps she might have fought it out of a peculiar malicious sense of humor. Although he —Steele—dreaded publicity, he wasn't willing to let her divorce him. But then Van always says he really wasn't a gentleman."

Marcia laughed and added, "I must get going . . . have to pack after supper and get an early start. I'll be interested in what you think, or decide, about Van when next you encounter her."

"She's asked me to supper Monday night."

"Oh? She must have taken a fancy to you. I've been no more than three times since I've known her, which is since I was a girl. There are people in Little Oxford who'd give both hands for an invitation and others who'd shudder at the mere idea and swear she'd serve pickled newts and fried bats or whatever. She has quite a reputation, our Vanessa."

Stacy went to the door with her guest. She said, "I think you underrate Mrs. Steele, and she told me you were an agreeable woman."

"Well, so I am," Marcia commented, "and she has the good sense to perceive it, but I'm not her cup of tea, or witch's brew. However, she absolutely dotes on Lee. I bet she told you he is a charmer."

"Now *you're* being a witch!"

"Not at all. She tells everyone that, including Lee. 'Bye. See you soon. You must come to dinner and meet your other landlord. I hope you speak Greek?"

"No. But I can learn," Stacy said, laughing. "Have a good trip."

She returned to the studio, made herself the long cold drink and went out on the small tree-shaded patio which opened from her bedroom. It was quiet and a small wind had risen to cool the late afternoon and blow away the insects. She sipped her drink, telling herself: "I think I'll be happy here"—and then erased the word, "happy" and substituted "content."

Happiness was dangerous. It was fragile and easily shattered. Like Humpty Dumpty, it couldn't be put together again. If you were sensible, you settled for less, much less, and perhaps found security.

"But," she argued with herself, "I'm not in love with Bob, not now. I haven't been for months. Why do I feel like this? Why did the clippings upset me?"

Where there'd been happiness, there was only emptiness, gray and cold as a winter morning; and that terrible sense of rejection, tearing like talons into heart, mind, guts. There were times when she was nauseated with it; she'd been that way all the weeks in Nevada . . . unable to eat or sleep, crying without volition, sometimes in front of strangers, the tears pouring down her face.

I should see a doctor, she thought, setting down her glass. The ice tinkled, and a bright bird flew by. This isn't normal; it can't be. Other women have been divorced against their will; other women have thought they were happy, have thought that they held the sun and moon and stars in their hands; and other women have awakened to find everything destroyed. Other women have been as stupid, not knowing, not guessing, wrapped in their own illusions.

No psychiatrist, she thought. I not only can't afford a year on the couch, but it wouldn't help me. The only person who can is myself—and I don't know how.

※ 3 ※

On Saturday, Stacy regarded her wardrobe with some misgiving. She should really buy more country clothes, she thought; it had been some time since she'd bought any clothes at all. She remembered her evening frocks, negligées, armfuls of delicate lingerie. She'd stored most of these in a trunk left with a friend, Sally Babcock, in Chicago and when, upon her return from Nevada, she'd spent several days with Sally before going East, she'd given everything away, lock, stock and barrel. Sally, who'd been in her art classes, was always broke and struggling; she could wear Stacy's size and felt no pain at inheriting secondhand garments. "Saved my life," she had said, hugging her friend.

Stacy had gone to Nevada with exactly what she needed for the climate and, as she had no intention of dining elegantly or making the casino rounds, her selection had been plain and practical. These came to the East with her, and she'd bought a short fur coat for herself, with her own money. In New York she'd acquired tweed slacks, shorts, shirts, and a few necessities, but Little Oxford demanded more.

She selected a pair of summer-weight slacks in brown. Amy had warned her, "Even if it's perishing hot, wear

22

slacks. Most of this bash will be outdoors and no matter how much Ben and his father fog with insect repellent, no one's safe this time of year. Of course, people will be running in and out of the house; if you can't bear it outside, you can eat with some comfort indoors. But Little Oxford is sold on patios, barbecues, clambakes and such. I'd ask our friend Ross Cameron, his wild kid, and his attractive wife to come and bring their swimming pool—it's a dilly—but they're not here now."

For the brown slacks, an orange and brown shirt; and on her small feet, elkskin moccasins. She hadn't much choice when it came to accessories—just the Indian silver and turquoise pawn jewelry her father had given her before her marriage, and a few bits and pieces inherited from her grandmother. One was a Russian chain, gold and black enamel, with a locket containing a miniature of an even more remote ancestress. That would have to do. The jewelry Bob had given her—and engagement and wedding ring, several bracelets, a watch and other trinkets—she'd left for him to dispose of. She doubted, however, that he'd present them to the second Mrs. Armitage, who kept most of her jewelry, Stacy presumed, in a vault.

When Stacy told her lawyer to give the leather jewel case to Bob, he had torn his scant fair hair and cried, "You're off your rocker. Who ever heard of such a thing? What's he going to do with it?"

"Former girl friends," she'd suggested. "I didn't know, until you found out, that there were several. Or, failing that, charity."

She put on the slacks, shirt, the old chain and the inexpensive watch she'd had to buy and looked at herself in the mirror. Brown eyes, widely set; long, heavy black hair, tied back; an oval face, olive-skinned but touched by the Little Oxford sun to rosy apricot. Her mouth was generous and full and drooped at the corners. She smiled in the mirror with determination. She didn't want to go to the Irvingtons, but she'd become very fond of Amy—something she hadn't believed possible. Getting in touch with Amy again had been an act of desperation and she'd regretted it bitterly, driving up that first weekend.

She'd envied her once. Now she envied her again: her marriage to young Doctor Irvington which was so obviously happy; her infant son; her delightful in-laws—Ben's doctor father, and his pretty mother. She thought now: She ought to get down on her knees and thank me because Bob tired of her and turned to me, and I, besotted as I was, married him.

The Irvington house was on Cherry Street. There was a one-story el, which contained offices for the older physician who had been known as Bing in Little Oxford since practically his birth, and his son, Benjamin. It had its own entrance and parking space. Tonight there was plenty of parking space in front of the big brown house; cars were already there and a large agile young man was running about directing the guests. Stacy asked, smiling at him, "What happens if all the space is taken, Amos?"

She knew him; he worked after school for the older Irvingtons and sometimes gave Amy a hand in her garden.

"Well," said Amos, "they can drive around back. There's acres. It's a little rough when you get past the porch and lawn but usable unless you go too far downhill into the pond and swamp."

Where the mosquitoes live, thought Stacy accurately.

Amy was at the door. She was as pretty as a blue-eyed apple tree in bloom, and her mother-in-law, Letty, with the frosted yellow curls, was there in back of her.

Amy said, "You look smashing," and Letty touched Stacy's shoulder and said, "Amy was afraid you wouldn't come."

24

"She knew I was scared; all those people," said Stacy.

They were steaming around, in and out of rooms, and Stacy heard the laughing from the big old-fashioned back porch, and beyond.

"Did you remember to bring a sweater?" asked Amy.

Stacy shook her head and Amy said, "Letty can lend you one. Later, after dark, it gets cool, thank God."

"Bing's set up the bar in the library," Letty told her, "and he's actually behind it."

"Ben isn't," Amy said sorrowfully, "I wish he were thirty years older and could take some time off."

"Well, I don't," Ben's mother said. . . . "Oscar, for heaven's sake."

Oscar was a beagle; he'd come up to stand beside her and woof gently at Stacy, who had met him before. She stooped to pet him. "Hi, feller," she said.

"Don't encourage him," Amy advised as Oscar regarded their guest with large, loving eyes and waved his erect white-tipped tail.

Letty said, "Here come the Bankses. Amy, take Stacy around and do the introductions; after all, it's her party."

People in the wide hall, in the big living room and in the library dominated by books, a big desk, a small fireplace, Bing Irvington and the bar. Amy made her way through with Stacy's hand in hers. She said, "Don't look so petrified. I'm real; they're real; you are too up to a point. No one's going to eat you, idiot."

Stacy said almost inaudibly, "I've been scared of masses of people ever since I was born. I had to get used to them when Bob and I———"

She stopped. Amy said briskly, "Well, get used all over again."

Dr. Irvington, when they finally reached him, was dispensing drinks and advice. "You know gin disagrees with you," he was telling one large, well-cushioned female. "How about dry sherry?"

"Hi," he said, "my favorite daughter-in-law."

"I may add, your only one," Amy said severely. "Give Stacy a drink; she's got the shakes."

"Stacy's smart," said Bing. "Anyone who braves a Little Oxford Welcome to Our Village Party should shake herself right into a quiet corner and stay there. You look better than you did earlier this summer," he told Stacy, smiling. "Must agree with you here."

"Forget the bedside manner," Amy advised, "and give the poor girl a belt of something."

"Vodka and tonic, light on the vodka, masses of ice," Bing decided and Stacy asked, smiling as he mixed it, "How did you know?"

"Very simple diagnosis; also a good memory. Where's Oscar, Amy?"

"Greeting all comers, as usual."

"Fool dog," said Bing fondly.

As they made their way out of the library, Amy said, "Pop Bing has fallen in love again. For years it was Tinker; and when Tinker died, he swore no more dogs. But now there's Oscar. . . . Hey back to the living room. You've met the Bankses, I think. But I saw Rosie Niles out of the corner of my intelligent eye."

Steered into the living room, and toward Mrs. Niles, who was drinking straight tomato juice, Stacy looked at her with interest. You couldn't be in Little Oxford even for a weekend and not hear about her; small, dark and burning like autumn leaves.

"This," said Amy, "is Stacy Armitage, Rosie."

Rosie gave her a small, rather ugly but firm hand. She said, "I missed you the weekends you were here."

"You're never home," Amy reminded her.

26

"Oh, now and then." Rosie regarded Stacy with big black eyes and Stacy thought: She's much too thin.

"Do you sing?" asked Rosie abruptly.

"Good heavens, no."

"She paints," said Amy. "I told you about her."

"That's right. Somehow," said Rosie, "you look as if you sang, and, in a curious way, you look a little like me."

Both dark, both small, both smoldering, thought Amy. There the resemblance ends.

"Where's Benjy?" Stacy asked Amy.

"Out on the porch, in a padded cell—I mean playpen— under a mosquito net, and surrounded by adoring and doubtless germ-bearing people. Let's go." She added as they made their way there, "The Palmers are late; Katie had a client."

The porch had its customers, but many had gone into the big yard, fringed with trees, and were already attacking the laden tables with paper plates and plastic utensils. Amy said, "No barbecue, thank heaven. It's too darned hot. Grab something and we'll find a place. I recommend the porch."

Stacy set her glass down on a table and went toward the lavish provisions of the usual nature—salads, beans, cold meats, deviled eggs, the works. Amy was still on the porch talking to her son. Stacy heard her say, "Suppose you go to sleep. You know you can sleep through fire alarms. Don't let all the attention go to your head. When your father gets here—if ever—he'll take you upstairs and put you to bed in the spare crib."

A man materialized beside Amy and asked, "Suppose I carry all that for you. In which direction are you headed?"

"To the porch," Stacy said. "Thank you."

"You a tourist?" he inquired as they made their way and Stacy laughed, "Well, I suppose so," she told him. "I've rented a studio here, and moved in about ten days ago."

"Then you're Stacy Armitage," he said, seemingly pleased. "I'm a classmate of Ben's—Fred Arnold."

"Doctor Arnold?"

"Nope. Couldn't take it. When people hurt, I hurt; when they're sick, I'm sick. Ben and I started medical school together; he finished, but I went into my grandfather's business. It's fertilizers. I don't know if there's any connection there."

Amy was signaling from the porch. "The Palmers," she called. "Come hold my place while I get some food. I'm starved. Hi, Fred. You've met Stacy?"

"I picked her—and her plate—up."

"I saved you a chair right by Benjy," Amy told Stacy.

Katie and Jeremy Palmer had found a small table and a couple of chairs, and Stacy said uncertainly, "You know Mr. Arnold?" "I should," Katie said. "I sold him a house a month ago. . . . Hi, Fred, I haven't had time to stop by since you moved. This character is Jeremy, my husband."

Stacy relaxed in her chair and Fred Arnold said, "Eat. That's what we're here for." He had found a wicker stool, and sat on it warily, a heavy, amiable man with an engaging smile. "May I get you a drink? Yours looks unhealthily diluted."

"It is. I've been carrying it around. But it's still cool. Thank you."

"I've tried to get over," Katie apologized, "but what with one thing and another . . . and Jeremy and I spend every free minute at our property. They're started to drill the well."

"I think with the friendly relations now established, the drillers are trying to reach China at," said Jeremy gloomily, "an astronomical price."

"Lee will be home soon," Katie predicted. "He'll hold your hand and make soothing noises."

"Lee Osborne?" asked Stacy. "He'll be home sometime Monday."

Katie regarded her with reverence. "How come you know that?" she asked. "No one else does. When I call his office, no one knows anything. All they say is he's expected back. I just assumed before the first snow."

Stacy laughed. "I saw his sister yesterday," she explained.

Amy toiled back, and Jeremy and Fred went to her rescue. She asked, "Hasn't Ben showed up yet?"

"No. But your child is in good hands."

"I hope he isn't in anyone's hands. No, he's asleep——" She broke off. "Oscar," she added, sighing.

Oscar, marching on his small paws, came and settled down by the playpen. He yawned and went to sleep too.

"He's elected himself Benjy's guardian or perhaps, uncle," said Amy. "Where in the name of St. Luke is Ben?"

"Probably taking some beautiful woman's pulse," Jeremy suggested.

"First time I catch him," Amy said austerely, "his will stop."

Half an hour later Ben Irvington, tall and redheaded, arrived, loped onto the porch, greeted his friends and said to his wife, "Don't tell me, let me guess. Have you changed him, I hope?"

"Interminably," answered Amy. "Take him away."

Ben scooped up his small, but equally redheaded, son and disappeared.

Amy said resignedly, "I think that kid will grow up to be a barfly or else take monastic vows. You never know the reaction. Anytime an Irvington throws a party he's there."

"Also, when the Palmers do," Katie reminded her. "I've started to condition him so when he's twenty-four he'll know what sort of a house he wants."

People drifted about into the fields, still faintly flushed with the afterglow—as were a few of the guests—into the house or out to their cars. Inside someone was playing good jazz on the piano. Ben came back and asked, "Any food left? I haven't eaten in a week." He ran down the steps and returned with a laden plate. "Missed some of the specialties," he said sadly, and Stacy, drinking the coffee Fred had brought her, asked idly, "I suppose you all know Mrs. Steele."

A chorus responded, consisting of Amy, Ben and the Palmers. "Vanessa!" they exclaimed in unison.

"Who else?" asked Stacy. "She came to see me Thursday."

"Did she bring Shadow?" Jeremy inquired.

"She did."

"Don't let Oscar catch you fooling with that gigantic cat," Amy warned her. . . . "Well, yes, we all know her, except perhaps Fred who's Johnny-come-lately. She's rarely ill—I think she nibbles herbs—but if she is, she's Pop Bing's patient."

Jeremy said, "Occasionally she comes to the bookshop to consult me. Usually I have to order what she wants. Not that it's as far-out reading as it used to be. In her own way she's probably the most intelligent woman in Little Oxford."

"Thanks," said Amy, and Katie snorted. She said, "Anyone who wants a book not in stock and makes Jeremy hunt for it, he believes is brilliant. When his own book comes out, I'm leaving town."

"What book?" asked Stacy.

Between them Katie and Jeremy told her. The book he and Beth Cameron had put together from an ancestral Revolutionary War diary. It would be published in the spring.

"Lovemay's?" Stacy asked.

"No, another publisher; a friend of Beth's husband, Ross Cameron."

Amy said, "To get back to Vanessa, the only one in this group who really knows her is Ben."

"Since I was a child," said Ben promptly. "But in those and later days she came and went, rather like a cat herself, now that I think of it. She's Dad's patient, but she's tolerated me a time or two when he wasn't available. She came to see Amy after Benjy was born—as a matter of fact I think she was at the wedding."

"She was," said Amy, "and sent an antique silver spoon——"

"I know her by osmosis," said Katie. "I wish I could get my hands on that house. I've never been in it, of course, but I'm sure it's haunted—always a pretty good sales pitch."

Amy said, "I like her, though I was a little apprehensive she might put a spell on Benjy."

Bing detached himself from a listening post at the doorway, and remarked, "I wish you'd stop this chatter about an old woman who has never done anyone a gram of harm but herself. Stacy, Letty's father came in a while ago. He'll go back to the guest house presently—he's really not up to parties. He said you promised to show him something."

"I forgot," said Stacy, stricken. It seemed to her she was always forgetting. "Where is he?"

"In the library."

Ben said, "I'll come along; haven't seen Gramp for a couple of days. Anyway, I could use a drink, but not large enough to alarm the answering service."

They went in together and Remsen Lovemay was there, old, frail and delightful. Stacy said, "I forgot the sketches, Mr. Lovemay. I'm so sorry."

"Gives me an excuse to come by the studio soon," said Lovemay, "when it's a little cooler. I'd like to look at your work in peace and quiet and at my leisure. As I told you, I do like what I've seen . . . the book jackets."

"A little brandy?" his grandson suggested.

"No. Bed, I think." He smiled at Stacy. "I walk a good deal," he told her. "I'll walk over someday. You've a phone?"

"I should have by sometime next week," she said. "I do hope you will come, Mr. Lovemay."

Not long thereafter Rosie Niles was saying to Stacy, "Come see me. Phone first. I rarely know where I'll be until I get there, if then, but I think I'll stay home until fall anyway," and Stacy was telling the Irvingtons what a wonderful time she'd had and how kind they were and Amy, going with her to the door, said, "Fred will see you to your car, and I think Amos is still around." She added, "You really stood up very well, Stacy, hating every minute of it!"

"I didn't hate it."

"You can't con me," said Amy. "Anyway, you know a few people now, owing to an invitation you couldn't refuse, and there'll be lots of others."

"I doubt it. Unattached women are only too plentiful."

Amy ignored that. She said, "From now on you can refuse. . . . Fred, see that she gets safely to her car."

Fred obliged. He asked, as they walked across the parking lot and people waved and spoke, "Did I hear you say you're unattached?"

"Yes."

"But I thought it was Mrs. Armitage?"

She said shortly, "I'm divorced," and Fred beamed—

she could feel it in the darkness. "So am I. I'd like to see you again," he announced predictably.

"That would be nice," Stacy said. She got into her car and, thankfully, drove home—alone.

4

Stacy took a sleeping pill, reluctantly. She had relied upon this temporary oblivion too often during her stay in Nevada and even before that, when the sky fell and the earth shook, and she and Bob had had several arguments, counter arguments. She tried not to think of those weeks; of the shock, brutal and totally unexpected, or of her own pleading tears and incredulity. But for some time now she had rarely resorted to the capsules.

Tonight she was tired, and still under the sense of unreality which came from being, once more, with a number of people, most of them strangers, and with the effort of being agreeable, seeming interested and vivacious.

Sleeping, she dreamed, first of the Pump Room. She could see herself and Bob, like figures on a moving-picture screen; she saw them joining other people whom they had come to meet; a middle-aged man, his elegant wife, and his more elegant daughter, Winifred. Bob's firm had recently been engaged by the company which Mr. Harvey headed. This had been a big fish; a big company, with solid, old money.

There it was, fixed in time, the small bright picture, moving across her mind, behind her closed eyes; and she woke, shaking, and said, looking at the illuminated clock,

"How much longer must you be a fool?" But one can't control dreams, awake or asleep.

She wished she hadn't given up cigarettes. Perhaps one would help. She had an old pack, unopened; she'd had it ever since she returned East. It was in the bedside table drawer. She turned on the light and went barefoot into the studio, found an ashtray and matches, and returned to sit up in bed, shivering. But the cigarette was dry, stale and harsh and she stubbed it out, went into the bathroom, brushed her teeth and looked in the mirror. Her image, she thought, was a little wild, even distraught.

She got back in bed, beat her pillows with a small fist, pulled the sheet over her, switched off the light, and turned over on her right side. She thought: I'll stay awake the rest of the night; but did not. Toward morning, she dreamed again, this time of faces: small faces clustered together like a huddle of dark stars, angry, hating, malicious, resentful, drawn with grief, profound and unendurable; vicious faces, which laughed, without humor; faces sodden with fatigue, faces steeped in the bitter water of humiliation.

She woke a little late. She had pledged herself to work today, but she was too tired. This last dream was a recurrent one, although she'd not experienced it since coming to Little Oxford. She'd done everything she could to exorcise it. The faces were as clear as her own in the mirror. She'd drawn them over and over again, hoping for a kind of catharsis.

When she had showered and put on a light robe, she made coffee and, sitting at the counter, drank it, looking from the windows. It was very hot and had been since sunrise. The mere thought of working was enervating and she was in advance of her deadline. But there was all the long day ahead.

Sometime after ten o'clock, on an inexplicable impulse, she dressed in a thin shirtwaist frock, took a handbag and a light sweater and drove, just before eleven, to the church presided over by Gordon Banks and to which she had been, twice, with Amy and Letty Irvington during her weekend visits.

When she reached the church area, she found a parking space on the quiet residential street, walked a block or so to the steps which led to the big stone church. People stood on the grass, talking before going in; children held their own small conversations; the church door stood wide and the organ was playing.

Going into the comparatively cool darkness—light streaming in only from the doors and the beautiful windows—she indicated to an usher that she'd prefer to sit in the back and, as she entered the pew, someone touched her arm.

"Hi," said Rosie Niles. "May I sit with you?"

"Of course," Stacy told her.

"Letty and Amy went in ahead of us," Rosie said. "I don't know which one's prettier."

Someone behind them said, "Hush," in an unhushed voice.

They stood, sat, knelt, bowed their heads and shared a hymn book. Stacy murmured docilely along, listening to the true, husky voice of the woman beside her, remembering what she'd heard: A very young singer with her husband's band in supper clubs well over thirty years ago. She could imagine faintly what it would have been like to hear Rosie sing the songs of that period in a small crowded place. But Stacy's knowledge of that era came only from nostalgic movies, records, radio. . . .

Gordon Banks was a powerful speaker, and Stacy acknowledged to herself that what he said made great good sense. But he said nothing which evoked a question or an answer from her. She listened gravely, admiring his striking appearance, his voice and delivery, and thought her own thoughts.

When the service was over, they went out to the vestry and Rosie said, "You're improving, Gordon."

"How, exactly?"

"Oh a little more human," Rosie told him carelessly, smiling her urchin smile. "Jessica here?"

"Of course. She'll be along presently."

He greeted Stacy with every show of pleasure and said he hoped he see her often. Then Rosie led the way out. "Want to wait for Amy?" she asked and Stacy shook her head. She said, "No, honestly, I'd better go home and get to work. I meant to this morning, but last night was a little too much for me."

"Like to swim?" Rosie asked and Stacy, astonished, answered, "Why . . . yes."

"What you need is cool water and a cold lunch." She put her hand on Stacy's arm. "Got a bathing suit?"

Stacy nodded and Rosie said, "I'll follow you—it's the Osborne studio, isn't it? We'll pick up your suit and a robe —not that you couldn't in a pinch wear mine—and slippers if you have them. Then I'll take you to my house. I let my good couple off on Sundays and scratch for myself. I'm a pretty good scratcher. I was brought up in restaurants. Come on."

Stacy went docilely, got into her car and Rosie said, "I'll catch up with you by the monument."

On the way home, Stacy tried to think of an excuse. A headache. Actually she had one. A pressing engagement? No. She hadn't. And the long afternoon lay before her, lonely and futile.

Rosie reached the studio shortly after Stacy and said as

they went in together, "I've never been here. It's attractive. May I look around?"

"There isn't much to see," Stacy told her. "Portfolios full of sketches, some paintings stacked against the walls. I haven't hung them yet. I don't know that I shall."

She went into her bedroom and pulled out one of the drawers built into the big closet. The smaller closet she kept locked. After tossing things about, she unearthed a bathing suit—cherry red—and slippers and took from the bathroom her terry-cloth robe. She came back into the studio and found Rosie looking at the painting on the easel. "Haunted," said Rosie.

"I hope so," Stacy said, laughing. "It's for the dust jacket of a Gothic novel."

"Scary," Rosie commented, "but it will sell the book, even if the author doesn't."

"Oh, she will; she's wildly popular," Stacy assured her. "This is very kind of you, Mrs. Niles."

"Rosie," Mrs. Niles corrected. "Or, if you can manage it, Roscika. A few people do—Jessica Banks and Bing Irvington, for instance, and only when I upset them. . . . Leave your car here. I'm coming back to the parsonage after lunch. Jessica has a girl coming up from the city and wants me to hear her sing. So I'll drop you off on my way there."

The first time Stacy came to Little Oxford she had had the impressive Niles house pointed out to her by Katie Palmer.

"I think it's marvelous," Katie had said, "all that wood and glass. Lee Osborne hates it."

"Who's he?"

"An architect; ours in fact. He's designing the house Jeremy and I are going to build. We wouldn't have quite so soon," Katie had told her, "except that we're having a premature baby."

"Premature?"

"Well, just let's say a sooner one than I'd planned. ... About the Niles house. Rosie isn't here now or I could take you inside. Lee doesn't like most contemporary houses, though of course he builds them. He'd have to starve otherwise. His firm can't just build churches, condominiums, libraries or what have you all the time."

Stacy remembered this going into the Niles house—big, comfortable, air-conditioned.

Rosie said, "Sit down. Those chairs look like some form of medieval torture, but they'll fit. This is the library. Can I fix you a drink?"

"No thanks," Stacy said, smiling, looking around at the books. "It's too early for me."

"You're a sun-over-the-yardarm gal?"

"Yes, and sometimes, nothing, yardarm or not."

"You're lucky," Rose told her. "I can't drink at all. Or if I do"—she shrugged—"but such lapses are growing further and further apart, thank God. ... Like music?"

"Yes, of course."

"What kind?"

Stacy said, "Most anything except rock and, I'm afraid, the less comprehensible classics."

"Sad, I bet," Rosie diagnosed. "Minor key. What we once called torch songs, blues." She added thoughtfully, "Also schmaltz."

"I'm afraid so."

"Put your feet up. I'll get you music and also some iced tea and you can listen and drink while I fix lunch."

"May I help?"

"No."

Stacy said, "Do you have any of your own recordings, Mrs. Niles?"

"Rosie, please. ... No, I destroyed them years ago. I'll find you something better."

Later they swam in the bright pool and Rosie said, "You don't sunburn, I'm sure, but it's pretty damned hot. Here's your robe. I'll go haul out trays; here—under the umbrella."

They had a cold lunch: crabmeat salad, an avocado, thin bread and butter, and then hot coffee.

"My father always said, 'No matter if it's a hundred degrees outside you have to have something hot in your belly.'"

Rosie Niles was, Stacy thought, remarkable—this small, too-thin woman with the mop of black curls and enormous black eyes, sitting there in her black bikini suit and orange robe, talking of the town, the way it had been, the way it was. She asked no questions, she exhibited no curiosity. She said at one point, "I never thought I'd be happy here, but I am. I hope you will be." She added after a moment, "It takes time, Stacy; it took me too long."

Driving home Rosie said, "I suppose you know Mrs. Steele?"

Stacy said, "Vanessa? Only in a manner of speaking. I've met her only once."

"I was born in Little Oxford," Rosie said, "and when I was eighteen or so, I left. After Bill and I were married we came back at intervals to see my folks. Long intervals. I didn't return for good until a few years ago. Vanessa arrived here after I'd left, and bought the old Northrop house. I'd known it forever; used to play with the Northrop kids. There were two of them—a tepid little girl and a precocious boy. Mr. Northrop was a carpenter. He bought the house after one of the banks foreclosed and amused himself rebuilding it. So it's an elderly house, and incidentally, a small one. Vanessa Steele came occasionally from wherever her travels took her. I understand from the grapevine that she was apt to turn up anywhere in the world, like Henry Kissinger. Well, anyway, she returned here to live about fifteen years ago. When I see her on the street, she speaks to me, and I met her once at Jessica's. I'd venture to say that she can't stand Gordon but likes his wife. Now, I expect, as you've met her—how, exactly?"

"She came to see me."

"That," said Rosie, "is a feather in your cap. What kind of a feather I don't know. Of course Mrs. Steele's as curious as a cat. She's not really interested in everybody, however, but everybody's interested in her. I suppose you know her background? Most of Little Oxford does. I heard it first from Si Wescott. He's the publisher of the local weekly paper. I daresay she herself gave him the material. I've heard she's by no means averse to talking about herself. Adam, her grandson, is a very attractive boy. He was here when Gordon's church put on a play by Cynthia Lovemay, Letty's mother."

"I worked at Lovemay's," Stacy said. "I never met Mrs. Lovemay though."

"I helped with the play," said Rosie. "Jessica got me involved. Adam turned up at the performance, without his grandmother."

They arrived at the studio, and Stacy got out. She said, leaning into the window near Rosie, "Thank you so very much." She opened the back door and took her terry-cloth bundle. "I enjoyed it."

"Come again," said Rosie. "I liked having you."

"Give my best to Mrs. Banks," Stacy said.

Rosie drove away. Lonely, she thought, and uptight, wary of people. Temperament. I'd like to see her work. Perhaps Jessica will make it a project to get to know her. Jess is balm to any wound. I might suggest it, she thought. If it weren't for the presence of Vanessa's cat—good heavens, he must be fifteen years old! I remember at the Bankses that day, she said she'd brought him here with her as a kitten—if it weren't for him, I'd like to be a mouse in a corner and hear what Stacy and Vanessa have to say to each other.

On Monday, before six, Stacy walked around the corner to the Steele house. She had hesitated before dressing. She thought: I used to be able to make up my mind promptly; now the smallest decision throws me. Certainly Vanessa's calling costume had been informal in the extreme, but, Stacy thought, I'm going to dinner. She didn't say, 'Come as you are'; she didn't say anything except just 'Come.'

She'd put on a pale green dress with a full short skirt, clasped an Indian belt—square silver links—around her narrow waist, slid her feet into green play shoes, picked up a sweater and small purse, and hoped she'd do.

Even without the mailbox marked Steele, it would have been impossible, Stacy thought, to mistake the house. It was frame, shingled and charcoal gray; the door was red. The roof looked like a hat, pulled down over the eyes of the small upstairs windows. There was a front porch with rattan furniture; it was shaded by lush vines that crept from the supports to the screening.

Stacy went up the path, bordered with perennials, and knocked. No one answered, and she looked at her watch. It was five to six. Perhaps she's forgotten, she thought, and, to her astonishment, felt disappointment and dismay. She went down the steps and walked around the back, where there was another vine-invaded porch—this one, open—which looked across a scrap of cut grass yellowing in the heat to a rough meadow bounded by a stone wall. On the wall Shadow was walking with dignified stealth, stopping to sniff out a chipmunk or a field mouse, and

Vanessa, below him on the tall grass, was matching his tempo.

Stacy started toward them. Vanessa looked up, and called in her deep resonant voice, "Wait there."

She and Shadow advanced toward their guest, Vanessa wearing, Stacy noted, a dress which came to her ankles, patterned in black and red. She carried a cane.

"I'm sorry," said Stacy, "I'm early—or was."

Vanessa said, "I'm always on time, but I think no one else ever is. I apologize. Let's get out of the sun; back way's quicker."

Shadow looked at Stacy. He made a small sound, and, she could have sworn, smiled. She said so, finding herself inordinately pleased, and Vanessa said, "He's taken a fancy to you."

She led the way to the porch and through the small immaculate kitchen into a big living room with an old table, set for two. The living room was a chaos of color and a clutter of furniture. It was wildly untidy and scrupulously clean. Books were everywhere on wall shelves, the floors, and in some of the chairs. The furniture was a mixture of inexpensive, adequate and beautifully polished old pieces. Tables were laden with small pagodas, Kwan Yins, Buddhas, dragons, Delft, Staffordshire, Meissen—and where there was wall space there were shelves for more objects: beautiful patch boxes in Battersea, tortoise shell, silver and what looked like gold.

Good grief! thought Stacy.

"Drink?" asked Vanessa. "If so, what? I've everything. I recommend vodka and tonic or in bouillon."

"I'd like that," Stacy said.

"Find a chair," Vanessa ordered. "Throw things on the floor if you want to—cushions, shawls—and there are footstools."

There were, mostly petit point.

She vanished, but Shadow remained. There was no fireplace in the room, but in the corner an obviously old Franklin stove. Shadow settled himself on a huge round brass tray, supported by folding wooden legs and bearing the signs of the zodiac. His emerald eyes regarded Stacy thoughtfully. She felt a little uneasy. She would have liked to prowl around looking at the thousand and one objects from a dozen or more countries—that was an African mask hanging from a book shelf—but Shadow made her self-conscious. If she as much as touched anything, she felt he would have turned in the alarm. Over the back of the chair she finally chose to sit in there was a beautiful cashmere shawl, hot to lean against, but she did not take advantage of Vanessa's offer to throw things about.

"Don't worry, Buster," she told Shadow softly, "I won't disturb anything, not even the dust, if there is any."

Shadow spoke for a couple of seconds and then Vanessa appeared with a tray. She said, "Make yourself really at home. Shadow, while a guardian and a watchman, rarely leaps to conclusions!"

"I was considering looking around," Stacy admitted, "but I was convinced that he wouldn't approve."

"I'll take you on the tour after supper," Vanessa told her. She set the tray on a teakwood table. "We live in a vast disarray of trash, beauty, books and comfort. I've turned on the kitchen fan. Are you prostrate with heat?"

"No, it's quite cool," Stacy said.

"Attic fans, and during the day, drawn shades. I raised them just before Shadow and I went walking. The porches keep some of the heat out. And I've other fans. . . . Here's your drink. Cheese?" she asked. "Crackers?"

Shadow jumped off the brass tray and advanced on Vanessa, rubbing his head against her leg. She gave him a piece of cheese and to Stacy's amusement, took a saucer from the tray, poured a little of her own drink in it and set it on the floor.

"He's not an alcoholic," she explained. "Just civilized. If I have a drink before dinner—and I usually do—or tea in the afternoon, he expects to share. Even iced tea. He likes the mint. I grow it out back."

Her extraordinary eyes fastened on Stacy. She said, "This is social chatter time. Anything serious comes after you're fed. What have you been doing with yourself since Thursday?"

Stacy told her.

"The Irvingtons?" Vanessa nodded. "They'll be good for you. Church?" She lifted an eyebrow. "Can't abide Gordon Banks," she said, and then, "Rosie Niles? Someday I must go see her; she interests me. But it's too hot for such a long a bicycle ride now."

When they had finished their drinks, Vanessa said, "Walk around, look at what you want; just don't drop anything breakable. I hate sweeping up. Shadow and I will get supper."

She vanished with the tray—Stacy had refused a second drink—and Shadow went with her. Stacy walked about, looking. There was an old small box—Russian she thought—enamel and gold, which she instantly coveted. Standing there with it in her hand she found herself wondering about the scent in the room—not light, not heavy. She'd noticed it when she entered but had no knowledge of its source.

With the box still in her hand, she walked across the room and found it, a small ancient incense burner, with faint blue smoke rising from it.

Vanessa asked from the doorway, "You mind it? If so, I'll take it out of the room."

"No, I like it." She turned, still holding the little box, and Shadow's ears twitched. Stacy found herself stammering. "I-I was about t-to put this back where I found it w-when I decided to find out where the fragrance was coming from."

"You like the box?" Vanessa asked.

"It's beautiful," Stacy said. "Russian, isn't it?"

"Yes. Supposed to have belonged to Catherine the Great, which I doubt, but it's old, very old. Keep it in your hand if you like. I see you have a feeling for things like that patch box—we assumed it's a patch box. It was given to me by a friend a great many years ago. Sit down, put your feet up, close your eyes. There's nothing more relaxing than to hold something smooth and old and beautiful, and I believe you could do with a little relaxation. I'll be back presently."

Stacy sat down, put her feet on a stool, leaned back and shut her eyes.

She turned the box over and over in her hand. It was oddly cool to the touch. She smelled the incense which drifted toward her on a small breeze from the open windows. She heard Vanessa moving about the kitchen, she heard her speak to Shadow, and heard him answer. She thought: I should go help her; she has no business carrying heavy trays at her age. But she was comfortable and felt boneless. . . .

"Good," said Vanessa, standing over her, tall, thin, the white hair thick and short on her beautifully shaped skull. "You were asleep."

Stacy sat up. She said, "Forgive me, I was coming out to help you and"—she shook her head—"I've no idea why I——"

"You were tired," Vanessa told her, "but you feel better now—and supper's ready."

Stacy rose. She said gravely, "Mrs. Steele, I believe you *are* a witch."

"Sometimes," Vanessa replied. "And sometimes you can just alter the spelling slightly. . . . Mind if Shadow eats with us?"

"Not at all," Stacy said, thinking: Maybe I'm Alice and I've gone through the looking glass.

"He has his own table," Vanessa said. "Sit down. Soufflés wait for no man, and I think you'll like the wine."

❧ 5 ❧

Supper was delicious and whimsical. Vanessa said, as they sat down, "Candles are indicated, of course, but it's far too light, and candle flame is hot, as any intelligent moth will tell you. Personally, I like to see what I'm eating. . . . you'll find it good, I think."

Stacy was acquainted with soufflés and also with wine. But Vanessa's soufflé was exceptional and although the guest had no expertise when it came to vintages—Bob had tried to teach her; he liked to entertain, at home and out —she'd not proved an apt or enthusiastic pupil. However, Vanessa's choice, poured from a beautiful old decanter, was soft and smooth on her palate. There was a salad of exotic fruits in a sharp dressing and, for the sweet, very strong coffee, laced with brandy and crowned with whipped cream.

When Vanessa rose to clear the table, Stacy said firmly, "I'm not going to sit in the corner and drowse. . . . Tell me what to do."

"You were just tired," Vanessa assured her. "Think nothing of it. Now you're restored. I'm the one who should be 'old and gray and full of sleep,' I suppose. But I'm not—yet. Help yourself to a tray from the rack in the kitchen."

Stacy obliged. She said, when she carried it out, "I'm a good dishwasher."

"Of course, but there's no need. I have one, a contemporary affair. Shadow and I don't need it, but now and then I have guests and I don't want them offering assistance or sitting alone contemplating their navels. And when Adam's here with me, he eats at least six meals a day."

When they emerged from the kitchen, Vanessa said, "Put yourself at ease, with your feet up. I always suggest that, and if you show signs of drifting off, I'll stick a pin in you, or Shadow will scratch. Either will achieve results."

Shadow had been listening. When Stacy had made herself comfortable, he approached her, stalking, put out a paw, the claws retracted, and smote her on the shin. Vanessa shrugged. "Just a warning," she told Stacy, "but tantamount to being knighted."

For a short time they talked of Little Oxford and then, somehow, Stacy found herself listening to Vanessa's philosophies. They were plural and drawn from various sources. . . . And then into lively travelogues. Vanessa had most certainly been everywhere and seen everything. She interrupted an account of India to say, "My husband disliked traveling. My son does too, although he's compelled to the beaten airways of business. Adam, now, I think he'll probably hitchhike around the world after graduation—or even before."

Someone came up the front steps, knocked and called, "You there, Van?"

"I didn't hear a car," Vanessa said, "so that will be your demi-landlord, Lee Osborne." She called back, "Door's open."

When Osborne came in, Shadow advanced to meet him

and Vanessa said, "Such Old World manners! When all the lights are on, you know damned well I'm in."

Lee went to her chair, kissed the top of her head and greeted Shadow. "*Ciao*," he said, and Shadow make a remark which was extraordinarily like an echo. "Always thought he had Italian blood," Lee said.

"Another incarnation," Vanessa agreed. "His descendants inhabit the Coliseum. . . . This is Stacy Armitage, Lee."

He went over to take Stacy's hand. "I expected to find you here," he said. "Marcia told me you would be."

"Well," Vanessa remarked, "good of you to come by, if only to observe your tenant."

Stacy said, "Your sister has been more than kind, Mr. Osborne."

"We are," he said gravely, "of good stock, now rather depleted, but we mind our manners."

Vanessa laughed. Lee fished in a pocket, and dropped a twist of tissue paper in her lap. "Just to prove I thought about you while away," he said, "and you know it's my custom to check on you as soon as I return from wherever I've been. So I brought you a trinket."

Vanessa unfolded the paper, and held up something composed of four round blue beads, and a number of oval white ones, from which a small pendant dangled. "Worry beads," she said, with resignation. "I've a drawer full. Besides, I never worry."

"I know—three or four of those banished souvenirs were brought you by me; as for worrying, the day may come. You're an ungrateful, also shortsighted woman, Van."

"Give the beads to Stacy; she worries."

"Do you?" he asked, found a chair and turned his attention to her.

"Sometimes," Stacy admitted, grinning.

"Very well. By the next time I go to Greece, I'll know you well enough to deduce how much, how often, and how seriously. If it's indicated, I'll bring back your beads."

"Should we ask you, 'How was Greece?' " Vanessa inquired.

"Not necessarily, but I'll give you a brief rundown. It's still there; my friends are in good health; I made a few new acquaintances; the weather was perfection and the light, matchless. Also, I had a chance to go to the island of Thera. I've a friend in Athens who knows Professor Marinatos, the archaeologist, who is directing the excavations at Akrotiri—that's near the southern tip of the island. It was an unforgettable experience." He asked, looking at Stacy, "You've been to Greece?"

"No . . . not anywhere exciting, actually."

Bob had promised to take her one day. "Give me five years and we can afford the works," he'd told her. But they hadn't had five years.

"You've plenty of time," Vanessa told her. "Mine's run out, but it was splendid while it lasted. Tell us more about Thera, Lee," she ordered. "All I know about it is what I've read recently. But I'm fond of Greece. I spent two or three memorable months there."

Lee talked; Stacy listened; Vanessa interrupted now and then. Stacy was regarding Lee Osborne with interest. He was unlike his sister, except for the prematurely gray hair; his was almost white, and as Marcia had said, curly. He had blue eyes also, but darker, narrower than Marcia's and obliquely set. He was a lean, compact man, not much taller than Vanessa and he was deeply tanned. The contrast between the young brown face and the startling silver hair was striking. His voice was deep, his words unhurried, and his enthusiasm as controlled as his slight gestures.

Vanessa spoke suddenly to Stacy. She said, "I doubt you've heard a word—so have you made up your mind whether you like him or not?"

Stacy was startled into honesty. "No," she said, and appalled, fell silent.

Vanessa chuckled and Lee Osborne laughed. "No, you don't like me, or no, you haven't made up your mind?" he asked.

"No, I haven't made up my mind," Stacy responded, recovering.

"How long will it take you?" he inquired.

"I haven't the least idea."

"Candid," said Vanessa with approval. "Also you must make allowances for temperament, Lee. She's an artist. You should understand that, since you are too, even when you're building structures you despise."

"I don't despise anything I build," he told her. "It's my profession and also a living. So far I haven't found anyone who wants Greek revivals."

Stacy looked at her watch. "It's time I went back to the studio," she told Vanessa. "I have to work tomorrow. It's been a wonderful evening."

Lee rose. He said, "I'll walk her home, Van, and I'll see you soon. I've missed you. I always suspected you'd be an almost, if not quite, perfect traveling companion, however difficult."

"Thirty, forty years ago," Vanessa said, sighing, "I would have been incomparable, but you were born too late or I, too early. . . . I'll stop by one day, Stacy, and see if you've made up your mind about him. If you have your phone by then, I'll call him and tell him the verdict. I never keep secrets, being a generous person."

Shadow took them to the door, said *"Ciao"* again and went back into the house. Stacy and Lee went out into the cooling evening. The stars were crowded into the darkened sky and Stacy said, "I hadn't the least idea that it was so late. Too fascinated, I guess."

"By Vanessa, of course. She has that effect on everyone."

"You're fond of her?"

"Very." He added, walking unhurriedly. "It's always so strange to return. This is another world."

"And you like the ancient one better?"

"No—but it draws me, it always has—not just Greece, of course—since the first time I went to Europe. . . . Are you comfortable in the studio?" he asked. "I noticed you didn't say you were going home."

"Very. . . . It isn't home yet, of course, but I hope it will be."

"I too," he said courteously.

She thought: It won't be. She felt emotionally stateless, without roots. No place like home. That was it exactly, if in a different interpretation. Not in California or New York, and not, after the unthinking years, Chicago. So why Little Oxford?

When they reached the studio door, she asked, "Won't you come in, Mr. Osborne?"

"Thank you, no. I'm not even unpacked, but unless I see Vanessa within a few hours of my arrival, she ignores me for weeks. She's like the guy in the TV commercials—demanding. You'll find that out and get used to it." He added, "You forgot to turn on the lights."

"So I did. Wait a moment." She took her key from the little purse, unlocked the door, went in and touched a switch which illuminated the carriage lamps over the door and the flagstones. "There," she said, smiling.

"Turn on a light in the studio," he directed. "You know, there was once a time in this village when nobody locked a door."

They looked at each other and he said, "Well, good night, Stacy," and she thought: What a very odd town! I expected New Englanders to unbend by degrees. And he said, "By now you surely know we're on first-name terms here."

"But New Englanders . . ." she began.

"Half the people in the village are transplants." He added, "It's pleasant having you as a neighbor," and was off, walking without haste toward his own house.

Stacy having put on one studio light, went in and sat down, remembering what Vanessa had told her: Lee Osborne was a charmer. She reflected soberly that he probably was. But he doesn't charm me, she thought. Quite the contrary. He was too controlled and remote and it seemed to her that there was a strange, subdued, but hard, glitter about him, like an aura. Vanessa probably knows all about auras, Stacy thought, but I certainly won't ask her about Lee Osborne.

She couldn't deny that he was attractive, but, she thought, he's almost inhuman, like one of those science-fiction invaders from outer space you see on the TV screen, or read about. How different from his outgoing sister.

She rose, went into the kitchen to fill a thermos with cold water, went to bed and almost instantly fell dreamlessly asleep.

On the next day before noon, Marcia turned up. She said, "I'm on my way to the village. Need anything?"

"No thanks," said Stacy. "I'm well stocked."

"If this heat wave doesn't end soon, I'll kill myself,"

Marcia told her. "It doesn't seem to bother Lee, fresh from sun, sand and water. Are you free to come for drinks on the terrace this evening, about six? Lee has a dinner date and I have to go to a Guild meeting, but do come for an hour or so. Don't dress—just drag yourself over, and cool off."

"But isn't it too soon? Mr. Osborne just came home."

"He suggested it," Marcia said. "He told me he liked you, but that you didn't like him. He wants to know why."

"Oh, for heaven's sake!" Stacy said, exasperated. "Vanessa asked me whether I'd made up my mind about him or not, and I said 'No.' "

"Yes, he told me that too." Marcia wandered over to look at the painting on the easel. "Van does things like that deliberately. She tries to trick people. Pay no attention to her. We don't. . . . Do come over."

Marcia had a most appealing smile, candid as a small child's, and Stacy said, "You twisted my arm. All right. Six o'clock, Mrs. Boyd?"

"Good. Lee will spend most of the afternoon tramping over the Palmer property with Katie and Jeremy, but he'll be back in time to change and sit awhile before he has to go out again. . . . I do wish you'd call me Marcia, you make me feel a hundred years old."

Stacy said hesitantly, "Perhaps I can explain to your brother that I simply can't make up my mind about people on first sight—Marcia."

No. Never before Bob, or since. But she'd known Bob for approximately three months before she was in love— quite hopelessly, she'd thought for some time.

"Lee takes a lot of knowing," Marcia said thoughtfully. "Yet he didn't, as a kid, and you're smarter than I. I'm crazy about people or I hate 'em. Instant reaction. Then

I spend months trying to figure out why and if it's been a mistake, which it often is." She smiled at Stacy. "See you at six," she said. She went out, got into her car and, almost literally, buzzed off.

A very nice woman, Marcia Boyd. Stacy had made her mind up about Marcia when they signed the lease; she'd met her briefly prior to that. And by now the Irvingtons and the Palmers were no longer strangers. It hadn't taken long to decide about Vanessa; she'd decided last night. Vanessa was somewhat fey and unpredictable perhaps, but Stacy was aware of a hard core of common sense and strength. She also felt that Vanessa was lonely; possibly this accounted for her shock tactics. She was in no way terrified of Vanessa, but frankly, Lee Osborne made her uneasy, she admitted. He seemed, she thought further, like a man in hiding.

When she walked over to the Osborne house at six, the sun was still blazing gold on the grass and trees, but there were lazy clouds, altering shapes, drifting across the blue. Perhaps, she thought hopefully, they held beneficent rain. Stacy liked clouds; a cloudless sky was not interesting. She also liked trees in winter, their bare branches making patterns against the gray or blue of the heavens.

Approaching the big house, she heard voices coming from the back, clear on the still air. She and Katie had been to the house for coffee after the signing. It was big and many-windowed, with a Victorian front veranda; and there were a great many trees, old bushes and flower borders. Beyond the terrace for which she was headed were the gardens in which Marcia, with the help of a part-time gardener, worked constantly. The scent of late-blooming roses seduced Stacy's senses; Marcia grew all kinds of roses, particularly old ones; the moss rose was her favorite.

As Stacy walked around the house to the flagstone terrace, Marcia and Lee came to meet her. He looked tired,
Stacy thought, and Marcia said briskly, "Come, collapse.
Lee has; he's been on the Palmer safari and I daresay
they've walked or crawled every foot of the precious
two acres a dozen times. I hope it's all right for
Katie."

"Katie," said Lee, "is like a sturdy bloodhound. . . . Why
don't you sit here, Stacy, in the chaise, under the umbrella? And what will you have to drink?"

"Nothing alcoholic, please," Stacy answered. "It's too
hot."

"Iced tea—coffee—soft drink?" Marcia inquired.

"Iced coffee, please."

Lee went to the back veranda where the ice bucket,
glasses and bottles stood on a cart and came back with her
tall, cold glass and a plate of cookies. Stacy shook her head.
"I'm still replete," she said. "Mrs. Steele—Vanessa—is a
superlative cook."

"Wait till she introduces you to some of her more fantastic recipes," Lee warned. "Half the time you don't
know what you're eating and you don't dare ask."

He talked about the Palmers and the house he was to
design for them. "Jeremy's easy," he said, "but Katie's a
mind changer." He looked over at Stacy and smiled
slightly. "One minute, it's to be on one floor—very contemporary; the next, split level, also contemporary—lots
of glass and sun decks, a sort of miniature Niles house.
. . . You've seen that?"

"I was there for lunch Sunday."

"Well, it's a good house if I may say so reluctantly."

"You were the architect?"

"All of us, really. I'd just come into the firm. I don't

approve of it, but it's good in its way; it won a number of awards. Jeremy," he added, "would really like a simple colonial—perfectly suitable for the setting, and certainly most habitable. But not Katie. She told me today she thought a Japanese house would be wonderful. I'll try to keep her to the split level."

Later Marcia said, "The weekend after next—over Labor Day, the Hardens are coming. Remember, I told you we were to meet old friends in New York when Lee flew in. On that Monday, we're having a small dinner party and we'd like you to come, Stacy. Just the Hardens, us and you—and, I think Fred Arnold. I don't know if you've met him or not."

"Yes, at the Irvingtons'," said Stacy.

She thought dismally: The unattached woman for whom the hostess has to scurry around to find the unattached man.

"Why not Remsen Lovemay?" her brother asked. "Stacy would enjoy him."

"I do," Stacy said, but Marcia shook her head. "He's a darling, but he goes out very little. He's quite frail, Lee."

"Then we'll settle for Fred; he's harmless," agreed Lee carelessly.

"I'd ask Vanessa," Marcia told them, "and Si Wescott —his wife's away—but Vanessa wouldn't come."

"Why not?" asked Stacy. "You're such good friends."

"She can't stand Elaine Harden. And when Vanessa goes out, she doesn't like competition."

"I wouldn't think she'd ever have any."

"No one," said Marcia firmly, "looks at anyone but Elaine."

"What about listening?" Stacy inquired.

Lee gave her a strange, sidelong look. He said lightly, "Who cares about listening when you can look?"

Marcia frowned at him, "You're making Elaine sound mysterious; she isn't. She's just extraordinarily beautiful. She's a distant cousin, Stacy," Marcia explained, "born and brought up in Washington, D.C. She used to spend her summers with us. She's younger than I and a year older than Lee. About ten years ago she married Gerald Harden, a San Franciscan."

"Stacy will think he's a monk," Lee murmured.

"Far from it. He was born in San Francisco; his business takes them all over the world. When they come east, we see them. This time, they're driving through New England and into Canada where he has a business meeting. You'll like them, I hope. Gerald's a very good sort."

"Gerald," said Lee, "is just an industrial giant."

"As for Elaine," Marcia went on ignoring him, "you'll want to paint her."

"Everyone has," Lee remarked.

Stacy said, "I'm not a portrait painter, Marcia."

"You," said Lee, "are a painter of dreams. . . . Katie told me . . . fantasy . . . Gothic. . . ."

"Stacy does beautiful work," Marcia said, "and she simply must have an exhibit. We'll get Rosie Niles on it, and you can help, Lee," she told him.

"I—well," said Stacy helplessly. "I hadn't considered— and I've been in Little Oxford so short a time—it seems like about twenty minutes."

"Spring's the time," Lee said, "for exhibits."

"I wish it were spring now," Marcia told them. "So does Elaine. She said she'd give anything to be here in spring or early summer."

"Certain seasons," said Lee, "are becoming to her."

Stacy looked at him. His face was closed against all expression, like a fist. But she was aware of the friction between him and his sister. Walking home, she thought: I wonder what Vanessa doesn't like about this woman, and why Lee and Marcia are so hostile? He doesn't want these people to come here, that's plain. But why?

A faint interest stirred in her and she found herself looking forward to Labor Day weekend.

⚝ 6 ⚝

Stacy's telephone was installed that week and she called Amy, who said, "Well, it's about time," and added distractedly, "Hang on. I think Benjy's swallowed a button. . . . Call you back."

She did so, saying, "I didn't ask your number, had to get information——"

"What about Benjy?"

"Found the button; one off Ben's plaid jacket—I really must take up sewing again—anyway, it was on the floor. I spend my time thinking Benjy's swallowed something besides his frequent meals. He eats like a horse. . . . Look, Stacy, last night Grandpa Lovemay said he wanted to bicycle over and see your work, but it's still so hot. I promised to take Benjy to the senior Irvingtons this afternoon. Letty's having a few female friends in for tea and wants to show how he's grown and how much he looks like her side of the family, also Bing's. Suppose I throw him in at the door early and leave him there to be cackled over—he's a ham; he loves it—and take his great-grandpa to see you—about three, maybe? How does that grab you? Or doesn't it?"

Stacy said it did, so Amy and Remsen Lovemay arrived a little after three. He said, "My dear, I hope it wasn't too short notice—I reminded Amy that you might be working." He shook his white head, "I'm a little out of breath," he admitted. "Amy drove with her usual skillful abandon."

"I wasn't working, and I'm glad to see you," Stacy told him. "Shall we make the tour—that is, if you feel up to it. You may need all your strength." She showed him the completed painting on the easel and the unframed pictures, which she had put out on one of the couches, a big table and some chairs.

"Someday I'll get around to the framer's," she said. "Meantime they're gathering dust. Here's a portfolio of sketches . . . most of the others are not for anything especially."

Lovemay was looking, as was Amy. "You haven't shown me these before," she said, "just the book-jacket sketches. Do you realize I'd never seen anything much of yours until you moved here? Just some of the book designs when we were slaving in Grandpop's former factory? It's all fabulous, Stacy."

"You mean fantastic," Stacy corrected her. "All this Gothic business, castles in fogs, boiling seascapes, vague figures drifting around in sinister settings, haunted gardens with menacing trees and weird flower faces."

"Imagination," Lovemay said, "sensitivity. You're very good, Stacy."

Amy said, "Personally, I'm a natural wide-eyed happy-hearted chick, so I wouldn't want any of this around, except on dust jackets, but I've been looking at the sketches for the children's books. I'd love to have some originals—or if you don't have them, the sketches—to frame for Benjy's bedroom. I'll save what's left over from the household money, if ever we get to a place where we can save. . . . I'm crazy about these pandas and koalas and that magic mushroom circle is something else."

Amy declined tea, saying, "Letty would kill me. Pearl's made an angel cake. You give Great-gramp a cup and then I'll whisk him away."

Lovemay said, drinking his tea, "I'm not your great-grandfather, Amy, just Benjy's."

"Well, of course. I get confused, dear—so when it comes to the seniors, I settle for Letty and Bing, and they like it. I'd better just skip the grandparent and great-grandparent bit."

"You won't have to explain me to Benjy yet," he consoled her. "He's a sensible infant; just says 'Hi' to anyone. . . . Stacy, do you go into the city often?"

"I've been here less than—what is it—three months?" she reminded him, "and I daresay I'll never go except to make the publishing-house rounds, but I do have to see Jim Swift at Lovemay's, soon."

"How about next Monday?" he asked. "I have to go in for a director's meeting and they're sending a car for me. Would you care to come along and hold my hand en route? Director's meetings—seldom as they occur—have begun to scare me. Actually, I just have to make an appearance now and then, like a smiling but silent ghost. Those bright young men and women terrify me."

"I'd like to go," she said, "especially to hold your hand, and it would be a lifesaver. Driving out here was bad enough, but the thought of driving into town gives me the megrims. Also I'm not enthralled by the idea of trains, particularly during commuting hours."

Therefore on Monday, Remsen Lovemay called for her in an impressive, air-conditioned limousine driven by a uniformed chauffeur and before they reached the office building, he said, "I'll just about make my eleven-o'clock appointment. . . . After the meeting I'm taking the few people I still know to lunch. Can you amuse yourself?"

"Of course. . . . Jim offered me lunch, Mr. Lovemay."

"Good—that is, I hope it will be. I'll have us picked up at, say, three. I'll meet you in the lobby and we'll head out before the traffic gets really rough."

"It's a deal," she said, smiling.

Jim Swift was waiting for her in his office. He said, "I canceled a dull date when you telephoned. I'm glad to see you, Stacy. Lemme see what you've brought me."

He approved of the painting and the sketches for the next jacket; they talked for a time and he gave her two manuscripts to take back with her. "Leave them here," he said, "till we get back."

"I'm meeting Mr. Lovemay in the lobby at three," she said, "so I'd better take them with me now, Jim."

At lunch, he said, "You look very well, Stacy. Village life must agree with you."

"Well, it's not exactly Mrs. Gaskill's village, but it will serve," she told him.

"Are you happy there?"

"So far, I like it very much. . . . This Egg Benedict dish is marvelous. I must really try to do some inspired cooking again."

She was a good-enough cook when she married, but a better one before her marriage was dissolved. Bob fancied himself a gourmet.

"Nice landlord?"

"Two—one male, one female. They're very amiable, and live next door, if not within shouting distance; they have a good-sized property. He's an architect. The studio I rent was built for him and it's exactly what I wanted— neighbors, but also privacy. Next door Lee Osborne and his widowed sister, and around the corner a woman named Vanessa Steele, who is completely incredible, but I like her."

"Not really Vanessa Steele!" Jim said, raising his eyebrows. "I don't believe it."

"You know her?"

"Not I—my father did. My mother used to twit him about it. I gathered he was one of Mrs. Steele's unsuccessful followers. The woman's a legend. She crops up in fiction now and then, not too well disguised. I'd heard she'd returned to the States to live, but had no idea where. Is she still beautiful?"

"No, yet the basics are there. Incidentally, she has a cat I yearn to paint. . . . Any kitty-cat books coming along?"

"Could be. Lois Winchester writes cat-and-kitten books sometimes. Actually she hates cats and has none, but she decided years ago that dogs and wild animals have been overexposed. So she writes about adorable playful kittens and their mamas and papas—always legal by the way, no out-on-the-tiles business."

Stacy sighed. "Shadow would never sit for her hero. He just ain't a cozy cat."

"Stacy," Jim said over coffee, "I'm afraid I may have done something you won't like."

"You couldn't possibly, unless you offer me a rejection, which you'd do so pleasantly I'd hardly know it was one."

"It's about Bob. He telephoned from Chicago recently —he and his wife are coming east in the autumn, when the foliage starts to turn, on a tour of Canada and New England, I believe. He said—we were pretty good friends once—that if Joyce and I were around at the time, he wanted us to have dinner with them somewhere—in the country perhaps. Well, that's quite a long way off."

"Not too far," she said. "It will be Labor Day first thing you know and the fall foliage starts in eastern Canada earlier than here."

"Well, he asked if I'd seen you. I said yes, and then he

asked where you were living. Seems someone told him you'd left the city but not where you'd gone. So I told him, without thinking."

"He likes to be considered what he calls 'civilized,' and I quote," Stacy said steadily.

"He could have asked your lawyer."

"He made a settlement, Jim, and after that there was no need for communication between our lawyers."

"I'm sorry, Stacy," he said miserably, having watched her face tighten and her color fade.

"It's all right, Jim. I doubt they'll get to Little Oxford. The most that can happen will be that he might telephone."

It wasn't all right. One reason—perhaps the only reason—why she had moved was because twice she had seen Bob Armitage walking ahead of her, briskly and alone, on Madison Avenue with the quick long stride she remembered. And once he had telephoned to say that he and his wife were in town and would she come dine with them. When she'd said no, he'd remarked that he'd hoped she'd become civilized. "I'd like to see you, Stacy," he told her, "and Winnie would too. She liked you very much."

Stacy had thought: Yes indeed, she must have been crazy about me.

"Don't worry, Jim," she said, "a lot can happen before the leaves turn."

"I wish to God you'd get over whatever it is you aren't getting over."

"So do I," she answered after a moment. Stacy met Remsen Lovemay as arranged; the car was there within a few minutes and they drove back to Little Oxford.

"How was your lunch?" he asked her.

Stacy said, "Fine, if too much—but the air conditioning was like a deep freeze. Do you know," she added, "even after such a short time away from the city I found myself confused and uncomfortable—heat, hurry, all those people. . . ."

"I know. When my wife and I went to France to live, the quiet of the countryside kept me awake . . . not that we had lived in town, we didn't; but I had to work there, and she went into the city frequently. Was your business talk with Jim Swift—I remember him; a nice man, and gifted—satisfactory?"

"Very, and I have a hurry-up job—also a jacket. The man who was to do it is ill; they kept waiting for him to recover, but, unfortunately for him, it's going to be a long hospitalization. So I'm to do it. I've brought the manuscript with me, and Jim's notes relating to it."

"Fantasy?" he asked, smiling.

"No, a romantic novel, and contemporary. . . . How was your meeting?"

"Pleasant, occasionally argumentative. I just listened. I'm afraid I disapprove of much of the Lovemay list, but I'd simply be a shaking voice crying in the wilderness of permissiveness, pornography—though no one has really defined what that is. Anyway, it's all progress, or so they tell me."

"We," said Stacy gravely, "are a couple of old fogeys, you and I."

"Definitely square," he agreed.

"Do you think this heat wave will ever end?" asked Stacy, sighing.

"It always has," he assured her. "I remember years ago, ten days or more culminated in the hottest Labor Day weekend I'd ever experienced, but on the last night of that weekend the temperature dropped almost thirty degrees to the discomfort of residents, guests and tourists, who had been dragging themselves around—there was an open-air concert, I recall—in what was, in those days, considered daring undress. Cynthia and I had house guests, but it wasn't until the next morning we discovered that the summer blankets had been pulled up and even bath mats resorted to in the middle of the night."

When they reached the studio, Stacy told him, "I'm most grateful. I don't think I could have endured the train."

"It was my pleasure," Remsen Lovemay said, "and if you have to go to the city again, maybe I can manage a car for you. The present firm humors its former president. I find that, nowadays, being very young or very old has peculiar rewards."

During the time between then and Labor Day Stacy was busy; her first consideration was the dust jacket. "She's one of the last of the romance writers," Jim had said of the author, "contemporary, to a certain degree; she hasn't lost touch with current reality, but she's gentle, decent and rather charming, and believes in the happy ending. When I discussed this with Bill Folger—you never knew him, did you? He's a good artist—I suggested landscape, flowers, that sort of thing; effective if not blinding. Mrs. Hammond doesn't need a shock-treatment jacket for her books. She has a following and her name is really sufficient."

So Stacy painted for Mrs. Hammond—her name above the title which was "Midsummer Magic"—a blue sky with drifting clouds, a sweep of meadow, an old stone wall. It looked rather like Vanessa's meadow and wall, but on the wall and in the foreground, over a picket fence, there were roses—white, pale yellow, deep pink and a startlement of red.

She telephoned Jim as he'd asked; he sent a messenger out by train, and called her within a day and told her, "It's fine Stacy. Thanks very much."

She saw people infrequently during that period. Amy once, and one afternoon Katie coaxed her out to look at what she called The Estate. Lee Osborne was there, talking to a contractor. And one day, just before the weekend, Stacy heard a scratching at the door, went to it and regarded Shadow. *"Ciao,"* he said cheerfully.

"What in the world are you doing off your leash?" she demanded, but he stalked past her into the studio, jumped from love seat to love seat, then sat on the hearth and contemplated a corner of the room with unnerving fixity. Stacy, seizing a pad and charcoal, began to sketch him as he sat, prowled or jumped. Then Vanessa knocked on the door crying, "Stacy, have you seen Shadow?"

"He's here," said Stacy, and Shadow looked at her with reproach.

Vanessa came in. She said, "I was about to take him for a walk. We were going Lossing Lane way; I had the leash because of that damned dog. Then suddenly, while I wasn't looking, Shadow vanished."

"Does he do it often?"

"Oh, yes. I let him go by himself to the meadow and actually I don't worry about his coming your way. No dogs. Shadow, apologize to Stacy. You weren't invited!"

"He's welcome any time," Stacy said, and displayed the sketches. "I've been dying to draw him—paint him, eventually. Do you mind?"

"Of course not, although he'll get a very swelled head; not that it isn't out of proportion now. But he's never still for long except when he's at home."

"I like him in action."

"Very well. Since he's adopted you, he can come and go as he pleases, if in this direction. Are you celebrating Labor Day? These long holidays are an affliction."

"I'm celebrating having had and fulfilled a rush order," Stacy told her.

"Good, but I meant socially."

"Just dinner at Marcia and Lee's. They are having guests . . . people named Harden."

Vanessa said shortly, "He's not a bad type. She makes my skin crawl."

"Why?"

"Too beautiful."

"But that's not possible!"

"In her case, it is."

"You weren't going to say beautiful and dumb, were you?"

"No. That cliché went out before you were born. Dumb, she isn't. Mute in a way, but it's of her own choosing. Back of that lovely brow there's a busy little brain," Vanessa said. "You'll see. Or maybe you won't," she added thoughtfully. "Artists are, I assume, concerned mainly with outward appearances; not many have tried to paint the inner man or woman. Oh, some—the greats of all ages, I suppose, but in my era a portrait painter, for example, particularly those specializing in females, who tried to capture what was beneath the fine skin and bones was not commercially successful, save for a very few whose names commanded big prices and hence respect."

She rose. "Tell me what you think of Elaine Harden," she suggested. "I'll drop by after Labor Day . . . Shadow too. Come along, Wretch," she said severely. The leash was in her hand, but she did not attempt to put it on his collar. "One of these days you'll give me a heart attack," she told him, "but perhaps that's been your ambition all along. You could then return to whatever jungle you sprang from and live to be thirty surrounded by your bastard brood."

She added unnecessarily, "I never had him altered, you know, which means a lot of policing on my part. For years a great many cats in the neighborhood have borne some resemblance to my dissolute friend."

On Friday, Katie telephoned her. "Unscheduled al fresco, mainly boughten, picnic in the backyard," she said. "People will drift in. That's Sunday, six on. Jeremy would like to relax, of course, with company. I asked Lee and Marcia, but they have guests, and had made plans. The contractor's coming with the wife and kids; also the people next door. You remember Frank and Olive and the terrible twins? Fred Arnold's coming too."

Stacy was inclined to refuse. She had that odd, half-resentful, half-guilty feeling one sometimes suffers when it seems that people are going too far out of their way to be kind. She thought: I can't repay all this. I hate giving parties.

Bob had enjoyed giving parties; at first she hadn't minded. He was her husband, her lover and teacher, her mentor as well, and to please him was of great importance. Small gatherings were good for business, he said; those in their own home, better than the bigger bashes which had to be thrown now and then at a hotel or supper club and at which actually one's wife felt like a nominal hostess. After about two years Stacy realized that the intimate, fairly expensive home parties not only brought in business but kept Bob busy, smiling and happy. Later, looking back, wincing, touching the lesser sore spots, she'd realized that after the first year he had not been amused or content to be alone with her, at least not for long. After a week of evenings together, he'd say, "Let's ask the Smiths and the Joneses—or whomever—to dinner next week. We haven't seen them in a long time."

Well, better to go to Katie's and endure Fred Arnold's rather reproachful, and open, admiration—he'd asked her to go out with him several times since they'd met; as yet, she had refused—than to sit at home looking at the studio walls afraid to sleep . . . perchance to dream.

Fred Arnold telephoned Saturday. "Understand you're going to the Palmers' tomorrow," he said. "I'll pick you up."

"Thanks," said Stacy, "but I'd rather not. I don't know exactly when I'll be able to get there." She added mendaciously, "Nor how long I can stay. I expect friends from New York to stop by—time indefinite."

"You're quicker with an excuse than my eighteen-year-old son," he commented. "Okay, see you—on Monday too."

She'd forgotten that he was to be at the party for the Hardens.

If persistence was the key to success, Fred Arnold possessed it. No pressure, no painting the opponent into a corner, simply the erosion method and an attitude of patience, even cheerfulness, but a gleam in the eye which could not, it seemed, be quenched.

On Saturday afternoon a motorcycle came roaring up the driveway and stopped. Stacy was working, and the noise and unexpectedness annoyed her. A salesman? What salesman would employ this form of transportation, unless perhaps, he was selling the vehicles and so arrived at one's door on a sample?

The doorbell. She muttered, went to the door, opened it and looked at a tall, lean boy, who, snatching off his helmet, said, "I'm Vanessa Steele's grandson. May I come in?"

"You're Adam," Stacy said.

"Not anyway Eve," said her gentleman caller. He looked around and added, "Gran said the studio had improved since you moved in." He added, "You'd improve most anyplace."

Stacy smiled. She said, "Sit down. . . . Are you here for long?"

"Not long enough. I have to get back to the expensive brain washing."

"You look like your grandmother."

"Sure. I don't look like my father or mother. I suppose it's essential to look like someone—all those genes and stuff."

"How about iced tea or coffee or Coke? It's too early for anything stronger."

Adam shook his head. His hair was very dark, curled slightly, and he wore it in a compromise, neither long nor short. He also wore jeans and a mind-boggling shirt. His eyes were the color of Vanessa's, his rather long face as brown as hers, his nose almost a replica, but the mouth and jaw were his own.

"Thanks," he said, "when I get to Gran's, she'll feed and water me. She gets upset if I don't eat my weight—after all, I'm still a growing boy."

"Does she know you're coming?"

"Of course not," he answered, mildly astonished. "I just arrive. She likes surprises. May I look around some more?"

"Be my guest."

He wandered about, slouching a little, whistling now and then. "She wrote me you had talent," he told her, "but wow—you're really something else. Also, she said you were, and I quote, 'more than pretty.' An understatement."

"Well, thanks."

"I'm hung up on older women," he told her gravely. "My current chick is a graduate student."

Stacy laughed. She said, "You're not exactly as I'd thought."

73

"Gran feels that way too," he informed her. "Before I was even through high school she was hollering about long hair, pot, girls." He shrugged. "When I got into college—God knows how, also why—she was convinced I'd be smoking something exotic in a water pipe, growing my hair to my waist, shacking up with every female—or maybe male," he added carelessly, "within miles. A lot of that exhibitionism went out a while back. I even wear a collar and tie when it's called for. I expect to join the system, via my father, when the time comes. In between I'll do a little horsing around, when I can con the bread out of him. Travel—that's it, summers and after graduation."

"From what your grandmother has told me about herself you inherit that urge."

"My parents," said Adam, "go to Florida now and then, or take a cruise, or even make the scene—or so they think —in Europe. First-class of course; suites, the best restaurants, the compulsive sightseeing." He shook his head. "The works, packaged. Gran, now . . . she's been an adult delinquent ever since she married my grandfather, I think." He added, turning his brilliant regard upon Stacy, "You would have disliked him intensely. Gran did, anyway. . . . Look, I stopped by before a formal meeting— don't tell her, will you? It's more fun for her if there's a presentation—to ask you to look after her."

Stacy said, startled, "I've never met anyone more capable of looking after herself, Adam."

"That's what she thinks. I worry about her. Alone in that demented house, except for that incredible cat."

"You don't like Shadow?"

"I can take him or leave him; he sort of likes me, I think, which is fine. If Shadow approves, your stock goes up. But really, Stacy," he added without apology for the use of her given name, "Gran's a real nut, if not certifiable . . . slightly on the weird side. My father pulls out what's left of his hair when he discusses her and my mother cries. They even added an apartment for her to their Westchester mansion—it's early Shirley Temple, you know—but she wasn't having any. Of course if she even decided to live with us, my parents would find themselves climbing the walls. But they're short on imagination and long on duty. So, keep a sharp eye out. . . . Naturally Gran's subsided in the last ten or more years, but I have a feeling she could break out, like measles, any minute. So, I worry." He grinned. "That's a switch. She no longer worries about me—I worry about her. I wish to God she'd have a phone. But she won't. . . . Well, thanks; be seeing you."

Stacy went with him to the door. She said, "I'll do my best, Adam, I promise."

He seized her in his strong young arms and planted a kiss upon her forehead. "You'll do," he said, released her, leaped on his waiting monster and went off, emitting sound and fury.

Stacy went back to work. She was smiling. She thought: Vanessa will never need my help—or anyone else's—unless she's ill. I hope she knows how lucky she is. That kid, she thought fondly, feeling extraordinarily old, really cares about her.

7

Stacy arrived in the Palmers' shared backyard around seven, and left before ten. She explained to Katie, her hostess, "Little Oxford's social life is beginning to catch up with me, and I have to be out again tomorrow night."

"Where?"

"Next door. Marcia and Lee, to meet their guests."

"Find out if they're in the market for a house—tactfully, of course. Just ask carelessly, 'Have you a place to live . . . healthy, charming, in a growing community with good neighbors, where there's still land to buy and room to build, or, delightful ready-made surroundings? Commuting too.' "

Jeremy spoke from the depths of a dilapidated chair. "My wife, the realtor," he said. "I expect that on the delivery table she'll be bugging the doctors and nurses."

"Perhaps you'd rather I sold them a couple of books on what to do with your newborn child? Incidentally, you haven't brought home any information on the subject. As I slowly cease to harass prospective clients, I'll have to do something; the radio won't take up all the slack and daytime TV scares me."

"You can get your information from Ben," advised her husband. "Maybe you can persuade him to write a book."

The next-door twins appeared on their own back porch with a guitar and an accordion and Katie said, "Ordinarily, I can't wait until our own house is built, but I often wonder how much I'll miss Baker Street, including the twins and Lancelot. Incidentally, I think he's growing bigger," she said and reached to touch the head of the twins' large and friendly dog.

Stacy, eating, drinking, talking, was aware that in her private mind she was reflecting upon the generations. Now and then she permitted a thought to surface. She said to Amy who, with Benjy but without his father, was briefly present, "I met Vanessa's grandson this afternoon."

"Did she bring him—Exhibit A? She dotes on that boy, or so Ben tells me."

"No, he came alone, on his way to see her. I'm sworn to secrecy; he wants her to have the pleasure of introducing him."

"Some secrecy," said Katie.

"Forget I said it. . . . He's a nice boy," Stacy remarked.

"Does that surprise you?"

"In a way, yes." She thought: Maybe grandchildren are more satisfactory than children even in this era. I suppose you suffer with and for them, but you don't have the responsibility. No one in the group around her was likely to have grandchildren for a very long time—well, Olive and Frank, if the teenage twins decided upon early marriages—and in order to have grandchildren, it was necessary that you first have children.

She made her apologetic escape and went home to read awhile, watch the eleven-o'clock news, and go to bed with her radio on. She thought: After tomorrow, I'm not accepting invitations—not, that is, where there'll be lots of people. All of her friends, from adolescence on, had

77

counted the day lost which didn't see them at a movie, a hamburger joint, an ice-cream parlor, or in cars. School nights were as painful to them as a broken arm; Fridays and Saturdays, as beautiful as an escape from a dungeon.

Freedom, that was the operative word. Stacy had all the freedom in the world; nothing could limit it except the practical boundaries of income and work. So what was she doing with it?

Amy had once suggested that if time ever hung heavy on her hands, she could do volunteer work at the hospital and Stacy had repudiated the idea with some violence. She hated hospitals. They frightened and depressed her; besides, she was useless in illness.

"I'm not asking you to become Miss Nightingale, but you're a free-lance artist——"

"I have deadlines."

"Oh, I know, but you can arrange your own working hours more or less. There are lots of community projects —environmental problems, today's kids and senior citizens."

No, these very admirable efforts to clean up air and water, alleviate pain and boredom, grapple with the difficulties of old and young were not, as she assumed Adam would say, her bag. All Stacy had wanted until her early twenties was to develop what talent she had and after that to be married to Bob, have children, and work when she could. That, for her, was the fulfilled life; home, husband, children and the exercise of talent.

Katie had once spoken to her about a Women's Liberation group, now voluble in Little Oxford and Stacy had looked at her in astonishment. "Do you feel unliberated?" she'd asked.

Katie had laughed. "Only occasionally. I have a job and anyone less tied to the kitchen you've never known."

"Only because Jeremy's a good cook."

"And so neat it sometimes sets my teeth on edge. However, I was lucky, I picked the right man—for me, that is. How about politics?"

"What about politics?"

"I belong to the League of Women Voters——" began Katie.

But Stacy shook her head. "I don't understand politics," she said firmly.

"Perhaps you could learn. . . . No? . . . I give up," Katie had said after a moment. "Incidentally, I suppose I'll feel constantly unliberated if ever I have this baby. I doubt if Jeremy will take on child care, or if so, not often. . . . What do you want from life, Stacy?"

And Stacy had answered, "To be free, I suppose, but in my own way . . . to work, also in my own way; to have good friends, like you and Amy."

"And to be let alone?"

"Not entirely," Stacy said, smiling, her face suddenly and vividly illuminated.

On that particular night Katie had said to her husband, "What a waste!"

"Waste?"

"Stacy. I can't get her interested in anything. I've tried. So has Amy."

He'd said gently, "She's been badly hurt, I think, and her instinct is to creep away and lick her wounds. All her friends can do for her is stand by."

On this Sunday night Stacy, listening to her FM, was thinking of Katie Palmer saying, "Your friend and neighbor, Lee Osborne, is next to impossible. No matter what I suggest for our house he vetoes it—and Jeremy backs him up. Men!"

"What's wrong with your suggestions?" Stacy had inquired.

"Oh, they're either impractical, unheard of or too expensive. And I suppose," she'd added gloomily, "that he's right. But it maddens me. He always explains in simple terms so that even a retarded child like myself can grasp his objections. He knows all about plans, blueprints, closet space, kitchen appliances, dirt, air, shade or sun. . . . He knows all about building, and the people who do it. He's very upsetting . . . and just about the best there is around here. He and Jeremy spend hours in discussion and I either tramp around my myself, or sit in his office, or at Baker Street totally ignored. And I have to live in that house too."

"You'll like it," Stacy had assured her.

Recalling tonight's conversation and those which had preceded it, she thought: Perhaps I was born too late. This is certainly the generation of the doers. After the baby's born and is old enough to leave with proper help, Katie will go back to work full time. She and Jeremy will have added responsibility—the child, the house. Amy's already saying that by next year she'll be able to leave Benjy with a suitable baby sitter and go back to the hospital to do whatever she can—secretarial work, coffee shop, anything, on a volunteer basis—to help out. They're so short-handed. I can't blame her or Katie; they're young, they're alive, they find time somehow to be useful. . . .

She envied them.

Suppose Amy had married Bob?

She wouldn't have; she'd have seen through him before that or if she had married him, she'd have left him in less than a year, Stacy thought. But she didn't marry Bob; she married Ben, a man whose life she can share. I married Bob, for better or worse. So it was worse.

As she often did, she thought of talking to a doctor— Ben, or his father, or both. Perhaps they could tell her why. Oh, the classic pattern was there; even she could see it: a rather introverted child with a so-called father image and a mother who cared only for herself. "Maybe I've become like her," Stacy told herself. A shy girl who came to New York to escape her surroundings, determined to become an artist, a girl who fell—at first forlornly and then ecstatically—in love, and whose husband had tired of her long before she realized it. "There are thousands of women like me," she told herself, drifting off to sleep.

The next evening was still very warm when she walked over to the Osborne house. She had gathered that this was not an occasion for shorts and shirt, or a bright cocktail frock or an it-will-do dress. She had two long dresses, the only ones she'd kept. The one she wore this evening was pale yellow, simple and becoming. She carried an evening sweater, and wore her prettiest sandals.

Lee came down his steps to meet her. "You look cool," he said, smiling.

"Don't believe in appearances."

"Marcia tried to pressure me into a dinner jacket," he told her.

"White, with cummerbund, or have they gone out?"

"I wouldn't know; never owned one."

Going up the steps, she said, "I didn't realize Little Oxford liked going formal."

"Just infrequently. But the Hardens are special— they're so accustomed to it that I believe they even dress for"—he hesitated and then said—"breakfast. And of course Marcia, who is quite besotted over our distant cousin, would appear in a tutu if Elaine demanded it. Tonight we're not eating outdoors, but in the dining room which, I hope, will be reasonably livable. I couldn't centrally air-condition this old barn of a place, but with units in the bedrooms, living room, kitchen and dining room, it will suffice."

Marcia was at the front door and they went into the big living room and Stacy met Elaine and Gerald Harden.

They were halfway through an excellent dinner cooked by Cora and served by a temporary helper before Stacy had the least idea of what Gerald Harden looked like.

Accordingly, to describe Elaine would have been impossible. You could say that she was wearing a transparent caftan, over a pale green slip and that it was loose and flowing, with a barely indicated waistline. You could report that she was as tall as Lee, that her hair was the color of a copper beech with the sun on it, and parted in the middle, drawn back into a knot on her slender neck. You could state that her eyes were widely spaced and gray, and that her skin and her every feature were flawless. But you couldn't convey to a listener the extraordinary sense of tranquility which surrounded her. She was a quiet woman; she spoke, like a good child, when spoken to; she listened gravely. Her voice was low and almost uninflected. The shimmering caftan was shot with gold and pale green. She wore no jewels, except a platinum wedding ring and, on her right hand, a very large emerald.

Vanessa had said, "She makes my skin crawl." Why? But Marcia had said, "Vanessa doesn't like competition."

Stacy looked at her with artist's eyes and with the eyes of simply another woman. Elaine Harden belonged on the stage . . . if she could act; or perhaps she needn't act; she belonged on some distant throne, in a mythical land, she belonged in a gallery, or a book, or a ballad.

The talk went on, and Marcia drew Stacy into it. Had she ever been to San Francisco? . . . Yes, she had, a long time ago. Such a lovely city. And Gerald Harden said, "Not perhaps as lovely as it once was, with current pollution and progress, but we like it better than any other town in the world—that is, to live in, don't we, Elaine?" And Elaine inclined her head in agreement.

Then they talked about the world and its difficulties and Elaine spoke to Lee, "You must tell us about Greece," she said.

"I told you," he reminded her, "in New York. It's still there."

Perhaps Elaine belonged in Greece, Stacy thought, on a pedestal.

Her husband was a tall friendly man, who'd been putting on weight. He complained about it, and the business meetings from one end of the country to the other, and in Canada, and Europe. "Banquets," he said, "lunches, dinners; no wonder we drop dead young." He added, "I don't know how Elaine stands it."

Elaine remarked that really, she enjoyed it, and Stacy remembered Adam saying his parents traveled first-class. If there were a super first-class, she thought, the Hardens would have found it. She'd seen the Mercedes outside the garage and the chauffeur doing a little polishing before putting it to bed.

They had coffee on the big comfortably furnished side veranda. It was a little cooler now and Marcia said, "We're going to have a temperature drop according to the radio, Lee. Do fetch Stacy's sweater, just in case. . . . What about you, Elaine?" And Elaine replied that she was very comfortable, thank you, dear.

It was a strange evening. You talked, you laughed, Gerald told a pale blue joke or two and asked Lee what he was doing. Lee said, "Building houses," and Elaine looked up from her contemplation of whatever was unseen to the rest of them and said to Stacy, "Lee came out and built our house in the Valley. Five years ago. It's beautiful."

"I didn't really," Lee contradicted. "I wasn't an old hand in those days, but I went along for the ride as a consultant."

"More than that," Elaine told him. "You knew exactly what I—we—liked."

All very normal, old friends and a stranger. For Stacy had not even the consolation, such as it might have been, of Fred Arnold. He'd telephoned that morning, Marcia had said, down with the twenty-four hour bug, and it was too late to invite anyone else.

While Marcia and Gerald were having an animated conversation about the stock market, shortly before Stacy left, she happened to glance at Lee Osborne. His chair was in the shadows, the long evening light having declined. He was looking at Elaine. His face was as usual, unreadable, and remote, but his eyes were alive, and Stacy shivered. In all her life—except when she'd looked at herself in a mirror and then looked away—she had never seen such an expression of—what was it?—despair or desperation.

Then *her* skin had crawled, but in compassion.

Lee walked her home. It was cool and dark and he took her hand and put it on his arm with impersonal courtesy. He said, "Hang on; you might stumble." And then, "What do you think of Elaine?"

"She's incredibly beautiful."

"What else?"

Stacy answered after a moment, "I think that's all. I don't know her, Lee."

"You," he told her, "are like everyone else. That's all they know. She's beautiful. . . . Did you get a chance to talk to Gerald?"

"Only very generally, I'm afraid."

"He's one of the good guys. Don't be misled by the stupid jokes and the preoccupation with business. He is, of course, a very successful and astute man, with a great many interests. But he's unbelievably generous. He'd give you the custom-made shirt off his back. I doubt he's ever refused to help friends, or even a stranger. He does a great deal for charity. Elaine's on a number of boards. She doesn't lift a lovely hand, of course, but she's there. Gerry not only gives money of which he has more than enough, but his time, and he hasn't much over. I wish you'd been able to talk with him."

Curious, she asked, "Why?"

"I have a feeling you're a good judge of most people. . . . Mind the steps. . . . What silly shoes you women wear. . . . I'm happy to see you left the light on."

She said, "Thanks, Lee, it was such a nice evening."

He smiled and said, "Wasn't it? Good night, Stacy," and went his way without haste.

Closing the door, she dropped her sweater and small handbag on a love seat and sat down. She must have imagined it, for just a brief moment. . . . No, she had not imagined it. Whatever ate at his entrails had been there, for a split second, in his eyes. Love? Hate? Or both? Frustration? . . . Resentment? She did not know and in a way, she'd rather not know. But in that instant of time the entire picture she'd had of him dissolved and vanished.

What did she think of Elaine? he'd asked her. She did not know except that here was a woman without outward warmth. She was as cool as a cave, as cool as the sea, or the light from a star.

Was she? Or was it merely appearance?

Perhaps it was simply a façade, a protective coloring, a deliberate camouflage.

Think of the cool things in this world, or the things that look cool—the new leaf, the sailing swan, the gliding fish, the pouring of a snake over rocks. Think of the glittering iceberg, most of it submerged. Think of a brook, but a brook runs and laughs and challenges obstacles. Think of winter, but winter is stormy.

Think of shining pearls, of diamonds, or of an empty, beautiful shell.

"And we'd still be wrong," she told herself later, lying awake and pulling the summer blanket up from the end of her bed; before morning she'd need another. She went to fetch one from the blanket chest, returned still not drowsy. So went on thinking of Elaine Harden. There's no sense in being fanciful, she thought. You were enamored of fairy tales as a kid, and you still deal with them professionally. What you saw was an unusual-looking woman with a kind of enchantment about her. She's otherwise perfectly ordinary, being human. She may even be stupid, although Vanessa said she wasn't. Anyway, she's alive; she's flesh, blood, bones and hair. She can have allergies, catch cold, get the flu, suffer sometime from a chronic disorder—although she looks disgustingly healthy despite her almost translucent skin. So what! She can afford skin care; she may diet for complexion and figure and that shining hair. But I watched her; she didn't eat much, but she ate everything, so . . . Like the rest of us, one day she'll have a terminal illness, or a fatal accident. However, Stacy concluded, while she doesn't look quite human, she is. She was most certainly conceived, she didn't rise from the ocean or descend from a star. A woman had given birth to her. She had to have her diapers changed, her hunger stilled, she had to be toilet trained, and learn to walk and speak. Now an adult, she still must yield to physical necessities: she washes, bathes, brushes her teeth and, I daresay, experiences occasional discomfort.

Stacy found herself laughing aloud. All this nonsense because a woman guarded herself—against what, if anything? Perhaps she spent a great deal of time at her dressing table, giving herself facial treatments and doing exercises against wrinkles as well as brushing the one hundred strokes a day. She certainly had none of the lines most women acquired even before thirty; laughter or worry lines imprinted, however lightly, when you're young by anxious vigils, pain.

All very inconsequential, Stacy decided. Mystery-woman stuff and it was ninety-nine percent certain that there was no mystery about Elaine Harden, except, as far as Stacy was concerned, Lee Osborne's fleeting expression when he'd looked at her unaware of an observer. Vanessa's impression of Elaine didn't matter. Anyway, she, Stacy, would probably never see the Hardens again. Lee, she would see for as long as she remained in Little Oxford. Whatever Elaine was, or was not, Stacy was sorry for him, so sorry she could have cried—for the first time since Chicago, for someone other than herself.

❦ 8 ❧

On Tuesday afternoon about four, Stacy opened her door to Vanessa, Adam and Shadow. They'd evidently walked, as no bicycle, motorized or otherwise, was outside. Shadow came in first, perfectly at home, and unleashed.

"Saw your car," Vanessa explained, "so brought my grandson. Adam—this is Stacy Armitage."

"Hi, Stacy," said Adam, smiling.

"Hi," said Stacy. "Please sit down. I see Shadow's already found his niche in the Chinese bowl."

"Well—for a minute. . . . What do you think of him, Stacy? Seems damned odd to be an ancestor," Vanessa added reflectively.

"Neat," Stacy answered, "if that's still the right word."

"It's not obsolete yet, just a trifle passé," Adam told her.

"Educated," his grandmother remarked. "As for neat in its original sense, and not referring to a drink either, he's neater than a year or two ago. . . . What's your opinion of my new neighbor, Adam?"

"Super," he replied promptly. "I think that's still with us. But then I have a passion for females over twenty-three, provided, of course, that they're slender, but otherwise built; dark, of average or more intelligence and responsive to me as a human being, as well as a helluva attractive undergraduate."

"I wonder if you will graduate," Vanessa said. "Personally, I don't see how, unless all your instructors are women, dark, stacked—which is one of your less lovely expressions—and responsive. I assume they're over twenty-three and intelligent."

"Oh, I'll graduate," Adam assured her negligently. "That is, if I can keep my mind on my less important work. I'll be twenty next month," he told Stacy.

"Libra," said his grandmother darkly. "Don't trust them, especially the men."

"It's not too bad a record, so far," Adam went on, ignoring her, "so I've bludgeoned The Parents into letting me take a year off afterwards. The draft no longer looms. I'll take a look at the world, such as it is, poor thing, and return—if not murdered, jailed, hijacked or otherwise interrupted—and join my father's successful enterprises for as long as I can stand it. I'd like to write," he told Stacy, "like, of course, everyone else. And his office hours aren't too demanding——"

"You'll have social engagements," she reminded him.

"I can take or leave them, I think."

"Adam," Vanessa commanded, "go look around and admire Stacy's work. I want to talk to her."

Adam did as bidden—for the second time, his smiling glance reminded Stacy, and Vanessa demanded, "Now, about Elaine Harden. What did you think?"

Stacy shrugged. "What's there to think, except she's incredibly beautiful?"

"Hey," Adam interjected, turning the pages of a sketchbook, "what have I been missing?"

"Not in your league," said Vanessa. "A little older than you fancy, I imagine. No, I don't suppose so. She's ageless, really, which is one of the disconcerting things about her —anyway, she's married."

"I didn't know that counted——"

"Sometimes not," Vanessa agreed reasonably, "but in this case, yes. Her husband is loaded. Besides, they live on the West Coast."

"It's on my future agenda," said Adam. "How about a formal introduction?"

"I know the Hardens very slightly," Vanessa said, "and besides, you're apt to run into them in Europe—on, of course, a public street, as they go in for penthouse suites, yachts—rented, I think."

"How about bodyguards?"

"Could be. Stick to the lower classes, Adam. Much more entertaining. I know, having experienced all classes."

Stacy looked at a clock. "Tea? Wine—I've both red and white—Coke——"

"Tea," said Vanessa and Adam replied graciously, "A glass of wine and a biscuit, if you don't mind, and will join me."

"I keep forgetting it's legal," Vanessa said.

"More fun when it wasn't," Adam told her. "Then I used to sit in your curio shop and you'd teach me the facts of wines—bouquet, vintage. . . ."

They stayed until almost six and Vanessa said, "Come home with us for supper, Stacy."

She shook her head. "I've things to do, and I've been out more than usual. . . . Another time, Van; but first you must come here. Adam too."

"I'm off to my great institution of learning day after tomorrow. Not being a humble freshman, I will have time to make a few stops en route. . . . How about tomorrow night?" Adam asked.

"You might consult me," Vanessa said.

"Why? You rarely fill your social calendar. Your broom's dusty."

"What do you like to eat?" Stacy asked him.

"Anything, as long as it's steak."

"I," said Vanessa austerely, "do not feed him steak."

"She certainly doesn't—soufflés, casseroles, strange fish, fowl cooked in God knows what; stews stemming from France, Greece, Italy, or what have you, but still, stews. Now and then a man likes something simple. Make mine rare."

"Six o'clock?" asked Vanessa. "And I do apologize for my descendant."

Shadow removed himself from the bowl, spoke pleasantly to Stacy and followed his family out. Stacy thought: I'll have to go shopping. But she was pleased. She liked the relationship between Vanessa and Adam; she liked them, period. Shadow a little more than tolerated Adam, who, while Vanessa was drinking her tea, had asked for a saucer —"Priceless, if possible. He's finicky"—and had given Shadow an ample taste of wine.

Stacy called Katie the next morning and said, "If you aren't too busy at noon, how about lunch at The Pink Lantern, if the Boss permits? I have to go to the supermarket."

"What's up?"

"Just Vanessa and her grandson for supper."

At lunch Katie said hungrily, "I'm starved most of the time. In my own house, or anyone's house, or restaurants. Ben keeps me on a diet. He says, given my way I'd have a ten-pounder. So I consume in bitterness, small, adequate —so Ben says—portions of plain, nourishing food. You don't like to eat, do you, Stacy?"

"Of course, but I've never been a big eater." She thought of Reno when she ate only to live and didn't want to do that.

They walked down the street toward Colonial Way to

Katie's office and Stacy said, "I hope Mrs. Warner doesn't think I kept you away too long."

"Emily Warner," said her employee, "handles me with kid—forget I said that—velvet mittens. She's not letting me go out often with clients; talks about stairs or rough ground. If she knew how much I go to our own property with Jeremy and Lee she'd have a stroke. And I love to go out with clients. The baby's not due until spring—about the same time as Jeremy's book. . . . You know, about this child . . . you'd think it's royal or something except that royalty is permitted about six names each. Of all things Jeremy wants Charity if it's a girl . . . and I'm sure my mother wants Susan. She'll be down for the event, of course. I think I told you she remarried, some time ago. I know Emily Warner would like Emily—somehow I do too. Anyway, I'm sure she wants to be godmother and then there's Jeremy's cousin of sorts, Jessica Banks. So I hope it's a boy."

"Why?"

"Simple. Jeremy, Jr. . . . Come in with me and say hello to Emily. And if she mentions my delicate condition, assure her I'm strong as an Olympic wrestler, and that Ben prescribes suitable exercises. You know Jeremy wanted me to attend those classes in natural childbirth . . . with him, of course. I refused . . . as the Women's Lib gals say, 'I should have control over what I do with my body.' "

"But why didn't you go to the classes? Was it against Ben's advice?"

"No, just lack of fortitude. Stoic, I'm not. I resent pain, so I'd rather be knocked out, when it's permitted. I have a friend who took the classes, but unfortunately she was in an automobile accident and lost the baby. You haven't met her; she doesn't live in Little Oxford . . . which reminds me, I must call her. We had a little apartment together when I first came here, then she married and moved, but not far. Here we are—let's go in."

After a short visit with the formidable Mrs. Warner, Stacy went back to the studio. Despite Bob's constant instructions and gifts of dozens of cookbooks, domestic and in translation, she was not Little Oxford's Julia Childs. However, the dinner she'd planned would be simple and—if she watched her broiler and the clock—edible.

Vanessa, Adam and Shadow arrived at the appointed hour and Stacy, serving drinks, said apologetically, "If I fly into the kitchen, please be patient. I'm practically certain that Adam at least will oblige by eating—how do you two like your steaks?"

"Rare," they responded in unison.

"But you, Van," Stacy added, "will have to suffer ordinary food."

"That's good," Adam said, with his wide, engaging grin. "After a few days at Gran's, I return to the lowly hamburger."

"Well," said Vanessa, "don't fret, Stacy. 'Better is a dinner of herbs . . . than a stalled ox.' Now that I think of it," she added, "Little Oxford has gone into dinners of herbs somewhat overenthusiastically from what I hear. Not that I object to natural foods in moderation. And a stalled ox does sound tough."

The evening was relaxing. Vanessa at her best with incredible stories of her adventures, Adam listening with tolerance, saying once, "Don't be taken in, Stacy. Gran loves to stun an audience but, of course, the travels of Mrs. Munchausen are somewhat exaggerated."

Stacy had a small television set, so they watched a comedy of sorts until Vanessa said, "Must you?" and then listened to music on FM. Shadow went happily to sleep after he'd had his cocktail, a small shot of bourbon and water. Van rose early, looked down at Stacy from her greater height and said, "It was very pleasant, and your salad dressing—I must have the recipe. Where did you get it?"

"In Chicago," Stacy answered, remembering that Bob's future mother-in-law had given it to her, the first time they'd dined with the Harveys and their daughter at the magnificent apartment overlooking the Lake.

Adam kissed her. "Thanks," he said. "I'm off at sunup. I'll send you a postal from wherever I light."

"That will be on his head," predicted Vanessa.

"What's a mere concussion?" he inquired. "Thanks for dinner, Stacy. You broil a perfect steak and bake an elegant potato."

When they had left, she went into the kitchen to wash up, having refused help. She thought, smiling, of Vanessa's fantastic frock—using the adjective correctly. It was pure fantasy, a straight, ankle-length dress of patterned jersey, as the weather had turned cool, and of many colors— oranges, yellows, browns, reds, all bright and autumnal. "My grandmother, the gypsy," Adam had said when they came in. "She dazzles the eye."

Shortly after six A.M. door chimes sounded and Stacy, struggling from an uneasy sleep, called, "I'm coming." She got into robe and slippers and opened the door to regard Adam and his cycle.

"Is anything the matter?" she asked, but he shook his head. "Sorry to barge in at this hour," he said, "but I didn't have the chance to remind you last night to please keep an eye on our old girl." He thrust a grimy piece of paper at her. "My address," he explained, "and the phone number, in case anything happens or you get worried about her."

"She'll be fine, Adam, and she has lots of friends, remember, as well as your parents."

"They could be anywhere, and usually are, and you're the nearest to her. Besides, she likes you." He struck her a small, sharp blow on the shoulder and said, "Knew I could depend on you," leaped back into the saddle and roared off.

Stacy returned to her bedroom, smiling, and somewhat flattered. If he only knew, she thought. I'm about as useful as a chiffon handkerchief when the dam breaks. Bob used to say in exasperation, "For an intelligent girl, Stacy, you panic faster than anyone I ever knew."

She'd bet her very good eyeteeth that Winifred Harvey Armitage wouldn't panic no matter how grave the emergency; nor, for that matter, would Vanessa, who would simply give an order and wave a wand.

She went back to bed, but couldn't return to sleep, so got up, showered and dressed while the coffee perked, and then went resolutely to work.

To her astonishment, Lee Osborne came in that evening. "We saw your lights," he told her, "so Marcia sent me over with an offering. Look out, it's hot."

He held out a small pie plate, a small apple pie.

"I was out for dinner," he explained and followed her into the kitchen. "Marcia and Cora went into a convulsion of baking, as there's a food sale tomorrow at the church. . . . May I sit down?"

"Of course." She came to sit across from him. "The Hardens have left?" she asked.

"Oh yes, in a flurry of well wishes and a mountain of luggage. We'll probably not see them again for a long time."

"What was she—Mrs. Harden—like as a girl?" Stacy asked.

He considered that a moment. "Difficult to say. We've known her since she was a kid, of course. She was remarkable even then. No awkward stages, no braces on her teeth. We were all in love with her; Marcia, our parents, and I. She never said much, but somehow we all did as she wanted." He smiled and looked at Stacy with his clear regard in which she could find no shadow, nothing but friendliness and slight amusement. "Those were great summers," he went on. "Marcia was older than Elaine, but she tagged along just as I did. For a quiet girl, Elaine could get herself and us—mostly us—into the wildest predicaments. Then after boarding school came college and we no longer saw her, or not much. I had to stagger through my own education, Marcia ahead of me, and then Marcia married. We did have one winter holiday with Elaine and her family in the Bahamas—very exciting, we thought. Her parents had a place there, and I thought the setting was made for Elaine—the color of the water and the sky and the scent."

"Somehow," said Stacy, "I can't picture her having parents."

"Well, that's the impression she gives," he agreed. "But, yes, the full complement; they traveled a great deal, which is one reason for Elaine's summers in Little Oxford, and the boarding school. They're San Franciscans and when her father died, of some strange fever in Italy during Elaine's senior year, her mother came home, also to die, of a heart attack. Shortly after that Elaine and Gerald were married. Marcia and I flew out to the wedding. They'd known each other a long time——"

"May I offer you a drink?"

"You may, but I must refuse. We have a couple of new clients and now that we're breaking ground for the Palmer house, things are pretty busy around the office.

Katie keeps bemoaning the fact that it's impossible as things are now, to get her into her house by Christmas. Spring's the target, really, and I hope it doesn't conflict with the infant." He rose and said, "I hope you like apple pie. Marcia said she was sure you weren't watching your figure."

"I'm not."

"It's worth watching," he said lightly. "Good night, Stacy. We'll see you soon, I hope."

After he'd left, she thought about what he'd said. Thumbnail sketch of Mrs. Gerald Harden. She thought: So I imagined things. "No, I didn't," she contradicted herself. "Somewhere, sometime, somehow, he's been dreadfully hurt, and by her."

❧ 9 ❧

The days slid—or cascaded—into autumn. By the middle
of September, it rained steadily off and on, mostly on.
Cellars were flooded, roofs leaked. "I think," Vanessa said
one day, "that it's time to build an ark, but the original
directions would be a little difficult to follow, even for
Lee."

Shadow moaned, shaking wet paws and legs in his
kitchen. Vanessa seized a towel and dried him vigorously.
"He blames me," she added, "for everything. I've hung
your raincoat and hood to dry, Stacy. How about tea? I
recommend a touch of rum; old pirate blood," she concluded gravely. She looked from the windows at the rain,
blowing on a southeast wind. "The foliage," she predicted, "isn't going to produce its usual spectacular—
which will be bad for the bus trips and tourists."

But now and again the sun came out and for a day or
more banked fires smoldered and blazed into defiant
flame. "Good show," commented Vanessa, consenting to
ride in Stacy's car to Rosie Niles' house. She had asked
them for tea and to listen to recordings by two local young
people—the girl for whom she had provided European
training and who was now working in Hollywood as one
of a chorus which appeared on television and gave con-

certs across the country. The other, a young man, who was now studying in the city.

Vanessa had accepted the invitation because, as she had told Stacy who had been asked to convey it, "I'm eaten with curiosity, and besides, she asked Shadow. Your suggestion?"

"In a way, yes. Of course, everyone knows about Shadow."

"Not everyone welcomes him. Adam sent him a catnip ball last week. Actually Shadow doesn't care for catnip. His tastes, are, as you know, more sophisticated."

"Has he written you?"

"Adam? Yes, on his typewriter thank heaven. He reported that he was still hanging in there, and was involved with what he termed heavy discussions—Tolstoy style, I gathered—on war and peace."

Shadow, sleeping on the ledge above the back seat, yawned. He enjoyed riding, not that he often had the chance.

Stacy's life had settled into an agreeable mold; she had friends, she could order her social engagements as she wished—have lunch with someone, go out now and then to dinner. She'd gone twice in recent weeks with Fred Arnold and been extremely bored. She saw a good deal of Vanessa and of Marcia and Lee. Her lines were laid in pleasant places. She did not have the terrifying dreams as often, but when she did, there was another page in the sketchbook she was careful to bury in a drawer.

Also, when the weather permitted, she went with Katie —sometimes with Lee and Jeremy also—to observe the building of the Palmer house.

"I think I'll call it Procrastination Manor," said Katie, sitting on the tailgate of a handy station wagon, on one of the cool sunny days, eating a sandwich. "I don't understand blueprints, nor can I visualize what the house will look like, if it ever gets built—what with strikes, delays and material ordered, I assume, from Outer Mongolia. . . . Pass me another sandwich—they're good."

Stacy, who had made them, warned, "Easy on the carbohydrates."

Lee and Marcia had persuaded her to have her own show in the early spring at the Little Oxford Galleries . . . and to exhibit somewhat later at the local outdoor show.

Lee had said, "Spring's the time. We'll coast down the icy toboggan into it. You've never experienced a Little Oxford winter."

"I'm resigned. I once lived in Chicago."

"Spring is special. Look at the blessed events now scheduled. Katie's baby, the completion of the Palmer project, I hope."

On Thanksgiving Day, which was windy, cold and rainy, he had walked her to the studio from Marcia's open house. "Mud," he warned, "even a suggestion of ice. Take it easy."

"If I fall down, I won't be able to get up. I've rarely seen so much food."

"Wait until Christmas," he said. "Marcia will give her usual bash, so will the Irvingtons. You and Van will be asked, of course."

"We've already been."

He went into the studio with her. It was a dark glowering day and the wind screamed every now and then around the north side of the house. "Shadow," reported Stacy, "despises this weather. Me too. It's depressing, and makes me almost as nervous as the cat."

"He's not a cat," said Lee, occupied with the logs in the fireplace. "He's a watchdog, a reader of character, and a guardian—well, not exactly an angel."

Stacy had gone into her bedroom and Lee, after lighting the fire, wandered around the studio. "Anything new?" he asked.

"Preliminary sketches for a cat-and-kitten book. I've managed to slip Shadow in. I've a lot of sketches of him now—I gave Van some—but for the book he wears an unfamiliar benevolent expression befitting the kind father of a large family."

"He has," Lee remarked, "fathered a number of families. It's the talk of the village. But I cannot picture him as benevolent or kind—or even giving a damn. May I look?"

"On the big table . . ."

But when she came back into the room, he was looking through a sketchbook and saying nothing.

Stacy said, "I didn't mean *that* one!" She'd had her nightmare record out that morning, when pulling other sketchbooks and pads from the deep drawer. "I forgot to put it away. Give it to me, Lee. It isn't meant for anyone to see."

He gave it to her. She bent and put it in the drawer, slammed it shut and straightened up.

Lee said after a moment, "You poor kid."

She stared at him, her color fading, her eyes enormous.

Lee took her arm. He said, "Let's sit by the fire. Would you like to tell me about it?"

"No."

"I assume those aren't first sketches for a book on medieval demons," he said. He sat facing her, his hands on his knees, the firelight on his silver hair.

"You'll think I'm insane," she said, "but for a long time I've dreamed of those faces. So I get up and draw them just as I see them. . . . I thought if I did that, they'd go away and not come back."

"It's not that easy—the catharsis. I expect artists, writ-

ers and composers try to blast whatever terrifies them—
in their minds or bodies, their inside world, or even their
outside world—into their creative work. Other people, of
course, can't. Take me, for instance. If I had something I
wanted to conceal, yet at the same time get rid of, can you
imagine the sort of houses I'd build?"

He was smiling, but his eyes were grave. And Stacy
said, with an attempt at normality, "A chamber of hor-
rors?"

"Exactly. . . . Have you always had these dreams?"

"No. And if you tell me to go to a psychiatrist, I won't.
Not that I haven't thought of it."

"When did they start?"

"When I was in Nevada."

After a moment he said, "You've never told me about
your marriage."

"No."

"I'm not prying—but I—we—like you very much,
Stacy. . . . By the way, did you ever make up your mind
about me?"

"About what?" She remembered then, and tried to
smile. "Of course. Affirmative."

"When?"

"Oh, a while back," she told him evasively.

"Good. Stacy, perhaps I can help. Talking sometimes
works better than, say, drawing."

She said, "It's simple, really. Bob—my former husband
—tired of me long before I realized it. So he amused himself. I didn't know that either. I was happy; I thought he
was. I was stupid. Then he fell in love and wished to
marry and asked me for a divorce. That's all, Lee, except
that if he'd died, I could have borne it better . . . still
believing he'd been as happy as I."

"Not everyone bears it," he told her. "Rosie Niles, for
one."

"I suppose so," she said dully.

He commented after a moment, "Rejection's tough."

Her color rose. "I suppose it is that—which is, of course, completely egotistic of me."

"You're still in love with him?" he asked, to her distress.

She began to cry soundlessly, the tears pouring down. He watched her and did not move. After a while, she put out her hand blindly, and he put a large handkerchief in it. "I'm sorry, Lee," she said shakily.

He rose, came over to sit beside her, and put his arm around her shoulders—firm, friendly, undemanding. "That's all right," he told her. "Do you good."

She shook her head. "It never has," she said. Then, "I'll wash and iron this," and she sniffed and blew her nose.

"Okay, Stacy. I'd like to help if I can."

"Then go home," she told him unsteadily.

"If I do, you'll only sit here hating me for finding the sketches and yourself for telling me——"

"No. I'll take a sleeping pill and go to bed."

"Will you do something for me?"

"What?"

"If and when you dream again at any time, show me what you've seen."

"Why?"

"Perhaps the nightmares may change; perhaps there'll be an interpretation." He rose and stood looking down at her. "You're a very talented girl," he said. "I like being with you."

Stacy smiled a little. "Van told me I wasn't to get any notions about you," she told him.

Lee shrugged. "She's right, no notions. I'm immune to female wiles."

"Which is why, I suppose, women do get notions?"

"Possibly," he agreed. "However, friendship is not notional. Shake on it?"

She put her hand in his and, when he released it, said, "I—I don't fall into friendship; that is, I never have, yet in Little Oxford it's becoming easy."

She went with him to the door and after a moment, said, "Thanks."

"For what?"

"I don't know, exactly, nor why I said anything. . . . I suppose it was your finding the sketches. Katie's tried, Amy, Vanessa—I mean, to make me talk . . . not out of curiosity, except possibly Van—but from kindness, and like you, wanting to help."

"Why didn't you let them?"

"Katie and Amy are happy women," said Stacy. "They could never comprehend. Besides, Amy knew Bob. She was, in fact, my competition. She was lucky; she lost. As for Van, she wouldn't understand either. I don't know much about her life, except that I believe she'd always be the one to reject."

"That's the legend," he told her. "I think the closest she's ever come to the kind of love which was not exactly of her choosing, but which could wreck her if it went wrong, is her affection for Adam. Fortunately he won't leave her—except physically—not if I know him."

He opened the door, said, "Try to sleep," and went out to splash through wind and rain to his own house.

Later, lying in bed, listening to music, the wind, and the minute fingers of the occasional rain on her windows, she thought: Lee Osborne understands rejection. . . . Elaine, of course; it has to be Elaine; and reflected further: It would be hard to recover from her. I suppose anyone who looks like that is practically most men's dream woman. And if anyone really knows her, Lee must.

The rains stopped; it was cold and clear; Remsen Love-may died in his sleep ten days before Christmas. His daughter decorated the tree, and the house as he would have wished, but only her family came for Christmas. Amy, Ben and Benjy, and from California, her daughter, Cynthia. She'd come for the services; her husband, together with her small children, followed.

Stacy went to Marcia's and Van came with Adam, who was spending his holiday with her. His parents were in Palm Beach and he said soberly, "It would be a mistake to bask in the costly sun, and then return to my unheated attic surrounded by unread books. I'd get pneumonia, also get kicked out of school."

Stacy brought little gifts: for Van, a portrait of Shadow at his best—or worst—curled up in the Chinese bowl, looking regal and disdainful. For Adam the wildest tie she could find. "Because you sometimes wear one," she wrote on the card, "but I wouldn't want your personality submerged." For Shadow, a silver bell. "This is for the birds," she wrote. And for Marcia, a knitted hood which Stacy had seen her admire in Little Oxford's best boutique. Over Lee, she had hesitated, and wound up getting him the books which she'd illustrated—the two Alices, and the Mushroom Ring. The others were not yet published.

Giving him the package she said, "Sometimes it's fun to regress into childhood."

He said, thanking her, "But Alice, I understand, is a serious social comentary."

Gifts were under Marcia's big tree for her. Lee gave her worry beads of unusual charm. "I didn't wait to return to Greece," he explained. "By now I know you worry, so I sent for these. Use them in good health. They're almost guaranteed to drive away spells." Van's gift was a wood carving, an owl. "I picked it up somewhere," she said, "and Shadow has never liked it." Shadow gave her a soft toy, a black kitten; Marcia, a handsome casserole. Amy had sent over cocktail napkins; and Katie and Jeremy, also at Marcia's for dinner, brought her wine.

"I don't remember a lovelier Christmas," Stacy told Marcia. "Even the sun shone."

She remembered other Christmases: rather ordinary ones with her mother; lonely ones in New York, no matter with whom she spent them; and happy ones, her first with Bob, her second . . .

There was no snow, but everywhere the Christmas trees shone—in windows, in back or front yards, laden with light. Jeremy and Katie insisted upon driving her and her packages home via Baker Street so she could see their tree, a triumph of decoration, unlighted, but shining. "All the old ornaments," Jeremy said lovingly, and kissed Stacy under their mistletoe, to Katie's pretended indignation. "Old married men," she said, "should not go around kissing pretty women."

"Whom else should they kiss?" he'd inquired, reasonably.

Katie's mother and stepfather were coming for the New Year's weekend, before they went to Florida. "She has to see for herself that I'm not going to have twins." Katie patted her stomach, sighing. "Van says that I carry whomever it is, very well. Even Mrs. Warner thinks I'm still presentable."

Anyway, she concluded, Stacy would have to come New Year's Day and meet the family. New Year's Eve they were going to the Bankses after the service. "You come, too," she urged Stacy. "Jessica would love it. I'm certain Rosie Niles will be there and, of course, those of the Banks children who are within shouting distance."

Stacy said she'd see. After they had taken her home she thought, as kind as they were and as much as she liked them, she sometimes felt smothered. Van had warned her before Christmas. She'd said, "Everyone likes you so much, Stacy, you're gradually being drawn into families—the Palmers, the Irvingtons, Marcia and Lee's. It's not a gesture with any one of them, it's valid. They mean it; they want you with them. But, if, as I fancy, you're a rather private person, you'll feel the walls closing in. I've avoided it, which is why I go out very little, have few guests and these rarely—I make an exception of you—and then there's Rosie Niles. From the little I know of her, she has to get away, not entirely for the reason she tries to make obvious."

At the door, saying good night to the Palmers, Stacy had said, "I wonder what the New Year will be like?"

"For us," said Katie promptly, "a gas . . . a house and a baby, a welter of last-minute workmen, moving—maybe I'll be lucky and in the hospital—a newly furnished nursery and a whopping big mortgage."

"In that order?" asked her husband.

"Whichever comes first," said Katie.

"I'll tell you what it will be like," Jeremy predicted, standing on the steps in the cold, clear air, his arm around his wife. "Weather—all kinds, usually bad, but relenting occasionally; strikes, influenza, highway accidents, marriages, births, divorces, rising prices, inflation, wars, unemployment problems, a lot of trouble, and a lot of happiness. Year after year it somehow comes out even. The old cliché—even wisdom becomes that—the more things change the more they stay the same, or words to that effect. . . . See you New Year's Day, Stacy," he said.

When she was alone, Stacy put things away: the bright cocktail napkins, the yellow casserole, the two bottles of wine. She put the owl on the mantel, then she sat down, took her Christmas cards from the Chinese bowl and looked at them. There was one she hadn't opened. She had never before seen the handwriting, but there was a return address. She opened it now. It was a big card, quite charming—children, Christmas trees, stars, little animals—and engraved with the seasonal greetings "from Robert and Winifred Armitage."

There was a note, in Bob's handwriting. "Winnie and I had hoped to see you this past autumn, but because of her father's illness, we did not make the trip as we'd expected. We hope to see you in the spring." He'd signed it "All the best, Bob," and his wife had also signed, "Winnie."

She was about to throw it in the fireplace, but she'd left the fire well banked, so she tossed the envelope into a wastebasket and resolutely put the card with the others.

She took the worry beads and soft toy to her room and got ready for bed, with a glass of water and the sleeping pill on the night table. She picked up the worry beads and, sitting on the edge of the bed, ran them idly through her fingers which were not as one might expect long and allegedly artistic, but short, almost spatulate. Elaine's, she thought, were the prototype of long, sensitive, graceful hands.

The worry beads were polished and loosely strung. Sitting there, feeling them slide through her fingers, Stacy yawned. Maybe she wouldn't take the capsule. She took up the black toy kitten from the pillow where she'd put it, lay down, switched off the light and presently, with the worry beads slipping from her hand and the kitten against her shoulder, slept.

❧ *10* ❧

The New Year came in on schedule, and Stacy spent New Year's Eve with Vanessa and Shadow, having refused other invitations. Vanessa had expected Adam, but he telephoned Stacy to tell her there were complications. "Nothing heavy," he added hastily, "but now and then one has to make an appearance. In other words, I'm booked to escort my roommate's sister to our academic festivities. Just tell Gran that the roads up here are impossible—and I can't book a plane or a train. That part's true. And say I'll be down on my first free weekend. I'll catch a ride with someone."

Vanessa received the news cheerfully. She said, "I didn't really count on it."

"Come to the studio," Stacy urged her.

"No, you come here. At midnight, we'll lift our glasses —which is rather absurd, if you think it over—and Shadow will have his quota in a saucer. . . . Sure you don't want to go somewhere else?"

"No. . . . I'm scared of the traffic, and anyway I don't much like the standard New Year's Eve."

Bob had; the celebrations had been spectacular—people's apartments, hotels, clubs, funny hats, noise, indiscriminate kissing and drinking.

The night was cold and clear, but no snow. Stacy walked to Vanessa's wearing heavy slacks, a pullover, a warm coat and sturdy boots. When she went up the back steps, she was ready to apologize. On New Year's Eve, you dressed to the dentures, but Vanessa, in a long Chinese robe, approved. "Just as long as you're not sitting before the tube watching Guy Lombardo," she said, "you don't have to wear a ball gown."

They talked, listened to music and Shadow slept with one green eye open. Stacy said, "When the cat-and-kitten book comes out, you'll have my first copy, but promise me you won't show it to Shadow. He'll hate me."

"Not at all. I liked the illustrations; you have deftly delineated Shadow's better self. He must have one, of course, and he undoubtedly knows it, so he'll admire to see himself in a role he's never felt called upon to play."

Just before midnight Vanessa produced a cold bottle of sparkling Burgundy. "Although why I don't know," she said. "Tribal customs are ridiculous. It will be simply another day—I put on this robe to honor the Chinese despite the difference in dates."

As they waited for the hour to strike, Lee came in. He said, "The party you refused, Stacy, is going full blast. It's only a quarter to—they won't miss me. I'll be back on the stroke of midnight looking for ghosts and such, but I just came over to wish each of you whatever you most want." He kissed Vanessa's cheek, and Stacy's forehead and made his exit.

Stacy said, astonished, "He left the party!"

"He always does," her hostess told her complacently.

One of her numerous clocks began to strike as she said, pouring the Burgundy, "They're all a little off, but it doesn't matter. Time isn't what we think it is. . . . *Salud.*"

Shadow, fully awake, did justice to his portion, and then Vanessa said, "Now, go home. There's something purely psychological about a New Year. Each is very like the one before, but somehow there's always the foolish human hope. . . . I've a present for you, Stacy."

"But you gave me my owl and the black kitten," Stacy protested.

"I had nothing to do with the kitten," Vanessa said. "Shadow shopped for that." She reached over to the table beside her, picked up the Russian box and put it in Stacy's hand.

"I can't take this," Stacy said. "You love it."

"I want you to have it. Now go home."

She did not kiss her guest; she was not a kissing person. She merely closed Stacy's fingers over the little box and said, "Someone I loved for a while gave me this. I used to think of it as a talisman. Now I'm too old to believe in talismans; they are for the young. I was young then, by comparison. I hope it brings you as Lee wishes, what you most want; and I expect," said Vanessa, "that will be healing."

Walking home, Stacy thought: Healing? I'm young, healthy . . . She shrugged her shoulders, shivered a little, and quickened her step. Here and there, small puddles glittered, having frozen where the road did not drain well. She let herself into the light and warmth of the studio, took off her things, turned on the television, looked for a moment at the dancing and the merrymaking, then switched it off. She thought: Van didn't mean that kind of healing. She put the box, which she'd kept in her hand, on the bedside table. . . . "All sorts of talismans or whatever," she told herself, considering the toy on the pillow, the worry beads and the box. Healing . . . ? Of course. Protection from dreams, the hurt scarring, the humiliation fading, and the wounds she did not like to admit even to herself, those of resentment and absence.

Before she slept she thought of the lights along the

roadway, the Christmas trees, the radiance of man-made stars. Tomorrow—no, today, or soon at any rate—the lights and stars would go out; the ornaments would be banished to attic or basement; the trees denuded, dying, taken down, thrown in a field or on a compost heap or collected by the town or removed to a center for recycling.

Early in January, Stacy went to the city by train. There was still no snow, which would have frozen into chunks of dirty ice to endanger hurrying pedestrians. Jim Swift was home with the flu. Stacy saw his pleasant assistant, a woman she had not known until she came east, but refusing her invitation—"Jim said I must take you to lunch—" ate alone in the busy restaurant half a block from the Lovemay office. There was no assignment for her. Jim had told her, when he asked her to come in, that he expected to have a novel which would need a dust cover. But the assistant explained that there had been the usual delays. . . . "The manuscript hasn't come down from the editorial department yet. I'm sorry, Mrs. Armitage, I should have telephoned you, but we are in such a clutter of work after the holidays, I forgot."

Stacy managed to get a cab and to go to another smaller publishing house with which she had worked before, but there was nothing there either. The art editor told her, "Not at the moment." So she waited for another cab, this one with a maniacal driver, went to the station, waited for a train and came on home, her car being parked at the Little Oxford station. It was not a hopeful entry into the New Year, she reflected.

But there would be other assignments; the publishing houses would be working on the next autumn-winter lists; and she should spend some time looking over her drawings and paintings to select those to be shown in the spring. Lee had talked to one of the gallery's owners and he assured her of their interest. "I'll take you in," he said, "together with some material—which isn't exactly the right word—sometime after the New Year."

Before mid-January there were snow flurries, blowing under a sky first gray, then blue. The ponds and lakes were deep-frozen and there were skaters wherever there was solidified water. After the flurries, a little snowfall, not substantial but enough to powder the trees, roofs and meadows and perhaps freeze if the temperature went down, or melt if the sun came out.

On that day Stacy was working on a painting she had put aside. Perhaps she could, after the elapsed months, return to it with some assurance that she could complete it—not to her satisfaction; she had never been satisfied with her own non-commercial work. This was not a fantasy of castles and moats, or of elves and unicorns, or of hooded women drifting in mist toward some dangerous destiny. It was a landscape on the shores of a lake, in the distance factories, the urban encroachment.

There was a sound at her door—a crying she recognized and a frantic scratching—and she ran to open it. Shadow was crouched there, waiting, speaking. She said, astonished, "Come in," but he stayed where he was, still crying on a high, urgent note. "Wait," said Stacy, and ran for boots and a coat and then went out. "You're not lost," she told him. "You know where you are." He turned to take a few steps ahead of her, stopped, turned again and cried at her, this time in what looked like anger.

She scooped him up and he struggled, but she held him fast and ran to Vanessa's. As she started toward the back steps, relaxing her hold, Shadow jumped down. "Good," said Vanessa from the back porch. "That you, Stacy? I've broken my arm, I think."

She was lying on the porch floor, her left arm awkwardly by her side. "Don't touch me," she said sharply. "Hurts like hell. Came out to see if the mail had come, slipped on a skiff of ice on the steps . . . managed to crawl back. I sent Shadow for you. No one's been by and I'm freezing. There's an old blanket on the chair; throw it over me. Call Bing . . . I will *not* faint," she added through clenched teeth—and did.

Stacy ran home and called Bing's office. Elvira Jones, his nurse, said he was out on calls; Ben was at the hospital. She'd reach one or the other of them.

"I think she's broken her arm," said Stacy. "I don't know what to do."

"I'll call the ambulance," Elvira said. "You go back, stay with her and ride with her to the hospital. Either Ben or Bing will meet you there; in any case, she'll be taken to emergency."

Vanessa was conscious when Stacy got back to her. She said, "I'm sorry. Clumsy old fool. Thank God it isn't my hip. Did you get Bing?"

Stacy told her, "Yes, Elvira will get him or Ben—meantime an ambulance will be on the way."

"Always wanted to ride in one," said Vanessa, "as the main passenger—I've ridden with other people often enough." She put out her right hand and Stacy, sitting on the floor beside her, took it. "Well, hang on," Vanessa said. "Glad I'm right-handed. . . . Will you take Shadow? Not that I expect to be away long."

"Of course."

Vanessa gave her feeding instructions. She said, "He won't mind staying with you; it's better than have you running back and forth; anyway you'll be company for each other. He'll be all right here until you get back."

Stacy sat there, feeling helpless and angry at herself and even at Vanessa who had not only injured her arm but frightened her neighbor. She had known since childhood that illness not only terrified her, but made her angry. How dare anything happen to people she cared for? How dare they allow it to happen?

Bob had once told her, recovering from a virus, that her reaction to illness was perhaps the only masculine trait she possessed.

The ambulance came and Vanessa said, "Let Shadow in the house; don't lock the door." Shadow demurred and she spoke to him, "Do as you're told. Stacy will be back presently."

In the ambulance over the louder catcry of the siren, Stacy could hear Shadow's voice raised in unholy protest.

"We'll get her there as soon as we can," said the attendant. "I haven't any orders. We'll have to wait till we get her into Emergency." He added, "That's Mrs. Steele?" in a somewhat awestruck tone. "I've never seen her before."

Vanessa, who had been silent except for an occasional lapse into colorful profanity, said, "I never go to hospitals, young man, either as a visitor or patient."

Ben was in the emergency room. He took one look at Stacy and said, "Go up to the third floor, speak to the nurse at the station and then wait in the reception room."

"I'm supposed to be the patient," said Vanessa. "Where's your father?"

"On his way."

Stacy took the elevator to the third floor, stopped obediently at the station and the pretty young nurse handed her a paper cup of water, and in a smaller one, a tablet. "Dr. Irvington said you're to take this and then sit down and relax."

"I'm all right."

"He said you were shook," said the girl sympathetically.

Stacy swallowed the tablet and went into the reception

room. She should call Adam. . . . No, she'd better wait until she knew more. Maybe it wasn't just Vanessa's arm; perhaps it was more serious. She thought: Old bones, they're frail, and then shook her head. She had never meant to become emotionally involved with anyone in Little Oxford. Look at me now, she thought, sick about Van. And I suppose I'll worry over Katie almost as much as Jeremy will.

It seemed a very long time before Ben came into the room, and she could ask, "How is she?"

"Fine. Broken arm. She's had the works. X rays, setting, cast, sedative. My old man's with her. We got her a private room which is a miracle. You all right?"

"I suppose so. I hate anyone to be hurt or ill, and I'm of no use whatever."

She thought, remembering how she'd hovered over Bob, with alarm and also reluctance if he had as much as a headache: It's a good thing we didn't have a child. I'd have been tied up in knots every waking minute.

Ben said cheerfully, "All Van worries about is her cat."

"I'm to go back to the house, collect his food, and take him home with me."

"He'll probably be more difficult than Van," said Ben, "and what are you going to do if he catches his paw or tail in the refrigerator door?"

"Don't even mention it."

Bing came in. He said, "Hi, Stacy. Van will be all right; it's a clean break. She'll hate it, but she'll manage. I'm going to keep her here for a few days, however. If I hadn't sedated her, she would have murdered me when I told her."

"There's something else wrong?"

"She's old," said Bing. "She's had a bad shock. Trauma. She'll be fine. Essentially a remarkably strong woman, good heart, good lungs, and all the rest of her is in order. She demanded, naturally, to go home; I had to speak to her severely. She's tough, and she'll be a difficult patient." He added, "She takes care of herself, you know. She's never missed her complete annual physical since she came back to live here. She's not at all anxious to die before her time."

Stacy said, "I promised I'd call Adam if anything happened to her."

"She won't like that . . . or, maybe she will," Bing said.

Ben said, "Look, Stacy, I'll take you back to Van's, we'll collect the ambrosia or potions or whatever she feeds Shadow, and the big boy himself. Then I'll take you home and you can call Adam. Do you have his number? . . . Good. I'll talk to him too. The soothing voice of experience."

"May I see her for a minute?"

"She'll be asleep; just look in. After tomorrow I'll let her have visitors. . . . You called Lee?" asked Bing.

"I didn't have time."

"I'll call him. He's devoted to her."

Ben walked her to Vanessa's door, tapped on and opened it. They both looked in. Vanessa was asleep and a nurse's aide sat with her.

Ben withdrew his red head and pulled Stacy into the corridor. "We won't disturb the currently placid atmosphere," he said. "Everyone has instructions; she'll be looked after. She doesn't need specials. Can you imagine if she had to have them and didn't like them? Thank heaven this room was vacated around three. She'll be watched over as if she were an injured dove and not a hawk. I shudder to contemplate what she'd be like if she had to share a room."

"Probably wonderful," Stacy said unexpectedly, "if she

were with a very ill patient—and, I think, interested in anyone who wasn't. She'd tolerate them, briefly. You know her curiosity about people."

"I still wonder," Ben said.

He drove her to Vanessa's, where Shadow was howling and hurling himself at the door. When Stacy opened it, he flew past her in a flurry of black fur, calling. At the foot of the steps he looked up and down the roads, still crying. Stacy picked him up. He struggled, but she held him firmly. "Don't fret," she said, "she'll be home soon."

Ben cleared his throat and said seriously, "That's right, old man. I'm the doctor, or one of them."

They went into the house. Stacy put Shadow in a chair and went into the kitchen. Vanessa had a heap of treasured baskets and Stacy, peering into cupboards, collected what was needed.

"Litter box," she said thoughtfully, "also fresh litter."

"What about milk?" Ben asked.

"I have some at home. I'll reorder tomorrow."

"See if you can find an overnight bag or something; she'll have almost everything she needs at the hospital, but she might want her own toothbrush, and," he added, "hairbrush and comb, though she doesn't, I think, get much mileage out of them."

"Stay here with Shadow. I'll go upstairs and look. Nightgowns?"

"No. She'll have the hospital version."

Stacy went into Vanessa's good-sized bedroom for the first time. It, like the living room, was replete with pictures, mementos, small tables, clocks. She found the brush and comb—silver, and shining—and bedroom slippers, which looked Turkish, and took from a marble-topped dressing table a lipstick. "She doesn't use powder," she said aloud. Would she be able to wear a robe? Stacy didn't know, but found half a dozen, selected a warm one and on second thought, a cashmere shawl. She took from a drawer of the dresser, stockings, a slip, panties; and from another, handkerchiefs. She was not amazed at the quality of Vanessa's intimate apparel, but only by the fact everything was monogrammed. In the bathroom she found two toothbrushes.

Then she looked for a small suitcase, and found on the floor of the second closet in the room a mound of flight bags and, finally, a suitcase, which she packed and carried downstairs. Ben took it from her, and she said, "If she needs anything else, I can bring it to her."

They packed Ben's car and he said, "I'll help you with Shadow's necessities, and then go back to the hospital with Van's suitcase."

They drove to the studio and he took the baskets in. "You take Shadow," he said. "Sometimes he scares me."

They went in. Stacy put Shadow in his sleeping basket, and said, "I'll put the things away later—now I'll call Adam. I'm sure he'd rather speak to you."

Shadow leaped from the basket, prowled, muttered and returned to it, while Stacy, fetching her address book, dialed Adam's number.

He was called to the telephone, came to it and asked, "Who?"

"Stacy. . . . You're not to be upset, but your grandmother's in the hospital. Her arm is broken."

"I am upset. Who broke it?"

"She did. Slipped on the back steps. Ben Irvington's here; he'll give you the clinical details."

Ben talked, Adam listened, and then asked to speak to Stacy again.

"Stacy, tell Gran I'll get down next weekend. We're having exams now—but if she needs me sooner, I'll get a compassionate leave or something. I'll call you every night. What's the number? . . . Thanks. . . . Don't put me on. She's really going to be okay?"

"Yes. Shadow's staying with me. I'll let you speak to him."

Ben shook his head. "Contagious insanity," he remarked.

"Bring him over," said Stacy, "and hold him, Ben."

"Basically I'm a dog man," Ben stated, gingerly carrying Shadow. "Hold still, you!" He held the cat at the correct level and Stacy put the receiver to his pink-lined ear. Adam spoke, Shadow replied, and as Ben was restoring him to his basket, Adam said, "Thanks, Stacy, Shadow and I consoled each other."

"Good," said Stacy. "We'll be in touch." She replaced the instrument and said, "Now Adam's really reassured."

"I'll be damned!" said Ben.

At the door, he said, "Don't forget to feed yourself as well as Shadow."

"If she's worse, if she needs anything——"

"I'll let you know," he promised, and loped off to his car.

Stacy sat down and Shadow came to lie in her lap. She stroked him, thinking: I used to believe cats really never cared for anyone but themselves, except with cupboard love . . . and that dogs were the one faithful die-on-your-master's-grave animals.

She was tired and had dozed off when the knock came. Lee followed it instantly, demanding, "Why don't you turn on the lights?"

"Shadow and I were asleep."

"It's been dark for some time. Who put on the outside light?" he asked.

"Ben. He brought me back here. We got Shadow, and——"

"Why didn't you call me?"

"I didn't have time. I was running to call Bing or Ben and running back to stay with Van till the ambulance came. Besides," she said honestly, "I didn't think."

He was walking around, switching on lamps, drawing shades. "It's nearly six," he said, "what about dinner?"

"I'm not hungry."

"I am. Marcia's out. I was contemplating getting something out of the freezer for myself when Bing called me. I was out of the house all day. Now I'll see what you have. Women who live alone rarely have anything edible until they have guests. Put your feet up. I'll forage, and when I've made up my mind, I'll fix us each a drink, including Shadow. He needs it."

She said, "I didn't know you were like Jeremy."

"I'm not. I dislike to cook, but I can broil a chop or scramble an egg and make superior coffee. Sit still, both of you."

Later, when she had cleared away, he sat opposite her and smiled. He said, "You never intended to fall in love with Van, did you?"

"No."

"Nor Katie nor Amy?"

"I never expected," she said, "to like anyone very much, I suppose. I mean, to get involved."

"Now," said Lee, "you're stuck with it." He rose. "Marcia will be running over here tomorrow and to the hospital if Ben lets her. I'll sneak in without warning. Van will be looking for me."

"Why?"

"Van's my kind of girl," he said, "and she knows it. If she were forty years younger, and I was, as the song goes, 'a rich man,' I'd buy a Greek island and take her there."

"As Mrs. Osborne?"

121

"Certainly not," he answered indignantly. "What do you take me for—a square?"

When he had gone, Stacy took Shadow for a brief, cold walk, came back and tucked him into his basket, and went to bed. But an hour or so later he was in her room, possessive and lonely, leaping up, batting the toy kitten to the floor, then settling himself on the end of the bed, where he went to sleep.

❧ 11 ❧

In the morning, Stacy looked after Shadow's needs, gave him a spoonful of her scrambled eggs, said soothingly, "I'm planning chicken tonight; you'll inherit a snack. I've noticed that Van gives you a moderate helping of whatever she eats. She says cat foods can be boring and that you're accustomed to things like paté and caviar. Sorry about that. I'm just a poor artist. This is an attic."

Later she took him for a stroll. . . . Thank heaven I remembered his leash. If he were to get away, Vanessa would murder me in hot blood—but then she wouldn't have to; I'd have a heart attack. . . . On their return he fitted himself into the Chinese bowl for a small nap and she telephoned Bing's office.

"He's at the hospital, but Ben's here," said Elvira, connecting her.

"How is Van, Ben?"

"In pain, naturally. Also bad-tempered; otherwise fine. She said to thank you for packing the case and added that as a rule she disliked having people paw through her things, but she didn't really mind you."

"May I see her?"

"Not today. Bing's ordered no visitors. He wants her kept quiet."

"I doubt that even he can manage that."

"We'll see. Amy wants to know if there's anything she can do for you. . . . How about supper?"

"No. I don't want to leave Shadow and I couldn't inflict him on you. Benjy would pull his tail."

"All right, but call Amy if there's anything . . ."

Stacy spent the day doing her personal laundry—the studio utility room included a small washer and dryer—washing her hair, and looking after Shadow, who had decided that, next to the Chinese bowl, he liked to sit under the big north light. While she puttered around, he washed himself, reflecting that she'd set an example, and thought his own thoughts, sometimes dark, sometimes sharp, sometimes philosophical.

His intuition told him that Vanessa had not really deserted him and his well-fed, pampered state caused him to regard Stacy most favorably. He was tolerant of her; she wasn't really a cat person by nature, but she was learning; he could find no fault. He would therefore, up to a point, behave himself, but he'd sure as hell take it out on Vanessa when she returned. . . . For a little while, he'd ignore her, refuse to eat, paw a few things off a table or mantel. But not for long because for the first time in whichever one of his nine lives this was he had been terrified. People with two legs had no business going around suddenly throwing wrenches into well-oiled machinery. For a considerable length of time Shadow's world had been, he'd thought, destroyed.

Blinking in the sunlight, he contemplated the approach of spring, every day a minute closer. There'd be the pre-Easter parade of willing girl cats; also the parade of young, hostile males. He could take them all on; he wasn't a boy, unwary and stupid; he was mature, cautious and very clever.

Stacy, looking up from whatever she was doing, said to herself: "I swear that animal is patting himself on the back!"

Marcia came over after lunch. Shadow looked at her, spoke in a dignified manner, and retreated into the bedroom and up on Stacy's bed.

Marcia, said, casting herself in a chair, "Such excitement . . . not that there isn't always something. We phoned Elaine last night, late. She's down with this new flu virus—they'd been away and had just come home. Gerald's worried about her. . . ."

"She looks fragile," Stacy admitted, "but I have a feeling that she's not."

"No, as kids, Lee and I were always down with something or involved in the usual accidents. Not Elaine. I don't suppose I'm really worried, but Gerald is. She's his entire world—comes way above his business interests, and I've thought for a long time that the reason he works so hard is for her."

"But wasn't he successful before they were married?"

"Oh, yes . . . actually, as Lee said, a few years later, he was as successful as he ever needed to be. . . . How about coming across the field for supper?"

Stacy smiled. She said, "Amy asked me too. Everyone goes out of their way——"

"Including Fred Arnold?"

"I haven't heard from him lately. I did go out with him a couple of times because it became embarrassing to refuse."

"He's the persistent type," said Marcia, "but he isn't yours."

"How did you know that?"

"I'm a fair judge." She got up and walked about restlessly. She said, "I doubt you've considered remarriage—"

"Good grief, no! Are you trying to tell me that our Mr. Arnold is the marrying kind. If so, you aren't as good a judge as you believe."

"I wasn't thinking of him . . . and I deduce that your marriage wasn't happy, from the simple fact that you're divorced. What I started to say was, I wish I could."

"Could what?"

"Remarry. You know, my husband was considerably older than I—and he died suddenly. Quite frankly, I've been looking for the past few years. Lee doesn't need me. We're very fond of each other, but I don't suppose I really need him either. You met Katie's mother, Susan Baines, didn't you—and her stepfather?"

"Yes, over the holidays."

"That," said Marcia, "is a happy marriage. Neither of them is young; he has several children by his first wife; Susy had only Katie. Susan's considerably my senior. I've taken a good hard look at Little Oxford and the area. No dice, no way. So what would you say if I went off on a cruise? Lee wanders abroad almost every summer; now it's my turn. Tropical islands, strange places, new places and people."

"That would be great, but from what I hear about those cruises, there are about twenty women—widows, single, and divorced—to one unattached man."

"Ah," said Marcia, twinkling, "but I'm younger than most of the seafaring harpies. I could get lucky."

"Have you spoken to Lee?"

"Not yet; first the travel agency, then Lee. But he won't mind. He'll simply say that I'll probably get into trouble, lose my traveler's checks, get robbed and rush around with the wrong kind of people, but he won't really mind. If I pull this off, do keep an eye on him for me."

Stacy thought: first Vanessa, now Lee. "I'm beginning to feel like a housemother," she said.

"Why?"

"Adam asked me to keep an eye on Van; a lot of good that did until the accident. I'm certain Lee can keep both eyes on himself."

"Well then, I'll tell him to oversee you. After all, he's your landlord. . . . I called the hospital; Van's not having visitors, Bing's orders. What do you think?"

"I don't think. I know she's fine," Stacy said. "I called too . . . which reminds me, I haven't heard if she wants anything else from the house. In the middle of the night I woke up—under a dark, heavy cloud—and thought I smelled cigar smoke. Then I realized Shadow was on my chest, weighing a ton, and that I'd been dreaming of Vanessa. When I packed for her, I forgot her cigars!"

"I'll tell Lee. He knows what she smokes; he can take some up to the hospital. He'll try to see her, but Bing probably has guard dogs stationed all along her corridor." She rose, "I'm going down to the travel agency. Gertrude —such a nice girl—will advise me. I need a clutch of folders and stuff."

"When do you want to go, Marcia?"

"Yesterday, tomorrow. It's impossible, of course—now we're into January—to get anything for next month unless someone goes broke or dies and therefore cancels. But perhaps in March. . . . Sure you won't come to supper?"

"Quite sure—but thank you very much. You see, I have to keep tabs on tabby (I hope he didn't hear that); he's my responsibility, if not for long. Actually, I like having him. When the next Gothic comes my way, I'll put a black cat somewhere on the jacket; of course, if there's none in the story, it might not be feasible."

Marcia laughed, went out and Shadow stalked from the bedroom and inquired, "What kept her here so long?"

"Oh, hush!" said his hostess. "She's a very nice woman, and I don't blame her for wanting to marry again. She rates a good, attractive, well-heeled husband and her own house. Maybe she and Lee will sell the big one. I wonder what will become of the studio?" She stopped, laughed, and added, "And she hasn't even gone on her cruise yet!"

At supper, she presented her guest with a small saucer of finely diced creamed chicken. He was happy. He'd had his drink, he was alone with a good friend—not of course his slave, but this one could easily become a minor vassal. Stacy looked down at him, washing himself after his little repast and said, "You know, I do like having you. I'll miss you when Vanessa comes home."

Shadow asked a question.

"I don't know—another few days. Stop bugging me. I wouldn't dare get myself a substitute cat, after you leave me. In the first place, there aren't two of you and in the second, you'd hate him." She added thoughtfully, "Not her."

Lee came in when she was reading, curled up in a love seat, with Shadow beside her. Shadow said, *"Ciao,"* graciously, and Lee said, "Move over, you two. I managed to see Vanessa!

"I said I had an important package for Mrs. Steele which she wanted me to deliver in person to the charge nurse on her floor. I know the receptionist downstairs in the lobby," he added, "so I exerted considerable charm and went on up, with Vanessa's cigars. But I lurked in the waiting room; they were busy on the floors, nurses and doctors coming and going. Then the one gal remaining on the station had a long telephone call and while that was going on, I slid down the corridor and went in Vanessa's room. I had asked the number, carelessly, downstairs."

"What happened?"

"She was alone, about to push one of those buttons to ask for something, or watch TV or listen to the radio. The walls talk, you know, and you can talk back. But she forgot what she wanted when she saw me—I hope it wasn't a bedpan. I gave her the cigars, said you'd thought of them, and she asked how Shadow was bearing up. I said, 'Tolerably.' I didn't want her to be jealous. Then she wanted to know why I hadn't been in before, at which point Ben came in, took one look at me and said, 'Out.' I outed."

"Coward."

"You don't know Ben as well as I do." He suffered Shadow to kiss his hand. "Shadow identifies," Lee said. "He knows I've been with Vanessa, if only close enough to hand her the cigars—I forgot to tell you she asked me when I had become a father—and to kiss the top of her head. She says you can come see her tomorrow; I'm to come, but at another time. Doesn't want anyone else."

"Imperious Caesar—I don't know the feminine of Caesar."

"Nor I, academically. But this one has far from turned to clay. I daresay she'll outlive us all."

"Why? Practically everyone I know in Little Oxford appears remarkably healthy too."

"No, we're all vulnerable. Katie's going to drive herself into early collapse, Jeremy will be devoured by silverfish. . . ."

Stacy was laughing. "How about Marcia?" she inquired.

"Marcia?" He twitched an eyebrow. "Oh, an exception, I think. As she grows older, she becomes younger."

"And you?"

"I'm rapidly evolving into an old, old man," he informed her, "ridden with regret."

"How about me?"

"Now you," he said vigorously, "need a lot of straightening out—being even more vulnerable than most." He shook his head. "It's a do-it-yourself job," he told her.

"I'm trying," said Stacy soberly.

"Good."

"Marcia came in briefly," she told him, "and speaking of people who really are ill, she told me Mrs. Harden is."

"We called her last night—it was her birthday yesterday—and Marcia always calls her if there's a telephone anywhere near—London, Paris, shore to ship. She's a telephone nut, also a compulsive buyer of greeting cards and unusual gifts. Elaine has flu; she'll get over it. I doubt the virus exists which would dare do battle with her determination to chalk up a victory—to say nothing of the cordon of doctors Gerry flings about her, if she sneezes. Actually, if she stands in a draught, *he* sneezes!"

He rose and looking down on her and Shadow reported, "Vanessa suggested you turn up about five. I'll go at the lunch hour. She seems to have made her own hospital rules. Her final words were that you could bring Shadow and leave him in the car, give him air, but see to it that he can't leap from a window. Also bring his blanket."

"Security?"

"Quite. Like Linus. If he has a blanket, he'll know he isn't going to become a castoff."

Dutifully, at the appointed hour, Stacy took Shadow and his blanket, and put him in the front seat. "If you don't behave, you'll be banished to the back," she told him. "I wish they'd make seat belts for people your size."

Shadow agreed, sat large and proud beside her, occasionally putting a paw on the wheel. "You can't drive," she told him. "It's against the law." But looking out the window, discoursing loudly when he saw a dog or cat or even pedestrians or other cars, interested him.

Parking, Stacy put him in the back seat, up on the ledge

with his blanket, and measured the amount of air she'd give him. "Don't speak to strangers," she admonished. "I won't be long."

She found Vanessa sitting in a chair. "This is Jane," she said, indicating the nurse's aide who was fussing with pillows. "I'll ring if I have a stroke, Jane . . . . Did you set out the ice and glasses? . . . . Good. Now, scoot."

Jane scooted and Vanessa said, "Over on the table—bourbon, ice, a thermos of water. It's time for the temporary escape, and be sure to give Shadow his drop of the creature when you get back. Now, fix us our drinks."

"Regulations——" Stacy began, astonished.

"Gone by the board, as long as your doctor prescribes. I had Jane telephone Lee this morning, so he brought the bottle. Anyone my age needs a brief expansion of the arteries. Bing approves. . . . Thanks. Cheers," said Vanessa, "which is an idiotic expression, as everyone over twelve knows that alcohol first exhilarates, and then depresses."

Stacy negotiated her very light drink, and said, "I suppose you feel ghastly, Van."

"Not really. When I hurt too long, I holler and someone comes a-running. I'm going home tomorrow afternoon. High time, for as long as they have me here, Bing insists on tests and they've taken enough blood to satiate Dracula, and enough urine to dehydrate me."

"May I take you home, Van?"

"Ben's going to. He wants to lecture me all the way there."

"Then may I come stay with you for as long as you need me?"

Vanessa said, "House guests unnerve me, even Adam."

"Adam's coming down on the weekend. You really will need help."

"Not at all, but he can fetch and carry, do errands. I

suppose he'll get a ride down with someone. He can use your telephone to order things—the pharmacy, my grocer and butcher delivery. He can borrow your car if he needs it," Vanessa said blithely. "Or he can walk."

"But——"

"I can read your mind. Adam can cook. I taught him. He can also make his own bed, for heaven's sake. And I'll see that he waits on me. There are compensations in everything. But you're a good girl, Stacy, and I appreciate it. How's Shadow?"

"He seems quite willing to stay with me until you return," Stacy commented, thinking: I'd better not tell her he also seems contented. "But of course he misses you."

"You're feeding him properly?"

"I think so." Stacy listed the menus and the extras.

Vanessa nodded. "No upset, no furballs?" she inquired.

Stacy said, exasperated, "I give up."

Vanessa was laughing. "Just testing," she said. "As a matter of fact, I know you're spoiling him and he loves it. But when I get home, he will punish me for my defection."

Stacy remained her allotted time, promised to be at Vanessa's at three-thirty—"Just wait with Shadow," Vanessa ordered—and then went down to her car. Shadow was half asleep. He spoke to her and Stacy said, "She's fine, Shadow. In fact, in better shape than I am."

Around noon the next day, Lee drove up, came into the studio and thrust two green-wrapped, damp parcels in her hands.

"Roses for Vanessa," he explained, "from me. Jonquils —forced into bloom, poor things—for you, from her. Arrange suitably. Van told me yesterday morning that she intended to command you to be at the house when she returns."

He followed Stacy into the kitchen and watched her put the flowers into separate pitchers.

"She won't let me stay with her, Lee."

"Of course not."

"But she can't look after herself!"

"She has her right hand," he reminded her, "and a plethora of curious garments into which, I'm sure, she can insert herself." They went into the living room and he picked up the Russian box. "I meant to ask you about this before. Vanessa gave it to you?"

"You thought I'd stolen it?"

"No, but I've been tempted to. Anyway, this is comparable to being knighted, or whatever it is, by Elizabeth the Second. Van's prized this for years."

"I know," she said, "it was given to her——"

"Yes . . . on, I might add, a Greek island, which I don't suppose the gentleman owned. She's never told anyone—or at least not me—who he was. But while she had a number of lovers," Lee said, "over a long period of time, I think this was the royal favorite."

Adam called, as he had each night and Stacy made her report. "I'll be there before supper. Tell Gran I'm bringing steaks," he said.

"You've come into a legacy?"

"No. Sometimes I gamble . . . poker, craps, horses—take your choice. You're invited to share the winnings."

"I think not. Your grandmother would much rather have you to herself."

"She'll run me off my feet; if you're there, you can share that too."

Stacy made a trip to Vanessa's in her car, leaving Shadow, who didn't complain. As he saw her carrying out his various belongings, he doubtless surmised his destination. She also took the roses. Shadow had spent some time admiring and smelling them, sitting on the kitchen counter. "They weren't," she told him, "sent to you." She shrugged, putting her hand on his neck. "I daresay you prefer orchids?"

She spent some time at Vanessa's. The house was aired, and as dusted as Stacy dared; she'd managed to get there for a little while each day. She found a vase—"Probably priceless," she muttered—and arranged Lee's roses, turned down Vanessa's bed and the one in the larger guest room, laid out a nightgown. I bet she never wears them, she thought suddenly, as it became apparent to her that of all the lingerie, the nightgowns appeared to have just come from a shop. She ran downstairs for a thermos of ice water, and up again. Then, as she drove back to the studio to collect her guest, she thought with astonishment: I don't suppose I've ever attempted to do as much for anyone—not that it's much—riding in an ambulance, going to a hospital, looking after a house and a cat. But it was unlike her. She'd never done anything for her mother which hadn't been asked of her; as for her father, he had been the doer. Only for Bob Armitage had she worried over housekeeping, cooking—and everything else. His guests, her own clothes, his comfort, his pleasure. But that had been engendered by the man-woman relationship which, she told herself, was now becoming outmoded; and it had not been spontaneous, but produced by—among other causes—subconscious fear of loss, of displeasure, of failure.

Now, parked in her own driveway she thought, for the first time: No wonder he tired of me and my touch of the Gothic, without the high spirits of some of the heroines.

She went in, got Shadow, put on his leash, walked to Vanessa's, and opened the door. Shadow explored, calling. He turned into the living room and directed his indignation at his recent hostess. "She'll be here very soon, Shadow," Stacy told him.

She was. Ben brought her and her suitcase in and Stacy ran to meet them. Shadow leaped, all four paws off the ground, approached her, looked up, decided all was well and hurried to dash a couple of china ornaments which broke, and a candlestick or two from the nearest laden table.

"Wholly in character," Vanessa said happily. "Stacy, will you fetch a dustpan?"

Ben helped Van into a chair and put a footstool in front of it. "Broke my arm, not my leg," she remarked. "Ben, you have calls to make. I have my medication, and warnings. So thank you, and good-bye."

"Dad will look in on you later," Ben said.

"I don't need him, or anyone," Vanessa said, but Stacy contradicted her firmly. "I'm staying till Adam gets here. Then I'll leave."

"It's pitiful," Vanessa remarked, "to be old and helpless at the mercy of friends and relatives. . . . Shadow, stop sulking!"

✥ 12 ✥

"I'm a rotten nurse," Stacy apologized, "but perhaps I can manage to make you more comfortable."

Vanessa's mouth twitched. She said, "You're not the Nightingale type; I'm not either. However, I do have a couple of traits which make me useful in a sickroom or around an accident."

"Such as?"

"Courage, efficiency and common sense; that's three— and don't excuse yourself because you're an artist. All artists are supposed to be, as they say, sensitive. That includes, I fancy, musicians, writers, dancers, actors—I could cite you any number of examples disproving that more or less accepted theory."

"Give me one."

"A lot of the males fought wars," Vanessa said, "and the females worked in hospitals, were fire wardens and"—she laughed—"I can't state with any authority a specific example, not now. I'm tired. I wish you'd go home."

"No. You might need something. You might want to go to the bathroom."

"There's a lavatory on this floor," Vanessa reminded her. "And I can still walk. You can get me a glass of water," she added, as the clocks began striking, not quite in unison. "I'll take one of these silly tablets. Here, on the table, where Ben left the bottle."

Stacy obliged and Vanessa said with resignation, "Don't prowl. Sit down. Talk to me."

"What about?"

"Cabbages and kings—your opinion of modern art, also pornography. What makes you tick, if anything? Ask me for a recipe. Do you know that I am proficient in Greek cooking? Also Italian and French, and I make a wicked blintz. Ask me what I think of men."

"What do you think of them?"

"Infuriating, often stupid, but indispensable—even when you're old enough to be historic. Sometimes they're a danger. Sometimes an escape. You should have seen me when I was young, the daughter of the president of an obscure college, which had one well-heeled alumnus, who came occasionally bearing a substantial donation—and my passport to a very much larger territory."

"Mr. Steele?"

"Of course."

Stacy said after a moment, "But you weren't in love with him, Van."

"Certainly not. I liked him; he was a reasonable and literate man. Also I was, for a time, grateful. . . . What's Shadow doing?"

"Sitting in a corner."

"He'll keep on ignoring me for a while, except when hungry. Then he'll forgive me. . . . I hear a car," Vanessa said.

Lee came in and said, "I see you have returned to your cauldron, Van."

"Yes. Sit down. We're expecting Adam. Stacy volunteered to baby-sit until his arrival."

"How do you feel, Van?"

"Puny. The cigars are over there—light one for me. I couldn't ask Stacy; she'd choke to death."

Lee found the cigars, lit one, and coughed.

"So she would. These are on the strong side," he said. "And I'm sure, very bad for you."

"Bing's sure too. Also Ben, but if I shorten my life somewhat, it's of no importance. Also, I didn't take up smoking until I was fifty—and in Spain. Thank you for the roses. Did you bring me any interesting gossip?"

"I rarely hear it; I live in an ivory tower. News, yes. Marcia's going off on a cruise."

"Well, bully for her," Vanessa commented, "as one of the few Presidents I've admired, might say. When?"

"March, she tells me."

"I hope she finds what she'll be cruising around for," Van said. Stacy looked at her with respect and Lee asked blankly, "What's that?"

"Fresh air, new people and places."

"Oh! . . . What's wrong with Shadow?"

"Malice aforethought. Absence does not make his heart grow fonder."

"It does mine," Stacy said, "because I'll miss him so much. I've even thought maybe I should get myself a cat."

"Not if you value my friendship!"

"Why?"

"I couldn't bring him to call; he'd murder an intruder."

"Suppose it's a girl cat?"

"No. You're a very conventional young woman; you'd see to it that the offspring were legitimate."

"But I could have her spayed."

"I don't approve. It's against nature for people with four legs. I'm not as sure about the two-leggeds."

There was a commotion outside, audible shouting, cries of "Have fun!" and "Be seeing you" and a car which had stopped with a crash, went off in a clatter. "That's Adam," said Vanessa.

Stacy went to the back door. Adam was coming up the steps. He had a flight bag, an overcoat, and some bursting parcels. "Hi," he said, "how is she?"

"In good form. May I take some of those packages?"

"Take the books." He thrust a heavy burden in her arms and she staggered back. "Some are for me to study," he said. "The others are for Gran. Right up her alley; ghost stories, witches, ESP and a couple of rather dirty, but well-written, paperbacks. I'll keep the steaks, they could drip."

They went in; he said, "Hi, everyone." Shadow muttered and remained where he was and Vanessa said, "Don't ask me what's wrong with him."

Adam kissed her cheek. He said, "Why should I? I know. How are you, Butch?"

"A term of endearment," Vanessa explained. "I'm frail, that's how. . . . What's in the packages?"

He told her and she said, "Well, unwrap the books and take the steaks into the kitchen."

"Stacy can help me," Adam said. "I've had a horrendous drive; my companion is practicing for the Grand Prix. We got a ticket. He has to show up in court Monday, or forfeit bond."

"You're staying until Monday?"

"Certainly. I'm cutting a couple of classes."

Stacy had opened the books and now followed Adam into the kitchen. He said sternly, "She looks washed out."

"She is. She hated the hospital, and the fall was a shock, but she'll be all right."

"Are you going to cook the steaks?"

"No, you are. I'm going home. I think she'd like to have you alone tonight so she can order you around, make you work, and also so that you can fuss over her a little. Did you ever read *Little Lord Fauntleroy?*"

"Good grief! No, sounds nauseating."

"There's a nice line in it—relative to a seven-year-old boy—or maybe six, I've forgotten—and his aged grandfather."

"So what's the line?"

" 'You could lean on me you know, I'm strong. I'm seven, you know.' I'm probably paraphrasing. One of my first illustrating jobs was a new edition of the old classic."

"Oh!" said Adam. "Let's go see our own old classic, shall we?"

Stacy and Lee left together shortly thereafter, Stacy promising, "I'll be over in the morning, Van, to see how you're getting on. Bing will stop by this evening."

"Seems incredible that a woman can't enjoy a broken arm in peace and solitude," Vanessa remarked ungratefully.

Stacy and Lee walked back to the studio, and she looked at her watch. "Have you time to come in for a drink?" she asked.

"Certainly. Marcia's going to be late. I think she's started her cruise shopping."

"You'll miss her."

"Naturally. But we're to look after each other come March."

"Who said so?"

"She did. . . . Here's your drink. . . . Of course, you know she is, like most women, a matchmaker."

Stacy laughed. "No flint," she said.

"That's what I told her."

They sat in comfortable silence, with the lights on and the shades drawn. Presently he asked, "What do you like to do, Stacy, apart from working?"

"Eat. Sleep. See friends. Read." She shrugged. "Listen to music. What do you mean beyond that?"

"Well, as we can look forward to spring, how about sports?"

"I was brought up in California," she told him. "I swim, and I used to play tennis, both adequately."

"I'll remember that."

Leaving, he said, "I'm not going away this summer— too much work on. You knew about the condominiums?"

"I've read about them."

"Business is picking up. . . . Are you going to decorate Katie's house?"

"What put that in your head?"

"Katie. She doesn't want a professional decorator and she doesn't wholly trust her own ideas. She says Jeremy will be interested only in the library he's planned, and the landscaping. She told me you had an infallible sense of color and proportion and she hoped you'd sit down with the plans and sketches and give her your ideas, not that she won't reject them if she doesn't approve."

"I'd love to," said Stacy, smiling.

The snow came shortly thereafter, starting on Monday evening. Stacy walked through the wind-blown flakes to Vanessa's, went in and said superfluously, "It's snowing hard."

"I know. I told Adam to telephone you when he got back to school. He didn't leave until about noon."

"I know. He dropped over to say good-bye. . . . Have you had anything to eat?"

"All I wanted."

"You're worried."

"Naturally," said Vanessa crossly, "and my arm hurts. I don't know if it's the weather or Adam."

Stacy went home and Adam telephoned half an hour

later. They'd had a flat, also the court bit took longer than expected and it was practically a blizzard by three o'clock.

"So run along," said Vanessa, when Stacy went back and reported. "I can get myself to bed. Come here, Shadow . . . mind my arm."

Shadow jumped on her lap carefully.

"He's forgiven you," Stacy said.

"Of course. He always does," Vanessa told her.

Stacy's first winter in Little Oxford was, the older residents told her, drawing on memory, quite normal. A lot of snow, a good deal of ice; a superfluity of wind. Trees and branches fell, occasionally the power went off for a while. "Nothing," said Marcia, "like last year; that was a terror." And Katie, who was also at Stacy's, having brought plans and sketches, said, "I'll never forget it."

But there was no blizzard that winter, just snow and darkness, dazzling sun and sudden thaws. Stacy had enough work to occupy her. She could use the mails to get work to Lovemay's, and if there were a deadline, a messenger came out. Also she had Katie's house to think about . . . the living room and dining rooms, the bedrooms and baths, the nursery and the enclosed porch—"Like a lanai," Katie insisted, "not that I've ever been to Hawaii" —and the sun decks. Stacy made color sketches and Katie went shopping for swatches of material.

In March, with a brilliant sky reflected in standing puddles of water which froze at night and melted by day, a number of events came about: Katie had her baby, a boy, so there need be no deliberation about a name. Vanessa, fully recovered, had predicted it. "An easy prediction," said Stacy, "either you're right or you're wrong; a fifty-fifty chance." Marcia went off on her cruise and Lee drove her to the pier with Vanessa and Stacy as passengers. Others came to see her off; there was a party and Marcia kept saying, "You have all the addresses for mail and cables, Lee? You'll keep in touch with Elaine and let me know. . . . she never writes."

He had, and he would. "Anyway," he said, "when you talked to her, she said she might be in Jamaica when you are."

On the way home, Stacy spoke idly of the brilliance of the mid-March day and Lee said, "Van would tell you to remember the blizzard of eighty-eight."

"She doesn't."

"Of course not. . . . What are you doing tonight?"

"Going to Katie's now that she's back in Baker Street. Her mother's still there, of course. I do like Susan Baines."

"Katie's extremely incensed that she can't get into her house before the end of April, and I'm impressed with your color schemes and the way you've indicated the placing of the furniture."

"It all belongs to Jeremy," Stacy told him. "The things in the Baker Street house, and some from storage; of course, there'll be new—the nursery, for instance—and mod pieces here and there, but good furniture, of whatever period, mixes like a perfect martini."

"Which, as a rule, you stir."

"Have it your way. I've given Katie the originals of the illustrations she likes. They're to hang on the nursery walls for Jeremy Jr.—animals, and the mushroom ring, gnomes and elves. No princesses or fairy godmothers—Amy's to be his godmother, incidentally—all strictly for the masculine taste!"

"Suppose the next time it's a girl?"

"Katie says, 'No next time.' "

"Absurd," said Lee, "if you're going to have a family, two's better than one; four's all right."

Stacy laughed. She said, "According to Katie, once is

enough. Jeremy says she has a very low level of pain. He told me when we were waiting at the hospital along with half of Little Oxford that she sprained her ankle during one winter——"

"Winter before this past one, I believe."

"And he said you'd have thought she'd broken every bone in her body."

"How's yours?" he inquired.

"Ankle or body?"

"Level of pain?"

"High, physically," she said soberly.

Leaving her at the studio, he said, "Wait. . . . Confetti in your hair."

She shook her head. "You'd think it had been a wedding."

"I'll keep in touch; mind you do the same. I promised Marcia," he told her.

Katie, Jeremy and their sturdy son moved into their new house after Easter, which was early that year. Katie's mother had come down again to help and Stacy was there constantly. Jeremy loped around unpacking cartons of books, Susan and Stacy tackled china and glass, and Katie —between hanging over Jeremy Jr., perfectly at home in the new crib and quite unaware of the nursery décor, and directing both volunteer and hired help—kept crying distractedly, "I don't know why we ever moved!"

"It was at your suggestion," her husband reminded her.

Lee, strolling in and overhearing, said soothingly, "Emily Warner can sell it for you by next week at a handsome profit, Katie."

"Sell it? My house!" cried Katie, aghast.

Stacy brought Vanessa up to see the house. They left Shadow lurking in the car, enraged because here were a couple of new acres, no doubt harboring field mice, chipmunks and squirrels, which he was not permitted to explore.

"Poor wretch!" Vanessa commented. "It's tragic the way cats, having become more or less domesticated, are forced to live in houses, particularly after nightfall. They're ancestrally creatures of the dark."

She approved of the house. "One of Lee's best, but I'm not coming to the housewarming," she said on the way home.

"Why not? They want you."

"Too many people. . . . Who did the landscape planting?"

"Ellsworth, I believe."

"Good, but too expensive," Vanessa said.

"By June," Stacy said, "it should be beautiful." She stopped and added, in astonishment, "I can't believe that I've been at the studio for months."

"When's Marcia returning? I can't believe that she'd jump ship."

"Next week, to your first question. As for jumping ship, when she reached Jamaica and found that the Hardens had preceded her and had a rented house, she couldn't resist."

"I know that. Beats me. She's such a sensible woman, most of the time."

Stacy was just getting her supper when the telephone rang. She answered it and a woman asked briskly at the other end of the wire, "Stacy? . . . This is Winifred. Bob and I just checked into the Inn—it's most attractive. We're on our way to my aunt's in Boston, and we'd like to see you. Could we? Bob has someone he wants to see in this area for lunch. Tomorrow we're going to meet him at the Freed place in Saltmarsh. Could we come by in the afternoon and say hello?"

I could make an excuse, Stacy thought, her throat dry,

but if I do, she'll think I'm terrified of seeing him—and her—which, God knows, is true. She said into the transmitter, "Of course, come for a drink—how about five?"

"Five," said Winifred Armitage. "Hang on a moment, I'll let Bob listen to your directions. I'm hopeless. I don't know my left from my right."

You sure don't, Stacy thought, and waited. The remembered voice came through. "Hi," he said. "How are you, Stacy? Tell me how to get to your place, will you?"

She told him; he said, "Got it," and "Good-bye," and hung up. Stacy sat down in the living room. She was shaking. She said aloud, "This is ridiculous."

After a while she rose and went back to the phone and called Lee Osborne's number. She thought: Please let him be there, please.

He was and asked, when she spoke, "Stacy, is anything the matter?"

"No . . . yes. . . . Could you possibly come here a little before five tomorrow, Lee?"

"If it's important, certainly."

"It is, to me." She began to stammer a little, something she did when embarrassed or frightened. "B-Bob and his w-wife and coming here, for drinks."

"Bob? . . . Oh," he said remembering. "All right, Stacy. I'll be there."

That night she made herself a stiff drink, ate very little, left the few dishes in the sink, tried to read, shivered her way to bed, took a capsule and slept heavily. In the early morning she dreamed. This time the faces were sly and smiling, illuminated by malice, alive with a shadowy, evil triumph.

⚜ *13* ⚜

It can be assumed that the average woman performs a certain type of ritual when expecting guests. Stacy straightened up the studio and vacuumed the one large rug, polished tables, dusted and then put two or three of her unframed paintings on easels. Those she had selected for the small exhibit were at the framer's. Bob would be certain to ask how, and what, she was doing; he would also have asked Jim Swift . . . not that he'd ever been particularly interested in her work. When she first knew him, his interest was purely academic—"How's the art department going?" Later when he lost interest in Amy Meredith and turned to Stacy, to her astonishment and gratitude, he appeared to share her small triumphs and disappointments. After they were married and moved to Chicago, he was tolerant of her wish to continue painting. "As long as it amuses you and keeps you out of mischief," he'd said, conceding that she was alone much of the time and the apartment no real chore, what with someone coming in to do the heavy cleaning. Later, he was agreeable to the art lessons. Some of her classes were at night and he was adamant that she take taxis back and forth. "Dangerous for you to drive around after dark," he'd said. When twice, there had been an exhibition of students' work, and she'd sold two paintings at one, and one at the other, he'd been pleased. "Someday I'll retire and you can support me," he'd said. "My wife, the artist!" Later, she reflected that he was impressed by success, in any field, and however trifling. And had further thought, looking out at the Truckee River, or driving to Lake Tahoe, Carson, or Virginia, City, courtesy of her lawyer's delightful wife, that he must have been very happy indeed with her art lessons; they gave him more time for his own pursuits.

She'd thought a great deal during these expeditions, talking from the surface of her mind to Mrs. Dayton, and looking with the blind eyes of a statue on strange places, mountains and lakes of emerald green or turquoise.

Not much had registered with her in Nevada, not the people she'd met, the women with whom she'd become outwardly friendly, or the strangeness and the beauty which was all around her. She'd continued to write to Lena Dayton, dutifully remembering her kindness and that of her husband.

Now she set out bottles and glasses and cheese sticks, and went to dress. She had some new country things, Katie having steered her to what she considered the best shop for these in Little Oxford.

Stacy put on a red shirt, and a tweed skirt of mixed white, red and black. She matched her lipstick to her shirt, and touched her eyelids with muted color. She brushed her heavy, shining hair and tied it back with red wool and wore country shoes, red and black.

She looked at her watch, went to fill the ice bucket and thought: Lee should be here by now.

He was walking across to the studio, noticing that only Stacy's car was in the driveway, and thinking of the peculiar ability of women to construct, torturously, their personal labyrinths in which they inevitably became lost for a period of time, long or short, but rarely forever. When he'd suggested to Stacy that she was still in love with Bob Armitage, she'd neither admitted nor denied it, simply taking refuge in tears. Pure grief he could understand, such as his sister's at the time of her husband's death, but she'd responded normally to the passage of time—eight years, wasn't it? Yet Rosie Niles was still in mourning. That, too, he could understand. But Stacy's category was difficult to pigeonhole. He had also suggested that she was suffering from rejection, and was certain he was right, but could this, alone, account for the nightmares? He had known a few women whose divorces had shattered them, but they had felt the tremors beneath their feet before the earthquakes. One had said to him not long ago, "When I began putting it together again, all I felt was hate, like a clean fire, destroying the rubble. But I got over that too."

He liked Stacy, he respected her talent, and was aware of her repressions. He knew a great deal about repression and not from the academic standpoint. He also suspected that her basic vitality could be expressed only in her work.

He was sorry for her and impatient with her. She had pretty much everything and didn't, couldn't, or wouldn't recognize it.

No one knows everything about anyone, he decided, which was scarcely an original conclusion, he conceded, laughing at himself.

He reached the studio door, knocked, came in and Stacy met him.

"You look," he told her, smiling, "alive, well and living in Little Oxford."

Stacy gave him a small, cold hand and said, "I know you think I'm an idiot. . . . Please come in, Lee."

"I'm already in," he reminded her. "Here, sit down with me. No, I don't think you're an idiot, really. You have people coming to see you, and you don't want to see them. It's as simple as that. So you asked me to come too, as moral support. What do you want me to do?"

"The drinks," she said. "I've everything set out I think —and well—just general conversation, I suppose."

"The attentive pro-tem host?"

"Something like that." She was silent for a moment and then she said slowly, "I don't seem to be able to face this situation alone, which enrages me."

"That's good. Anger at one's self is often a psychological antibiotic." He thought privately: Not that it has been for me.

"I'm sorry I nagged you into this," she told him. "I didn't know whom else to ask."

"Your female friends wouldn't have been of much assistance," he agreed. "Not even Vanessa, for obvious reasons. . . . I hear a car," he added and rose.

Stacy said, getting to her feet, "I'll go," but he touched her shoulder and said, "Let me cope."

He went to the door, and she heard voices and an exchange of names and Winnie Armitage came in ahead of the men, crying, "Stacy—this is absurd! Bob's asking, 'Mrs. Armitage?' with a question mark and I'm saying it with a period. Really, you should revert to your maiden name—not nearly as confusing. How are you? You look marvelous."

"I'm fine," Stacy said. "Hello, Bob."

He came forward then, smiling and saying, "This neck of the woods certainly agrees with you. It's been a long time, Stacy."

"Oh, yes—suppose we all sit down? Lee's offered to officiate."

"I'll take orders," said Lee. Scotch and water for Mrs. A., Scotch on the rocks for her spouse.

"Vodka?" he asked Stacy.

She nodded, and Lee went into the kitchen, thinking of Bob Armitage, the average, go-getting, personality-plus fellow. He was disappointed in Stacy; he'd expected someone spectacular. As for the second Mrs. Armitage, she was pretty, her fair hair curling under the small mink hat. He'd approved of the short matching coat he'd taken from her, and of her aquamarine dress, which matched her eyes and was shaped to her body. He also admired her pearls, and thought: I bet, a steamroller.

When he returned with the tray of drinks and the nibbles, Winnie cried, "Not for me. I'm terrified of gaining an ounce. You never had to worry," she told Stacy, exhibiting flawless capped teeth. "You've always been thin as a splinter ever since I've known you."

Bob said, "Nice place you have, Stacy," and Lee remarked, "I see to it that she keeps it in order. I'm her landlord."

"Such delightful country," Bob commented, lighting his wife's cigarette before Lee could make a move. "Haven't been in this area for years."

Winnie was telling Stacy, "We're building in the suburbs. You'll have to come to our housewarming, provided it's ever finished. I'm in a complete dither with decorators, builders and architects."

Bob asked Lee what he did.

"Just another architect," he answered smiling, and Winnie said, "I'm sure I wouldn't be in a dither with you," but Bob broke in to assure that Winnie had her own ideas and that each was a hundred and fifty percent original, but practical.

Lee thought, looking at Stacy, who was listening to Winnie: I wonder what she's thinking.

She was thinking, with incredulity, how much Bob had

changed. Oh, he looked the same, except for a few lines, and a slight puffiness under the eyes. His hair was the same, and the eyes themselves, his smile and his voice. But his hands were restless and when Winnie spoke to him, usually a statement, followed by, "Don't you agree, darling?" he agreed instantly. Also, he fretted over her. Was she certain she wasn't in a draught? he asked her twice.

When he remembered Stacy, he inquired courteously, "How's the work going?"

"Very well," Stacy answered and Lee rose to suggest, "How about a private showing? . . . I know, of course, that you've a dozen things at the framer's for your exhibition, Stacy."

"Exhibit? When?" asked Winnie. "Where?"

"Not until June," Stacy said. "The small gallery in the village is in great demand."

Now they were walking about, looking at the paintings. Lee showed them some of those still stacked against the walls, and Bob turned the pages of a sketchbook and said, "You've come a long way, Stacy."

Winnie cried, "But they're really very good!" and Stacy thought: If they don't go soon, I'll throw something.

They went—an hour and a half after their arrival—and Bob suggested, "Why don't you two come back to the Inn and have dinner with us?"

But Lee said promptly, "We'd like that, but as it happens, we have an engagement."

They left. Lee stood with Stacy at the door, his arm around her shoulder. And when the car drive off, she said, "I don't know how to thank you."

"Here sit. We don't have to be at the restaurant until seven or after."

"What restaurant?"

"Do you like Greek food?"

She said, bewildered, "I suppose so—I went occasionally to a place in New York, when I lived there."

He said, "This one is The Aegean. It's out toward the lake. Theo, the owner, is an old friend of mine."

"Lee, you're being very kind," she said, "but honestly, I'm not hungry." She wasn't. She felt vaguely sick. There was a hard knot in her stomach, another in her throat, and her head ached. "I'm sorry. Look, you go on home. I'll wash up and go to bed."

"You owe me something. Go powder your nose or whatever. We'll wash up when we get back. Isn't the laborer worthy of his hire? If I go now, you'll sit here and brood and probably break the glasses, which will upset Marcia."

She went without a word. He took the tray into the kitchen, put things away, washed the glasses and waited.

When she came back, he said, "You've been crying."

"Not very much. It was—just—such an awkward situation, and I'm not good in awkward situations."

"Get a sweater. It's cool," he told her. "We'll walk to the house, and get my car. The walk will do you good."

The air was fresh and sweet as lime sherbet, the April wind tugged at her hair, as they walked in silence. As they reached the house, he said, "If it's any consolation, your guests felt as ill at ease as you did."

"I doubt it."

"Was your former husband always so hearty? I expected him to smite me on the back any moment—and does his current wife always babble?"

She answered faintly, "I suppose so. Bob was always outgoing and Winnie——" She broke off, "I don't know, really. . . . I didn't try to sort things out. I just spoke when spoken to, mostly."

"It was a good idea," he said seriously, "under the circumstances."

On the way to The Aegean he told her about the people who owned it—Theodorus and his wife, Thalia; Charis, their daughter. "Pretty," he added, "and lovely; she now calls herself Cherry." Alexis, the son. "Clever boy," he said. "His father sent him to Cornell; he'll have a big place of his own someday. You'll like them."

The Aegean, on the Lake Road, was small with sturdy ample tables and comfortable chairs. The décor was simple and bright, the tablecloths and napkins, heavy linens, and it was spotlessly clean.

Lee was greeted with embraces; the introductions were made and Theo said, "This will be a celebration. But you should have come on a weekend, Mrs. Armitage."

"Dancing," Lee explained.

Stacy looked at the menu and shook her head. It was incomprehensible, and she wasn't seeing very well.

Lee took it from her and said firmly, "I'll order. No drinks, Theo, except a bottle of Rodity's Rosé."

Stacy looked up at the owner. She said, "I'm sorry, but I—I don't feel very well," and to Lee, "I just can't eat. I'll sit here with you and watch."

Why had she come? Her head was swimming. She had had nothing to eat since her breakfast of toast, coffee and juice.

"You needn't eat—I shall." He consulted Thalia—the family were all hovering around his table, and the few other diners watched with interest—and Thalia said, "Soup. The *avgolemono*—it will do her good."

Lee translated. "A happy blending of egg, chicken, lemon and rice. . . . A small salad," he added. "Easy with the fetá and anchovies this time. Me, I'll have the *moussaka* as usual."

When they were alone, Lee said, "You'll feel better, I promise you."

"I'll try. . . . I apologize for being so stupid."

Lee chomped thoughtfully on a Greek olive. "You'll be all right. Was it so dreadful—this afternoon?" he asked.

"Not exactly, just strange."

"How, strange?"

"Almost as if I were someone else——"

He beckoned to Cherry and she came, smiling. "Ask your mother if Mrs. Armitage may have her soup as soon as possible. She hasn't eaten all day," he said.

"Coming right up," said Cherry and went with the speed of light to the kitchen.

"How did you know that?"

"Deduction." He buttered a piece of bread. "Eat that, slowly. It's very good. They do their own baking here."

Cherry came with the soup and said anxiously, "Mama hopes you will like it."

"Try a spoonful," Lee said. "It can cure anything—well, almost anything."

"It's delicious," Stacy told him.

"Someday you must try other specialties. I'll forbear reciting them now. . . . Don't talk if you don't want to. The onlookers will just think we're married, or I'll talk, then they'll think we've quarreled. I'm ready for a reconciliation and you're just sulky."

He talked—about the restaurant, the family and where he'd met them—"Actually, they were struggling in the city, and I persuaded them they were needed here"—and of the Palmer house, of Marcia, and the village.

They were almost ready to go, having their coffee, his Greek, hers not—"Perhaps you'd better not embark on Greek coffee tonight"—when young Alexis came over. "Phone for you, Lee," he said.

Lee excused himself and went into the small waiting room to the left of the door. When he returned, Stacy asked, "Anything wrong?"

"Yes. I'll tell you on the way home." He collected his bill, said the farewells, promised to return and they went out to the car.

Stacy said, "I do feel better."

"Good," he said, and when they were in the car, "That was Cora. Marcia called. Gerry Harden has died of a coronary. I'll get the first plane out tomorrow for Jamaica."

She said inadequately, "I'm so sorry, Lee."

After a moment he said heavily, "I simply cannot believe it. Of course, he drove himself, but he is—he was—a young man. Marcia needs help. I'll call her as soon as we get home."

Stacy thought: Marcia needs help. Not Elaine?

When they reached the studio, she said, "Don't get out, Lee . . . and I'm so very sorry. And thank you again for everything."

"That's all right," he said abstractedly. "Try to get some sleep. It's over," he told her. "Try to believe it's over." And thought: For Gerry, anyway.

Stacy went into the house and made herself ready for bed. Her head no longer ached; she did not feel ill. She felt, as she had told Lee, strange. She could not have expressed why, had she wished to. It would have been impossible to put into words the change which she had seen, almost as soon as her unwelcome guests entered the room. Winnie was as she remembered her; she had always been talkative and animated; she was now perhaps even more assured than on that first evening in the Pump Room. She would never change, Stacy thought. The mold was there, and the pattern; appearance, style, mannerisms, a great deal of money and besotted parents. Yet, if Bob tired of her? He won't, Stacy thought. Perhaps she'll tire first.

The alteration was, of course, in Bob. Lee had dismissed him as "hearty," Stacy had softened it with "outgoing." He still was, but whereas the trait had been, since her first knowledge of him, as much part of him as his skin, it now seemed superimposed. The quality she had always associated him with was male dominance, a careless confidence, occasionally psychological brutal, often insensitive. She thought: He's in love with her, of course, but he's afraid of her.

She remembered Lee speaking to her of rejection; a cliché word nowadays. You couldn't write it off as vanity or humiliation. But why hadn't she seen what had happened to her natural awareness? She'd been so vulnerable to his shifts of moods, so sickeningly anxious to please, she told herself with a flash of anger. Cinderella and Prince Charming . . . or was that Sleeping Beauty?

She had really been out of love for a long time, except with herself, her self-centered self—out of love since the morning at breakfast when he'd said, "I want a divorce, Stacy," and told her why.

She reached out her arms in the darkness, feeling as if she had emerged from an imprisoning cocoon. Now she had wings. For the first time since that dreadful Sunday morning, she felt that she was on the way to becoming free.

Before she slept she thought briefly of Lee. Would he be free, she wondered, as Elaine was now?

❧ 14 ❧

Stacy was writing letters at the kitchen counter shortly before eleven the next morning. She had slept well and, if she'd dreamed, didn't recall it. She had awakened early, oppressed for a split second by her usual sense of futility, a formless misery, but a moment later, fully conscious, she was aware of a curious sense of emptiness. It was like a clean-swept, unfurnished room, barren of everything except the faint light which precedes dawn. Physically, she was conscious only of hunger.

She fixed herself a more substantial breakfast than usual, washed up, took stationery and stamps from the drawer of a table in the living room, and returned to the counter to write in the spring sunshine. First, a letter to Jim Swift; the manuscript which had reached her two days before was at her elbow. She had read it and had suggestions to make and questions to ask. It was more difficult to answer her mother's last two querulous letters: "The least you can do is to write me once a week," complained Mrs. Ware and Stacy thought: About what? The weather? The exhibit? But I wrote her about that last time. The occasional social activity?

The screened front door stood open and someone asked from the steps, "You home?"

Stacy left her high stool and went to meet Vanessa.

Shadow came in first, looked around to see that nothing had been altered, and padded into the kitchen to lie on the counter in the sun and idly roll Stacy's pen back and forth.

"Wherever have you been?" Vanessa demanded. She lowered herself into a big chair, pulled the scarf from her head and ran her fingers through her hair.

"Here, mostly. . . . I'm glad you came. I've a present for you."

"What for? It isn't my birthday."

"I don't know when your birthday is."

"I've no intention of telling you. I think people should stop having birthdays at, say, twenty-one. I was, of course, born on a cusp. What's the present?"

"Mary Renault's new book. I stopped at the book shop recently and Jeremy told me you collected her. I was going to bring it over this afternoon."

Vanessa, who disliked showing gratitude, except on rare occasions, nodded. "Well, splendid. . . . What am I interrupting?"

"I'm just doing mail, which I hate."

Vanessa settled herself in the big chair. She said, "Then you'll welcome my arrival. By the way, Shadow and I went past here—on foot and paw—yesterday afternoon and saw a car outside with Illinois plates, I think. My eyes aren't as good as they might be."

Her distance vision was excellent; she wore glasses only to read, and not always then, as Stacy knew.

She said, half amused, half annoyed, "Not much escapes you. Yes, an Illinois car containing my ex-husband and his wife, who were in the village for a couple of days and came to call."

"Interesting," Vanessa commented, "or I hope so. During the few times I was compelled to see my late spouse, I was either furious, bored, or both."

"Now," Stacy said, "I'll tell you something you don't know."

"Which is . . . ?"

"Lee left for Jamaica sometime this morning. I don't know the plane schedule."

"Jamaica? Anything wrong with Marcia?"

"No. Gerald Harden died of a heart seizure, and as Marcia was with him and Mrs. Harden, she sent for Lee."

"When?"

"Last night. We were having dinner together, Cora telephoned him at the restaurant. He brought me straight home and said he'd take the first plane out. I'm certain he'd want me to tell you."

"Of course," Vanessa said. Her extraordinary eyes, luminous in her lined brown face, were thoughtful. She said, "I'm sorry about Gerry Harden. I liked the little I knew of him. This makes for an interesting situation."

"That's what I thought," Stacy said, "though I have nothing to go on, really."

"You're jumping to what you feel is an obvious conclusion. You think that once the proper amount of time has passed, Elaine will graciously consent to marry Lee. After the tedious formalities are disposed of, she'll be able to marry anyone she selects. Well, you're wrong. I've known Elaine since she was a small girl—coming here as I did off and on. If it happened to be during the summer, she was here with the Osbornes. By the time I became a fixture around the corner, she was, of course, married, and I saw her only a few of the times she and Gerry stopped by to see Lee and Marcia."

"Okay," said Stacy, not really caring. "Maybe it's not obvious, but it seems so. They've known each other practically forever—she's unusually beautiful—and he hasn't married anyone else," she added triumphantly.

Vanessa shook her head. "Way off course," she said.

"Lee has never talked to me about Elaine; I daresay it's the only thing he hasn't—but I am convinced that he dislikes her."

"Why, for heaven's sake?"

"I don't know," Vanessa answered regretfully, "and it bugs me!"

"I'm surprised," Stacy said candidly, "that you haven't asked him."

Vanessa shrugged her thin shoulders. "The word is astonished," she corrected. "I'm astonished myself, but Lee has established off-limits areas, and those who know him are careful, if they value his friendship, to respect them—even, I imagine, his sister."

"How about a cup of coffee?" Stacy asked, after a moment.

"Thanks, not today. Shadow and I have an errand or two. How were your callers?"

"Who? Oh, Bob and his Winnie. Just fine," said Stacy brightly.

Vanessa said, "I assume that this was one encounter you dreaded. You're not like me; I was delighted to go to the mat as it were. But the circumstances were very different. . . . Adam writes he will be coming down some weekend. He's talking Europe, and his parents object. I must see my son and daughter-in-law," she added reflectively. "I think I'll write and tell them, now that they're within reach, that I'm feeling a trifle fragile. And once they discover I'm in good health, they'll complain about Adam, which is silly of them, as I'm on his side."

Stacy went out with her and Vanessa looked across the fields, the road and at the sky. She said, "I predict that we're going to enjoy a superlative May. We don't always; May can be wet or cold or hot or a mixture of these. You'll see," and added carelessly, "Let me know if you hear anything. I don't expect Lee will have time to communicate. Take a deep breath," she advised the younger woman, "before you return to your correspondence."

Shadow propelled himself into Vanessa's shopping basket with the book, and they took off.

Stacy went back to her letters, and then fixed herself a small lunch, after which she went out and walked across the fields toward the Osborne house. She thought: Vanessa considers herself infallible. I'm sure she thinks Lee dislikes Elaine because she does. If she's wrong and I'm right—if he's in love with her—I hope there'll be a happy ending.

She stopped to consider that she did not believe Elaine Harden could be in love with anyone.

She turned her thoughts away; she had become fond of Lee. He was, she thought, a good friend; all she could do was wish him well. Her own situation preoccupied her. You carry a burden for a long time; then it's lifted, your shoulders straighten, you experience a natural relief but are aware that something is missing. What do you do now? she thought. You work, you discard the nightmares, you *live*.

She had almost reached the Osborne house, when Cora came out of the back door, waving a dish towel. "Hi," said Cora. "Isn't it a lovely day?"

Stacy agreed and they stood there talking for a moment. "Did Mr. Osborne get off all right?" she asked.

"Bright and early. . . . Poor boy, he was very upset," said Cora, who had known Lee for many years.

"Of course. I was so sorry."

"Mr. Harden," Cora said, shaking her pepper and salt head, "was a fine man, and just about the best friend Lee ever had. Elaine—well, what a shock for her. You never know, do you?"

Stacy agreed that, no, you never knew.

"The Lord moves in mysterious ways. Poor Marcia. It must have been terrible for her too." She added, "Lee said he'd let me know their plans." She turned to go into the house, "If you need anything, holler," she added, "and stop by for a cup of tea or coffee when you can."

Ten days or so later Stacy was working when Lee walked in. She dropped her brush and stared at him. "When did you get back?" she asked.

"Last night." He looked very tired. "I was too beat to telephone except to let my partners know——"

"Marcia?" she asked.

"We took Gerald back to California," he answered wearily, "for burial. I stayed on a few days; Marcia's still there. I don't know when she'll be back. There are a thousand things which must be done—lawyers, the usual details. Elaine is competent to handle all this under direction, but Marcia doesn't want to leave her; and she's trying to persuade Elaine to return here with her."

He was walking about the studio, looking from the windows. "I don't know if she will or not," he added, "although she's often said she'd like to spend another summer here. . . . What are you doing?"

She showed him and he said, "I like it. It has light and a sort of gaiety."

"It's not a Gothic novel."

"Marcia asked me if I had looked after you."

"I hope you told her that indeed you have."

"Of course. I'll help where I can on next month's exhibit, fetch the pictures to the gallery, even hang them for you. Meantime, if you don't mind, I'll drop by in my guardian role and we'll take time out to drive around. I doubt you've been on all the back roads. We can also go calling on people, the Palmers—I've a good excuse there

—the Irvingtons, Rosie Niles if she's around, the Bankses. And when, presently, the Ross Camerons return to their ancient dwelling and contemporary swimming pool, we'll crash their parties too."

Stacy laughed, "Aren't you afraid of rumor?" she asked.

"Not at all; it won't be the first time. I enjoy it, rather."

"And you're very busy."

"Not most evenings, late afternoons, Sundays. . . . you're all right, Stacy?"

"Never better."

"Good girl. We'll have to go back to Theo's some night so that you can do justice to Thalia's cuisine."

"You haven't told me how you are."

"Tired. All the formalities, planes, and the legalities too. But I've great powers of recuperation. Now I'll get back to the office. . . . See you soon." He gave her a half salute and went out with his long, quiet stride. A short time later Stacy saw his car leave the Osborne house, headed toward the village.

May arrived on time, and much as Vanessa had predicted, in a small, creeping fire of pale green, which strengthened as the rose and ivory effervescence of fruit blossoms foamed along the streets, in backyards, bordered the parkways and illuminated the fields.

"Wait," said Amy, at the hairdresser's. "Little Oxford's dogwoods attract people from miles around. I stay home weekends. Go out of the village a little way and the roads are crawling with artists."

She and Stacy were shouting at each other under their side-by-side dryers.

"What did you do with Benjy?" Stacy asked.

"Left him in a playpen, with Mrs. Ferris. Of course, he can get out, but she has an unerring watchful eye. And she's willing to come whenever I need her, though, of course, Letty cries, 'What's wrong with Grandma as a baby sitter?' The answer is nothing, except her instant surrender to his charm and demands. But she's not always home. . . . Also Ben said if I didn't have my hair done soon he'd leave me." The dryers went off simultaneously and her last words were audible to various women having manicures, waiting for someone to pick them up or merely reading the lurid magazines which were available in great profusion.

Amy lowered her voice and said, "So that will be all over town in no time, flat. Comb outs now—and then lunch. This is an adventure. I'm so glad you called me."

"I don't come here often," Stacy told her. "I wash my own hair; it doesn't need setting, but it does require cutting and thinning."

At lunch Amy said, "You and Lee must come to dinner the first night I can be reasonably sure Ben will show up."

Stacy answered, "All of a sudden, we get asked everywhere together. It's pleasant, of course, but embarrassing."

"Well, you each might do worse," Amy said candidly.

"Lee has no intentions, honorable or dishonorable," Stacy said solemnly, "and neither, I must add, have I."

"Speculation is rife; Katie and Jeremy were saying so just the other night."

"Spare me," Stacy begged her, "also Lee."

"Is Marcia ever coming back? I miss her."

"Lee says before the end of the month. With Mrs. Harden."

Amy fell back in an exaggerated gesture of astonishment. "Don't tell me! The lily maid. . . . Speculations will run higher than ever!"

"I've always thought of *that* Elaine as blonde," Stacy said mildly, "and I cannot cast Lee as Sir Lancelot."

"Everyone," said Amy, "will give parties."

"She's in mourning, remember?"

"Yes, of course. Small, suitable gatherings—not an orgy among them," Amy conceded. "It isn't as if she were a rare migrant in these parts; she was practically a summer resident for years. Wait till I tell Ben. He'll have a minor convulsion."

"Why?"

"He thinks she's out of this world—her looks, I mean. He doesn't know her, of course. I certainly hope she isn't taken with some usual, or unusual, ailment while she's here. . . . How long is she staying?"

"Possibly all summer."

"Dear heaven!" said Amy dramatically. "I pray she'll prefer an older physician—Bing, for instance, or even the young new one."

"What new one?"

"Haven't you heard? Unfortunately, he won't be here until autumn—and by that time the fascinating Mrs. Harden will be off on a yacht or touring Europe or something."

"Tell me about the new doctor," Stacy said patiently.

"His name's Carstairs. I don't know where he's from. Served his time, as Ben puts it, at Hopkins—intern, resident. Then he practiced with someone distinguished, and has just bought old Doctor Melvin's house, with office. It's just within the village limits."

"You've lost me."

"Doctor Melvin," Amy explained, "retired before I ever laid eyes on Little Oxford. Then he died. He was older than the Charter Oak. His widow stayed on awhile, then went to live with children or grandchildren. Now she's in a nursing home. Ben met Dr. Carstairs here a couple of months ago when he was looking for a town which could support another doctor. He's an internist, but his specialty is allergy. He should build up quite a practice. It's not only food, smoke, poison ivy, cosmetics, newsprint or common things," she added. "It's people allergic to people, especially when married to each other. There's an RN at the hospital; she specials. I was talking to her the other day. She's Hopkins and she knows him. Seems when he was just out of medical school he married a woman considerably his elder, and loaded.

"Does Ben like him?"

"Ben takes after his father; he likes practically everyone. As to Doctor Carstairs, Ben doesn't really know him, of course; says he's attractive, quiet and clever." She looked at her watch. "Must fly," she said. "Mrs. Ferris, by this time, will be hallucinating. Benjy has that effect on people . . . especially when he condescends to converse."

They walked to the parking lot. "What a day," said Amy, "I can smell it." She looked rather like spring herself, Stacy thought, her apple-blossom coloring and blue eyes.

"I'll call you," Amy said, when they parted. "That's a threat as well as a promise. . . . Are you excited over your exhibit?"

"Of course."

Stacy went back to the studio. She'd been right. Anyway, it was obvious that friends and their friends' friends would take a vocal interest in her pleasant relationship with her neighbor. Next week, she was going with him to the Ross Camerons. She hadn't met Ross, but Beth Cameron had called on her recently, and among other things, had said she and her husband were entertaining a few friends. "I asked Lee to bring you. I hope you'll come."

After she had gone, Stacy reflected that Little Oxford had more than its share of beautiful women. This one was a glorious redhead, poised, friendly and charming. Stacy knew she'd worked for Jeremy Palmer and was the owner of the old diaries which she and Jeremy had edited, and which were shortly to be published. Also she'd married Ross Cameron, Jeremy's friend who'd been divorced and had one child by that marriage.

Stacy went into the studio thinking that all exurban or semi-suburban localities were probably very similar. Little Oxford was simply one example of varying income ranges and conditions, diverse landscapes—and all the same problems. But it was a life she'd never before experienced. In California she and her parents had lived in the small city in which she'd been born; it was within reach of a much larger one, but was self-contained. It had industry, for example, more actual poverty than most suburban places, and certainly more sharply defined social boundaries. She'd had no special feeling for it despite having had a good many friends during her average growing up. She'd forgotten many of the girls she'd known, and remembered only the boys who had been interested in her or she in them. She'd had no anchor there except her attachment to her father and her still-present dutiful concern for her mother. In New York, she'd had no roots, except in Bob; the same was true of Chicago. Now she felt that for the first time she was putting down roots—tentative, fragile and subject to a changing emotional climate which could encourage growth or destroy it. She felt as uneasy and as uncertain as a child who enters a strange locality and new school to attend classes under unfamiliar teachers and begins hesitantly and hopefully to make friends, but is also anxious and lonely.

❧ 15 ❧

Adam came galloping around the corner to the studio. He shouted through the screen door and no one answered, but a moment later he heard Stacy call, "I'm around in back."

There was a small flagstone patio, reached also from the kitchen. Stacy was lying on a lounge chair, which together with other outdoor equipment, Lee had brought from the Osborne barn earlier in May.

"Hi," said Adam with an approving whistle. "You are sensational in shorts. I can't wait for the bikini season."

"When did you get in?"

"Last night. The uncrowned queen of Little Oxford summons you to tea. My parents are there for a family conference about me, of course. Gran needs reinforcements."

"Why?"

"Well," he answered, collapsing on the flagstones, his arms about his knees, "four of us decided that a walking tour—England, Scotland—would be educational. All those beautiful British birds!"

Stacy laughed. "Your family won't permit it?" she asked.

"They can't prevent me. At eighteen I came into a small

income from my grandfather's trust fund, a mere pittance, naturally, until I'm twenty-one—but it will pay my second-class way, bicycle rentals and modest pubs or whatever."

"I thought you were going to invade Europe after graduation."

"That too. This is just a preliminary investigation. The other guys browbeat their families into consenting and also supplying the wherewithal."

"If you can afford it," Stacy asked reasonably, "what's the problem?"

"My mother cries and my father bellows a lot, in a well-bred way. They know that scenes revolt me. Gran, naturally, thrives on them."

He rose and seized her hand. "Come along," he said, "we need you."

"I can't come like this."

"Of course you can. You're overdressed for the heat wave."

Warren Steele, his wife, and his mother, were on the back porch. As Stacy and Adam approached, he said, "By the way, Mother hates cats, and of course Shadow is aware of this unpardonable flaw, so he spends his time bugging her. Malicious animal."

As they ascended the steps, Warren Steele rose, and Vanessa said, fanning herself, "About time. . . . Makings for a spritzer are on the table, also a pitcher of iced tea. I don't believe you've met my son and daughter-in-law, Stacy."

Warren smiled and took Stacy's hand in a firm, short, no-nonsense grip. He was a big man, twenty pounds overweight, and bore no resemblance to his mother or son, being fair and florid, his hair receding from a high forehead. The younger Mrs. Steele remained seated. She was a rather small, painfully thin woman, with artfully lightened brown hair and china-blue eyes. Stacy was entranced to see Shadow sitting at her feet, staring at her fixedly. He turned his head, looked at Stacy and, she thought, winked and then went back to his preoccupation with Emily Steele.

Emily Steele said, "How nice to meet you. Adam speaks of you often, that is, when we see him, which is rarely. . . . Mother, will you please call off that horrible cat?"

"He's just admiring you, Emily. . . . Shadow, make tracks," she added.

He made them as far as the porch railing, leaped upon it and crouched, staring.

Warren Steele spoke apologetically to Stacy, who was pouring a glass of tea, "My wife's allergic——" he began.

"Nonsense," said Emily. "I adore kittens. We've always had kittens around. But Shadow terrifies me."

"He thinks you're a mouse," Adam remarked, "but he couldn't be further off."

Emily turned to Stacy. "Perhaps Adam's told you about his hare-brained plans," she said.

"Just now," Stacy admitted.

"I do hope you have some influence with him," Warren broke in.

"I'm afraid not," Stacy said, sitting down near Vanessa. Anyway, I sympathize with him. When I was his age——"

"Hardly decades ago," Vanessa remarked.

"——I would have liked nothing better," Stacy concluded, and almost believed it. At Adam's age, however, she'd been in college looking no further ahead than to graduation and escaping east to find a job.

Adam's father said, frowning, "At Adam's age he should spend his summers until graduation serving an apprenticeship in the business world."

"Good grief!" said Adam. "The record's stuck!"

"Well, I did," said Warren. "My father had the right idea, but then," he added sorrowfully, "a good many young people respected their parents in those days."

Vanessa smiled and Stacy saw it, half-amused, half-grudging affection. Warren's father had not, of course, brought him up to respect his vanished mother, Stacy thought, and few could blame him. On the other hand, when Vanessa's son was of age, he had made his own decision. She concluded that he was a stuffed shirt, but that much of the stuffing was praiseworthy.

Adam said, "I do respect you and Mom—but if, as you point out, I'm to spend the rest of my life toiling in the establishment, grubbing away like a good boy, I feel I'm entitled to some freedom until after graduation. Say, a year after," he added, sliding his eyes toward his parents.

Emily began silently to weep, her face unmoved, but large tears coursing down her cheeks.

"Ma, for Pete's sake," said Adam, exasperated and Warren put a heavy arm across her shoulders. "Now, now," he murmured.

Vanessa said, "Give over, Emily. . . . Warren, fix her a spritzer; the wine's cold; so's the soda. You're old enough," she told Adam. "We'll drink to your holiday."

"You're such a bad example," Emily told her balefully.

Shadow growled and Vanessa asked, "When have I ever been a good one?"

"It's only for six weeks," Adam reminded them. "Then I'll come home, run errands, drive the car, turn up at the country club, seduce the Westchester maidens . . ."

Later, Stacy walked home, leaving the Steele family to argue over the supper table. Vanessa had urged her to join them, but she'd refused. She felt a certain amount of sympathy for Warren Steele, who had undoubtedly longed for a son exactly like himself with a touch of his conventional Emily, and, perhaps, a slight sharp seasoning from his own legendary father. Warren had not married until he was thirty, and had then made a very careful selection, Vanessa had told her once, adding, "Poor Warren! He hoped to dilute what was once known as bad blood."

Vanessa herself, at the table, listening to Emily's plaints and Warren's pronouncements, was thinking of this also. She thought: Adam inherited, I believe, the best of us all. You have to say of Emily that she's merely unimaginative and dull, but on the whole, kind and certainly devoted to her family. Warren's dull also, but good. Good men are rarely exciting, I suppose. As for Warren's father—she shrugged her mental shoulders, unaware that her son was thinking also of her. In a resentful way he both admired and loved her. She'd been an exotic and thorny blossom in the Steeles' well-tended garden; stubborn as a mule, wilful as the wind and also as ruthless and self-seeking as her husband, his father.

Before they drove home that evening, he'd given Adam, along with counseling and admonitions, his reluctant, parental blessing—echoed by a tearful Emily.

"Wow!" said Adam when the car drove off. "You've done it again."

"Stacy helped," said his grandmother absently, "but even without us, you would have prevailed."

"How come?"

"Youth," said Vanessa. "Growing old, that's the only thing I regret losing. . . . If there's coffee, bring it in; if not, make some. Put a slug of brandy in mine. Your parents wear me out. Then come and draw me a map of where you plan to go."

"I've told you."

"Not specifically."

"Oh, you mean where can you reach me and when? I dunno. Country roads, few conveniences, a look at the sea, a mountain to climb, a lake . . . Tim Rogers—he and Hank room next door to me—he's the planner. That is, he'll probably see that we don't tangle with the fuzz, have someplace to lay our heads and food at reasonable intervals. There should always be one practical guy along. And of course, there's always the American Express—London—Edinburgh—in case we're arrested or someone back home is inconsiderate enough to get murdered. You keep yourself in check for those six weeks, Gran, and don't fall down cliffs or back steps."

"I'll try," said Vanessa.

May foamed and flowered, the dogwoods bloomed and shortly before the Memorial Day weekend, Lee borrowed a partner's station wagon and took Stacy and her paintings to the Gallery, where she was to exhibit in the smaller of the two rooms for the month of June. She liked the gallery owners, a pleasant, knowledgeable man and his wife, and they were very helpful. The room had just been cleared; they could hang the paintings, and the Reynoldses would open the room again, June first. Stacy and Lee worked early that morning, then he went to his office and with the Reynoldses' assistance, the job was completed. "What do you think?" she asked them, looking disheveled, her hair flying, her hands grubby.

The Reynoldses said they were pleased. "You'll draw a good crowd," said Ed Reynolds. "We'll announce it in the local paper and others; we've already sent out cards . . . I think you'll do better than you expect. . . . Don't you, Janice?" he asked his wife.

She answered, pulling back the collar of her smock, "It's going to be hot, I think. We'll turn on the air conditioning." She stood back and looked around the room.

"Frankly," she added, "I'm a little tired of landscapes, seascapes, abstracts and portraits. Your work has great imagination, Mrs. Armitage."

"It needs more than that," Stacy said, scowling slightly, "and I'm so grateful to you both."

She took a taxi to the studio and took a long shower. She was half dressed and brushing her hair when the telephone rang. She reached for it, thankful there was a bedroom extension.

"Stacy?" said Lee. "How did things go?"

"Fine. Where are you?"

"Still at the office. You must be tired."

"I am, a little."

"I'll come by in an hour. Chad's driven me home. I left his station wagon in the parking lot. Anyway, I'll take you out to dinner."

They'd had dinner together a good many times these past weeks—at his house, with Cora officiating, here in the studio, at friends', and once again at Theo's.

"I'll fix something here."

"Nope. I'm in no mood for home cooking. Suppose we just go to the Inn?"

He called for her and they went in companionable silence. When they were seated and he'd ordered, he said, "Ed and Janice Reynolds are nice people. He's a frustrated artist, you know, and was also a critic in the city. She inherited some money and they came here and opened the gallery some years ago. Are you pleased with the exhibit?"

"Oh, yes," she told him and then her animation faded and she said, "I've been trying to think, since I saw everything hung, what's wrong with my work."

"Ed suggest anything?"

"No. He just nodded when his wife spoke of imagination. When I got home, I suddenly knew the answer."

"Which is . . . ?"

"It lacks strength," she said soberly. "It's—well, pretty, I suppose. It has charm, perhaps; but strength, no."

"But you have it in you."

"Where?"

"The nightmare sketchbook," he said, watching her.

Her color faded, as her animation had. "I'd almost forgotten," she said faintly. "I was going to burn the sketchbook."

"Don't."

"Why not?" she demanded, setting her wineglass down. "Those sketches are horrible. They're ugly, terrifying."

"They're all of that," he admitted. "But they're powerful; they express strong emotions, Stacy. Don't destroy them—not until you're sure. Perhaps not even then. Where are they?"

"Locked up."

"Are you aware of how much you've changed?" he asked.

She shook her head. "Yes . . . no . . ."

"Make up your mind."

After a while she said, "What do *you* see?"

"A woman who has awakened from a bad dream," he said, smiling. "Is that it?"

"I suppose so."

"When you were a child," he asked, "did you ever wake in the dark and see crouching, unfamiliar shapes in the furniture around you?"

"I expect every child does," she said.

"And when it's light again, then you're no longer frightened?"

"You're suggesting my marriage was a bad dream?"

"No, I'm sure it wasn't." He thought: Perhaps just a dream. "Not until after it was over."

She said, as the waiter came to take away the entrée and

salad plates, "Once you said something to me about rejection. That was, of course, right. I did feel rejected and—very sorry for myself. But when I saw him—Bob—again, it was he who had changed, or so I thought."

"Familiar furniture after all," he said, smiling. "Here come your strawberries and cream, one of the most becoming fruits a woman can ever eat. So eat those."

"Not familiar," she contradicted, "and, you must admit, in a different setting. I've really been an idiot," she said ruefully.

"We all have that tendency." He raised his glass. "Here's to change," he said. "And to Marcia's homecoming."

"Oh, good," said Stacy. "When?"

"Two days after the holiday. They couldn't get reservations before. She telephoned this afternoon."

"Mrs. Harden's coming with her?"

"That's right," he said, "for the summer—unless she gets restless."

🎋 16 🎋

On the first day of June, Stacy's exhibition was opened to as much of the public as cared to attend; and Marcia returned to Little Oxford with Elaine Harden. Lee met them at the airport in the afternoon; in the morning he had stopped briefly at the gallery, where he found Stacy looking nervous.

"Uptight?"

"Well, yes. . . . I promised I'd be here and again in the afternoon. So far no one I know has come. They're all being very courteous," Stacy said. "I wish I were home."

"Eventually you will be. . . . Here's someone you know."

"It was Rosie Niles with Mrs. Reynolds. "Don't bother, Janice. Stacy and I are old friends." She gave Stacy her hard little hand. "Congratulations," she said. "Now I'll look around. . . . Oh, hi, Lee—where's Marcia?"

"Due home today."

"I've been away. What's been happening?"

"Stacy can tell you."

"Don't come with me," Rosie told Stacy. "If I see anything I don't like, I'll mutter audibly, which could be embarrassing for us both."

She went off, flickering before the paintings like a small

intense candle. She spoke to a few people, returned to her starting point and went the rounds again, slowly.

Stacy said, "I hope she doesn't buy something just because she knows me."

"She's liable to," Lee told her.

"I wish she wouldn't. People shouldn't hang paintings to which they don't relate."

He interrupted. "In that case," he said, "she'll buy one and give it away. Don't put yourself down; nor Rosie."

He'd left by the time Rosie returned; a few more people had filtered in; now and then Stacy heard a snatch of conversation. "But who *is* she?" "Oh, recent; a friend of Amy Irvington's, I believe." "No, I don't know her." "The card said people who get here between four and five are to be introduced." "I like this, don't you?"

Stacy's face burned, and Rosie asked, "Where's Lee?"

"He has to meet Marcia and Mrs. Harden."

"Fill me in."

Stacy did so and Rosie said thoughtfully, "I'm sorry. I liked Gerald Harden, though I knew him very slightly. . . . Why in the world are you looking distraught?"

"I can't help overhearing comments."

"Good, bad or indifferent, don't let them get to you. I grew hardened to it. Bill always said, when, now and then, there was a heckler, drunk or sober. 'Rosie, always remember, you're the one who got the job, and who has the talent.' I like that painting—number eighteen, I think —the one with the fog rolling in, the houses barely visible, the shadowy figure."

Stacy said, astonished, "That's just the original of a book jacket, Rosie. I didn't have enough without using some of those and some of the illustrations."

"I don't care how it was conceived. I like it; spooky but restful. You could spend hours wondering whose figure, what's happening in the fog, what people are in the houses, back of drawn shades."

"You can read the book to find out," Stacy told her, laughing.

"I don't want to read the book. I'll furnish my own people and happenings. I've just the place for it in my dressing room. On the way out, I'll tell Mrs. Reynolds it's a sale. You can come help me hang it properly. . . . How did you make out at the Palmer house?"

"They were pleased, I think. I still have shopping to do for Katie. She's redoing some of the old furniture; slipcovers, that is. I'll take her swatches."

"I'll get there soon to see what I think of the house. It wasn't quite finished when I left. . . . I was in London and Paris," she said, "in case you hadn't heard."

"I heard."

"It's impossible to keep anything quiet here. This town is composed of eyes and ears—also tongues. Next time I'll go to Tibet. I'll call you soon, Stacy."

"Rosie, are you sure you like the painting?"

"Why else would I buy it?"

"To be kind," Stacy answered, "and then you'd give it away."

"Did you arrive at that conclusion all by yourself?"

"Lee helped."

"He would. Well, he's right. I often buy things from ceramics to paintings to books to folk art just to encourage the people who created them. And these I do give away to people I'm sure will like them. I don't have tag sales myself. But I also buy things I like and these I keep. I'm not being kind, simply selfish." She smiled not only with her generous red mouth but with her great black eyes. "I suppose it's natural to be suspicious of kindness, or what you think of as kindness—which translates into charity, doesn't it? Or a touch of condescension? God knows I once felt the same way. Take a chance, Stacy, even in tight, self-contained Little Oxford. Quite a few of us are un-motivated."

Some time after the noon hour Stacy returned to the studio to take a sandwich and milk to the patio, where she could lie back and smell the fragrant air. If it was polluted, she thought, she didn't know it. At two, she had to be back at the Gallery. This was customary, she'd learned. The Gallery thrived on modest showmanship. Artists didn't just go in and ask if—for a fee or simply a possible com-mission—they could be exhibited. And it wasn't like schools and banks which specialized in local painters and had exhibitions as a public service, or like the elegant shops which showed a few paintings in their windows, advertised them and, when there was a sale, collected a commission. The Gallery selected its exhibitions, and not all were local. They advertised, promised that on opening day the artist would be there at certain times and, for an hour in the afternoon, served sherry and made formal introductions. Granting that ninety percent of the resi-dents came out of curiosity, and village people came to look at the residents as well as the paintings, there were always those who were really interested, especially in the new and unknown whose work might increase in value. Those were the buyers, as a rule, and the Gallery had never been known not to recover the cost of advertising and good sherry.

When Stacy reached home, she'd sold two paintings in addition to the one Rosie had selected. And Mrs. Reynolds had predicted with evident pleasure, "This was only the beginning."

By evening Stacy was tired. After supper she went, as she'd promised, to see Vanessa and give her a report.

She'd also promised to take her to the Gallery during the exhibition. "Not that I intend to buy anything," Vanessa had warned her. "I haven't room left for a feather in this house and Shadow and I already have examples of your work for free. . . . When do I get his portrait study back?" she asked.

"I told you, Van, after the exhibit's over."

"I could drop dead before that. I hope it's labeled not for sale."

"It is, to Mrs. Reynolds' sorrow. She told me there are quite a few cat fanciers in this area."

"Then you can take orders," said Vanessa promptly, "to paint their inferior felines."

"I couldn't," said Stacy. "I never have done animals—"

"Watch your language!"

"——except when illustrating a book. Besides, Shadow isn't exactly a cat."

Shadow pricked up his ears and smiled. Extraordinary, the power he had over this fond and foolish female.

"Marcia home?"

"Lee was to pick her up this afternoon," Stacy said, yawning.

"Scat," said Vanessa. "You're out on your feet."

"I don't much like standing around looking vague," said Stacy. "Maybe I should look eager or hopeful, but it's sort of awkward. Thank heavens I don't have to, after today. I'll probably just go in briefly with you, or other friends, but then I won't feel as if I'm also on exhibit."

She went back to the studio and was ready for bed when the telephone spoke. She answered it half asleep.

"How was it?" Lee asked.

"Terrible—I mean, very nice."

"Sell anything?"

"Rosie bought 'Night Fog,' and two others were sold

this afternoon. I have the names of the buyers. . . . Tell me about Marcia. Is she all right?"

"Fine. Just a little tired. She and Elaine have gone to bed. She said to give you her love, and she wants you to go with her and Elaine to the Gallery in a couple of days."

"Are you coming down with a cold?"

"No. Why?"

"You sound hoarse."

"Women talk too much," he said. "Not you; I make the polite exception. I've been smoking too much——"

"With a pipe you smoke mostly matches."

"That's what you think. Glad about the sales—see you soon," he said. "Good night."

Marcia called the next morning. After the greetings, after Stacy remarked, "I missed you; so did Van," Marcia said, "Well, I'm back now. . . . Are you free for lunch day after tomorrow—that's Friday."

"Why, yes. . . . Jim Swift and his wife are stopping by Saturday. They're on a trip through the area."

"Suppose Elaine and I pick you up. We can have lunch and go to the Gallery."

"Why, yes," said Stacy. "I'll be so glad to see you. What time?"

"Say twelve-thirty."

But Thursday afternoon Stacy called the Osborne house and said when Marcia answered, "It's Stacy—about tomorrow——"

"Lee said you'd try to get out of going to the Gallery."

"It isn't that. It's Van. She just left. She came to use the telephone. Shadow's ailing. She called a veterinarian. She's to see him at ten tomorrow; I'm taking them——"

"Good heavens . . . is it anything serious?"

"I don't think so, and Shadow doesn't, either. But Van's worried."

"If he does this often," Marcia pointed out, "she'll have her own phone installed—not, of course, for herself, but for him."

"They're to be there at ten o'clock. You know how long you may have to wait in any doctor's office. Suppose I meet you? After lunch I have to do some comparative shopping for Katie."

"Don't tell me she's throwing out the furniture. . . . Wait a minute. She's asked you to pick up a few more transistors."

"No, they're already in every room in the house. Jeremy's decided she's a radio freak. I'm going to look at slipcover material. Where shall we meet?"

"Elaine likes the Inn; it's quiet."

"If I find I'm going to be late, I can call you there."

"Very well. And perhaps we'll just go look at the exhibit before lunch. Would you rather we did that?"

"Frankly, yes," said Stacy.

She took Vanessa and Shadow to the animal hospital. Apparently he could read because he looked from his window ledge and uttered a loud profanity. They did have to wait for some time and Shadow, who had submitted to the indignity of a large carrying case, thrashed about and moaned. Children with barking dogs were interested. One decided, aloud, that the lady had a sick raccoon. Women with large leash-held or small arm-clasped dogs were sympathetic. The poor thing must be in agony. Was it, one asked, a toy poodle? She adored toys.

Vanessa responded that, no, it was a cat, that he was by no means in agony, but simply spitting mad.

When their turn came, she said, "Come in with me, Stacy."

"To hold his hand?"

"No, mine."

They went into the examination room and Doctor Parker lifted Shadow from case to table.

"Watch it," Vanessa warned. "He's being far too docile. Either he's terribly sick or he's about to attack."

"We understand each other," said Doctor Parker, and dared to stroke Shadow's black head. "You're a big, handsome fellow," he informed him unnecessarily and Shadow closed his eyes, smiling.

At the conclusion of the visit (during which Doctor Parker's assistant, Mike, a good-looking young man, regarded with appreciation not only the patient but also Stacy) Doctor Parker diagnosed, "Digestive upset. . . . What do you feed him?"

Vanessa told him in detail, including alcohol.

"I'd cut out all rich table scraps, and also his cocktail."

Shadow's tail grew very large.

Vanessa said reluctantly, "All right. But he's accustomed to his very diluted drink before my dinner."

Mike chuckled and suppressed it, but the doctor said seriously, "I see. Well, suppose he goes on the wagon for, say, a week? Then you can report how he is generally. How old did you say he was?"

"I didn't, but he's going on sixteen—and a bit," she added.

"Very fine specimen," said the doctor. "Now, the carrying case."

Shadow aroused himself from the melancholy into which his suddenly delicate digestive system had plunged him. "Mike, give me a hand," said the doctor hastily, just escaping a good, deep scratch, but Vanessa ordered, "Let me."

She spoke in no uncertain terms to her familiar; he closed his eyes again, affected a swoon and was popped into the basket.

"Thank you," Vanessa said graciously. "You have my name and address? Will you please bill me?" and swept out.

"Well, I'll be damned!" said Mike.

"That," said his employer, "is Vanessa Steele. The old lady, not the cat."

"Who's the girl?"

"I've no idea. I'll tell you about Mrs. Steele sometime. I've been hoping to get my hands on that cat, not that I wish him a disaster. But when you hear about her, you hear about him. We had a cleaning woman once who worked for Mrs. Steele for a while; swears she's a witch."

"I wouldn't be surprised," said Mike.

"Okay, so it's Mrs. Godly's Pom's turn, and we may as well get that triweekly checkup over with," Doctor Porter said.

Stacy delivered Shadow, his medication, and Vanessa to their door and Vanessa said, "Good. I hope I don't have to call on you again. Shadow's always been so——Hell," she added, "I suppose he's growing old too."

"Van, Doctor Parker said not to worry."

"What does he know?" asked Vanessa unreasonably, and then laughed. She let Shadow out and he scooted away, grumbling. His dignity had been impaired. She said, "He'll come back. Run along. Give my love to Marcia and be sure to tell me how the widow is doing. Someday, Stacy, will you take me to Letty Irvington's? It's too far on the bicycle, and Oscar will cheer Shadow up."

"Oscar!"

"You didn't know? He's the only dog I've ever known Shadow to tolerate. Oscar, who has the disposition of a saint—although I suspect their dispositions weren't always that good—thinks Shadow's great fun, so Shadow humors him."

Stacy kept her appointment, getting to the Inn only a few minutes late and was conducted to Marcia's table.

Marcia, indicating her cheek, said, "Well, kiss me hello," and Elaine, smiling slightly, said, "How very nice to see you again."

Stacy sat down, refused a drink and said, after a moment, "I'm so very sorry, Mrs. Harden."

"We're going to be neighbors," Elaine told her, "so please don't call me Mrs. Harden. And thank you, Stacy. Everyone who knew Gerry, however slightly, is, I think, sorry."

She was unchanged. She was not in mourning, but wearing a beautifully cut dress of gray and mauve. "I could never have gotten along without Marcia," she added.

"Of course, you could," Marcia said. She had lost weight, Stacy noted, and she looked tired.

Their waiter came; they ordered. Elaine, a large salad and iced tea; Marcia and Stacy, omelettes. Before they were served, the conversation was desultory. Elaine said that Lee had told them how delightful it had been to have Stacy next door. "For company." she added, and then, "But I really want to speak about your paintings. They're lovely . . . I told Mrs.—Reynolds, isn't it?—that I want the one of the roses—the still life."

"Please," said Stacy, hating herself for feeling uncomfortable again. She was an artist, wasn't she, who hoped someday to make her entire living at it and to give Bob's contribution, if possible, back to him or to a charity?

"You mustn't feel——"

Elaine looked at her thoughtfully. The color she wore was somehow reflected in the gray eyes. "I want it," she said, "because I like it. Do tell her, Marcia, that it wouldn't make any difference who painted it. My best friend, my worst enemy, or a total stranger. I simply want it."

"You can believe her," Marcia said.

Stacy did. . . . Whether Elaine Harden loved, hated, or didn't even know you, if you had something she wanted, that was it.

Stacy said, "It's one of the few paintings I've done since I came here . . . the last of the roses. Vanessa brought them to me, and I put them in my Chinese bowl."

"I've a small living room off my bedroom," Elaine said. "Lee designed it for the view. From two of the windows you see a rose garden. Gerald masterminded that, over the heads of the landscape architect. He had a passion for roses, and said that when he retired he would grow them himself."

Marcia's eyes filled with tears. Elaine's did not. "He would have liked your painting, Stacy," she added.

☙ 17 ☙

Before noon on Saturday, Jim and Harriet Swift came to the studio for lunch, after which Stacy led them to the Gallery and her exhibit. Three of her paintings belonged to Lovemay's; one had hung in Jim's office. After the exhibit they'd be returned. The rest of the originals for jackets and illustrations she had been permitted to keep. After the Gallery, they walked back up Parsonage Hill to the parking lot and said good-bye.

"Have a good trip."

"We shall," Jim told her, "and see you, I hope soon after we get back." And Harriet said, "I wish you'd spend a weekend with us, Stacy. It's not very far."

"Good luck with the Gallery," Jim added. He was interested in the paintings which had not been Lovemay assignments, and had especially liked the still life. "Who did you say bought it?"

"A friend of my landlord, who is visiting them this summer."

"She has good taste. I don't think I'd want the 'Night Fog,'" he said, smiling, "much as I liked it as the book jacket. It has an eerie quality which is fine on a dust cover but not for a living room."

Stacy laughed. "Mrs. Niles—she bought it—said it's spooky, but restful."

"Curious combination of qualities," Jim said. "She must be a rather unusual woman. You know her?"

"Yes, though not well," Stacy told him. "She's a dedicated patron of local arts and artists. I'm sure I spoke of her to you once. Rosie Niles—her husband had first one, then several orchestras."

"I remember him now—and her."

When Stacy reached the studio, she parked and walked to Vanessa's. The oldest unmarried Collins girl was there; since Vanessa's accident, she had been coming once a week to clean for her and to take her personal laundry home. She was sweeping the back porch when Stacy came up and said, pushing her hair out of her eyes, "Hot for this time of year, Mrs. Armitage."

"Hi, Edna. . . . yes, I suppose it is."

Edna lowered her voice. "Mrs. Van's fit to be tied," she warned.

Stacy knocked and Vanessa said crossly, "Come in, Edna. You don't have to knock."

"It's Stacy."

"So, you come in."

Stacy went through the kitchen into the living room. Shadow spoke complainingly from his basket and Stacy asked, "Is he worse?"

"No. Just in a bad temper, like me. He's outraged by his restricted diet. I can't get it through his head that it's good for him."

"Why are you in a bad temper?" Stacy inquired. "And may I sit down?"

"Sit by all means. . . . It's that blasted boy."

"Adam?"

"Who else?"

"But what's he done?"

"Given in. He's canceled his trip; his friends, he says,

will have to get along without him. I had a letter from him today."

"Why isn't he going?"

"Oh," said Vanessa, "a girl, of course. Seems she's been up at the college for some weekend clambake or other and also she lives in the next town to Adam and is going to be home all summer. She'll work in the summer theater there, as an apprentice. Adam thinks he'd like to do that too—which is hardly entering the business world," said Vanessa gloomily. "And I doubt that Warren and Emily will see much more of him than they would if he were in England. But they're delighted, especially Warren, because Adam's promised that if he can't paint scenery, usher or whatever it is apprentices do, he'll get a paying job—office, supermarket, it doesn't matter to him."

"Why should that upset you? You'll see more of him."

"When he isn't busy emptying wastebaskets or putting cans on shelves or running around backstage. . . . Women!" She laughed suddenly, like a girl. "The bane of men's lives. Look at me!"

"I'm looking."

"But not, usually, for long," Vanessa added. "Shakespeare was right. Eventually men recover and when they remember, simply dig nostalgically through the ruins."

"I doubt that Adam is serious," Stacy began, but Vanessa interrupted in astonishment. "Of course not; he goes through this every year or so. It's expected and perfectly normal. Just makes me mad to think how I labored to bring his benighted parents around. . . . How was lunch?"

"Today?"

"Don't be wilful. Yesterday I thought you'd come by before or after supper."

"I was tired," Stacy said truthfully.

"And besides, you forgot."

"That's right."

"I forgive you—graciously. How's Marcia?"

"Thinner, a little worn."

"Ladies in waiting," said Vanessa, "are usually both."

"Elaine doesn't seem to me to be a very demanding person," Stacy said.

"That's the real trick. Quote, doesn't seem to be, un-quote. The operative word is 'seem.'"

"I've the impression that Elaine regards Marcia as a somewhat older sister."

"I don't think so, nor Lee as a somewhat younger brother."

Stacy said doggedly, "I think she feels they're all the family she has now."

"Douglas—Marcia's late husband—was extremely jeal-ous of Elaine Harden."

"But why?"

"Oh, the time Marcia spent on her and with her. . . . You call her Elaine now?"

"She asked me to."

"Watch yourself, Stacy. I'm not implying that our Mrs. Harden leans toward the girls, nor for that matter, toward the boys. Vertically, she casts a long shadow."

There was a plaintive inquiry from the occupant of the basket and Vanessa said, "Go back to sleep; I'm not talk-ing to you or about you. . . . Well, I've known a good many women in my time. I don't, of course, really know Mrs. Harden. I don't particularly want to. She reminds me, now that I think of it, of one of those beautiful underwater flowerlike creatures which silently devour anything that drifts their way."

Stacy laughed. She said, "That's a repulsive simile."

"Isn't it?" agreed Vanessa cordially.

Stacy said, "I didn't especially like her when we first met. I don't, actually, now. But I was sorry for her yesterday; and she has so much quiet charm."

"No," said Vanessa, "not charm. To me, at least, charm has warmth; sometimes that's all it is. I would substitute the word 'enchantment.' I've no idea what the dictionary or thesaurus dictates, but to me, they aren't the same quality. Let me know by summer's end what you think then."

When Stacy had left, Vanessa spoke to Shadow and he left his basket to leap with calculated languor into her lap.

"Don't put me on," she told him. "You're feeling much better. You're just emotionally upset because you can't have what you want. I wonder if Elaine Harden gets emotionally upset when she can't? And I also wonder why she feels that, possibly, Stacy could be of some use to her? Otherwise, she wouldn't bother; she'd just stay there underwater. Oh, well. . . ." She stirred and Shadow jumped down, annoyed. "I'll fix supper," she told him, "and as long as we can't share it, I'll drink my aperitif alone. Then I'll cook a nice, expensive, but nourishing lamb chop. You'll have your small permitted tidbit."

She thought going into the kitchen: I'm a tough old woman. I don't form attachments—well, Shadow, which only serves to show what an idiot I am—Adam, and in a way, Stacy. She's all I never was, including vulnerable to a large degree. I'm not; never have been, and she's just beginning to come out of a tunnel, as from a spell. I don't want to see her hurt by anyone.

June dreamed her way into July and the exhibition was over. Stacy had sold seven paintings. Jim Swift returned and sent her a manuscript. She went to town to see him on a sweltering day. She couldn't do it, she said; it demanded something masculine, even harsh. He agreed regretfully, and she went back to Little Oxford, just as regretful but not discouraged. "I know it's a hurry-up job," she'd told Jim, "but it isn't for me."

So you win some, and lose others. Someday she'd have to learn to make the attempt even when she couldn't relate to the subject, the narrative, or the thought which had gone into it.

She said as much when, that evening, she had supper at the Osbornes and Elaine asked, "You have to feel it, don't you?"

"I suppose so," Stacy answered, and leaned from her chair to retrieve Elaine's gossamer handkerchief, just as Marcia filled her glass of iced coffee for her and Lee adjusted the big umbrella over the table on the terrace.

"You pamper me," Elaine said.

"We always have," Marcia reminded her, "ever since you were knee-high."

"And now, Stacy," said Lee. "I thought she'd be immune."

Stacy looked off over the small green garden and sunken bird bath, hearing the others talking but not listening, as the birds, bright or drab, descended or rose to write their signatures on the wind.

"Stacy, are you asleep?" Marcia asked.

"No—just in a slight stupor," she answered, rousing herself. "I'm sorry—too potent a drink, too good a supper, too lovely an evening."

Elaine spoke in her low, curiously uninflected voice. "Sometime, Lee," she suggested, "you must take us all to Theo's. Remember last time? Gerry had such fun. . . . Is that pretty girl, Theo's daughter—I've forgotten her name—still there?"

"Charis? She calls herself Cherry now. Yes. But she won't be for long; she's getting married in the autumn," he said.

"Her parents will miss her," Elaine commented, but Marcia said, "There's a young cousin coming over—it's a big family."

"Lee will be heartbroken," Elaine predicted, adding, "Have you been there, Stacy?"

"Oh, yes. I like it very much."

Lee said, "Two or three times."

Marcia, looking from him to Stacy, said brightly, "Oh, good," and Elaine added, "Well, we must all go. Theo's a superb host. Besides, Lee has to watch his investment."

Lee made a small sound of exasperation and Elaine went on, "The wind's growing cooler. Lee, I left my sweater indoors."

Stacy and Lee walked back to the studio, he shortening his long stride to her shorter steps. The pleasant fragrance of pipe smoke hung in the air, which was now still. She thought: But it isn't cooler and the wind has dropped.

After he'd gone back to his house, she thought of something else Elaine had said. What was it exactly? . . . Oh, yes, after she'd spoken of Theo's, she'd remarked that it was unfortunate Lee hadn't planned a trip to the Greek islands this summer and added to Stacy, "Gerry and I were never able to connect with him. I always wanted to. This summer Marcia could have gone too."

And Lee had said shortly that this summer wasn't the time for him.

As Stacy came back from Vanessa's the next afternoon she saw Elaine Harden walking over to the studio. She met her at the front door, and Elaine said, smiling, "I almost missed you, didn't I? Marcia's off on one of her errands of mercy, so I went for a walk and thought I'd like to see the studio again. Am I interrupting?"

"No, do come in." She added as they went into the big room, "I apologize for the way it looks. I haven't picked things up. . . . I'd been working, and then went to Vanessa's around the corner to inquire about her cat."

Elaine cast herself into a big chair, and Stacy reflected that she couldn't make an awkward gesture if she tried. It was as if she had no bones. She said, "That's Mrs. Steele, isn't it? Grim old woman, and that horrible animal."

Stacy said, "I wouldn't call her grim. And Shadow is more of a person than a cat."

"I'm allergic to cats," Elaine said. "The one time I saw him—I assume it's male—he sat and stared at me until I was as nervous as cats are supposed to be. As for the fabled Mrs. Steele, it's difficult to think of her as the super siren of her era."

Stacy thought: I was wrong. Elaine has changed. One of the qualities I noticed when she and her husband were here was her silence.

Aloud she said, "I like Vanessa Steele very much."

"So do Marcia and Lee, particularly Lee," Elaine remarked. "Incidentally, he was annoyed with me last night —not for the first time."

Stacy regarded the tranquil face and said, dutifully, "I didn't notice it."

"Oh, yes . . . when I spoke of his investment in Theo's. But of course, his two outstanding traits are loyalty and sentiment."

She rose, without haste, in a single fluid movement and walked across the room. Looking at the Chinese bowl, she said, "You'll have this, Stacy, until it's stolen or broken, but I'll have it full of roses for as long as I wish."

Stacy thought, irritated: I wish I'd thought to say that painting wasn't for sale. "I suppose so," she said. "So has Vanessa—Shadow, in the bowl—it's one of his favorite places."

"The cat? I prefer roses. . . . I remember when this

studio was built. From the time Lee went off to the university at seventeen, his own studio was his dream—or one of them. His father built it for him from Lee's own sketches as a graduation present. When he returned from Greece, the foundations had been laid."

"He went to Greece after his graduation?"

"Yes—it was a five-year stint before he had his degree. Lee and a small group of his classmates went with one of their instructors. That's when he fell in love. Marcia was very concerned. She was afraid he'd never come back. She didn't know about the girl, of course."

"Girl?"

Elaine laughed. Stacy had not heard her laugh often. She said, "Naturally. The daughter of a great archaeologist—older than Lee and engaged to be married. Lee came home and worked for three years with a firm upstate, in order to get his license; then his own firm here was organized. The people at The Aegean were distantly related to someone in the archaeologist's family, so when he ran into them in the city"—she shrugged slightly—"I said he was loyal. I've always imagined that Theo's daughter looks a little like that other Greek girl." She added, "Lee doesn't know I know about her. Some years ago he told Gerry and Gerry, of course, told me. You won't say anything to him, will you?"

"I've no reason to," Stacy said shortly.

Elaine looked at her watch, which was encased in a golden seashell and fastened with a pearl. Stacy had noticed it before. She said, "What a lovely watch!"

"Gerry gave it to me," said his widow. "He had it made from Lee's design. . . . Marcia will be coming home; I must go."

Stacy went to the door with her and Elaine said, "I'm so happy you're here. Marcia has dozens of friends, I know, but you're next door—and Lee, ever since I can remember, appreciates a pretty woman."

Oil and vinegar, Stacy thought, like a salad dressing. "As long as you're here for the summer, Elaine, they won't need me," she said.

"Summers end," Elaine reminded her, "and besides, I may not be. You can't go back in time. We're no longer children, Lee, Marcia and I, nor teenagers. I'm accustomed to change—Gerry and I traveled so much."

Feeling self-reproachful, Stacy said, "You must miss him terribly."

"Of course. There were times before I left California that I considered selling the house and property—Gerry bought considerable land for investment. Marcia was horrified when I told her. I suppose she's right. If I went away, I'd have to have someplace to come back to . . . almost everyone does. I'm very fond of England and Europe, but I can't imagine living there for more than a few weeks at a time." She smiled and went out. Stacy followed her to the flagstone steps and watched her start walking, slowly, toward the Osborne house.

She thought: Why did she tell me that about Lee?

❧ 18 ❧

Toward the end of June, came publication day of the Charity Eaton Revolutionary diaries, owned by Beth Cameron and edited by her and Jeremy Taylor. Jeremy had flatly refused to hold an autographing party at his bookshop. If customers came in and asked him to sign a book or left word asking Beth a similar favor, he could hardly prevent it. But a formal—which meant an advertised—function was out of the question. And absurd anyway; neither he nor Beth had any part in the original and a bookshop could not be expected to keep a planchette handy for the author.

One evening, Katie explained this conduct to a group of their friends. "Despite the mortgage," she announced, "this costly shack, the various fees which accumulated—lawyers', Lee's—to say nothing of an expensive baby and Jeremy's recent purchase of a guardian dog whom he has named Saint Charity"—she gestured toward the mosquito-netted pram, on the so-called lanai, beside which rested a St. Bernard—"Jeremy balks at anything as crass and materialistic as giving himself and Beth a sendoff which might prove profitable. Even the window display, which he'll have to consent to, affronts him."

"Can I help it if I'm humble?" Jeremy asked.

Ross Cameron provided the solution. He gave the party, starting with cocktails and spinning over into a buffet supper. He had no qualms, he admitted about assisting his wife to earn a little pin money. "Correction," he added, "pen money." The living room, study and hall of the old house overflowed with stacks of books, shopping bags, and pens, lying around casually. "Of course," he told his wife, "this clambake will cost me more than you and Jeremy can earn in split royalties—unless the diaries become a classic. They could very well, you know. Libraries, universities, students of the period, Women's Lib—your Charity was quite a girl."

This highly irregular fiesta was great fun. Everyone came, including Emily Warner with the Palmers, and Vanessa with Stacy. Veronica was there, Cam's daughter, not yet a teenager, hence as she herself said, "Not yet obnoxious." She was hypnotized by Vanessa and said solemnly, "I hear you're a witch."

"Occasionally," Vanessa admitted. "Scared?"

"No. I bought some books on how to be one a while back, and tried a few spells at boarding school."

"Did they work?"

"Well, sort of . . . one of my classmates got the flu. Of course, there was a lot of flu last winter—but it maybe wasn't a coincidence, as I hate her. Another one got kicked out of school. Then Miss Ellery—she's on my corridor—caught me and finked. I was drawing—well, they call them symbols—and burning incense. I had to go see the Headmistress who gave me a lecture; a real blast and also about a zillion demerits. Maybe I should have concentrated on her and Miss Ellery," she added thoughtfully and then, "Stacy says you have a black cat, Mrs. Steele."

"Don't all witches—except those who keep ravens?" asked Vanessa gravely.

"I guess so. What's it's name?"

"Shadow. He's a warlock."

"You're putting me on," Ronnie concluded after a moment.

"So I am; and someone's been putting you on too."

When Vanessa encountered Stacy at the buffet table, she said, "Come sit with me. I'm unaccustomed to social activities. Mind if we go home early?"

"Of course not."

"Who's the woman who darts in and out like a dragonfly and casts a stern, shrewd eye on all proceedings? I saw her escorting one unsteady female guest away from the patio."

"The dragonfly is Mrs. Latimer, Cam's indispensable housekeeper and four-star general. . . . What do you think of Ronnie?" she asked.

"Ah," said Vanessa, "ours was indeed a meeting of minds. Hers is, if you'll pardon alliteration, marvelously malicious. Not that she exhibited any malice toward me, but it's written all over her. Precocious children interest me, if not for long. I was one. An only child, brought up by an obscure college president in even more obscure academic surroundings, either turns out to be an educated, respectable girl or, like me. If I'd had a daughter, which thank God I didn't—Warren may be dull but he's uncomplicated—she'd probably have been a second Veronica."

A number of Cam's friends came up from the city to attend the party and the firm of Mason, Jackson and Demerest was represented by the president, Mr. Mason— whose interest as far as books were concerned lay mainly in nonfiction—and an attractive young woman from the public relations department. Mr. Mason later in the evening managed to cut Stacy out of the herd.

Sitting by the pool he remarked that it was a good party and Cam's house a treasure; also his wife. His own wife, he explained sadly, couldn't come. She found little time for social activities aside from those over which she presided.

"Do you write?" he asked Stacy.

"No."

"You don't even try?"

"Not even that," she admitted.

"Extraordinary. Everyone else tries. What do you do then, apart from looking like a lovely gypsy?"

"I paint," Stacy answered.

"Really? What?"

"Dust jackets, end papers, sometimes; also illustrations . . . and other things."

"How clever of you," said Mr. Mason, "to compel my interest. We have an art department."

"I know, I used to work at Lovemay's."

"I understand Remsen Lovemay lived here."

"Yes, for a long time, before his retirement, and then, before his death."

"You knew him?"

"Slightly—and I know his daughter and her family. But I'm Johnny-come-lately in Little Oxford."

"How about lunch?" asked Mr. Mason, a big, amiable man with a big unamiable wife, both over sixty. "I'll introduce you to the head of the art department afterwards."

Cam strolled toward them, saying, "If you need a refresher, holler."

"Help," said Mason plaintively. "I'm trying to make a date."

"Give over, Quentin," advised his host. "Too bad you can't stay on, there are a couple more days left of Stacy's show at our local gallery."

The P.R. girl came up, breathless. She said, "Sorry to interrupt, Mr. Mason, but people are asking to meet you."

"Duty calls," said Mason brilliantly.

Cam lowered himself into a chair and said, "Quent Mason specializes in pretty women. They take his mind off his job of dealing with temperamental writers who in turn specialize in outspoken, overwritten autobiographies —also biographies of people long dead or recently demised, to say nothing of the thousand and one exposes of public officials, wheelers and dealers—you name it—and of course the spate of war books from those who have participated or observed. But he's a nice guy and quite harmless."

"I thought you came to rescue me."

"Not necessary. However, as an ex-menace, I try to atone by saving innocent maidens—for someone else. I thought Beth said the Osbornes were coming? . . . Where's my literary redhead?"

"Over there, talking to Vanessa."

Cam put two fingers in his mouth and whistled. Beth rose and came to sit beside Stacy. "What now?" she inquired. "I was busy."

"I come first. Where are the Osbornes?"

"They'll drop by later; they had to take their house guest to catch a plane."

"Elaine?" asked Stacy, astonished. "I didn't know she was leaving."

"Just for a brief visit—Boston, I think."

"I was looking forward to meeting her," Cam said.

"So you shall," Beth assured him, "provided I'm around to ride shotgun."

"Beth," Cam deduced sadly, "must have met her. What's she like, Stacy?"

"Beautiful."

"But not your type," Beth assured him. .

"What do you know about my type?"

"I'm it," said Beth, "and intend to remain so."

Mason came back and demanded, "Is that really Vanessa Steele over there?"

"It is."

"Fabulous. Do you suppose she'd consent to writing her autobiography?"

"Ask Stacy," Cam advised. "I wouldn't know."

"It would be sensational—names, dates, places—especially names. What do you think, Mrs. Armitage?"

"I think, no."

"What has she to lose at her age? . . . Beth, take me over and present me."

"You've been presented," Beth told him.

"But I didn't place her; besides one rarely hears anyone's name in a crowd."

Stacy suggested, amused, "Why don't you introduce Mr. Mason second time round?"

She and Cam watched, saw the introductions and a few minutes later, the departure of Mr. Mason, heading for the bar.

On the way home, Stacy asked, "Do you mind if I ask what you said to Mr. Mason, Van?"

"Not much, although certain replies surfaced, such as one Adam applies frequently, I understand, which is 'Bug off, buster.' But it hardly seemed courteous, although relevant. I simply thanked him, said no, and suggested he'd be wasting his time if he tried to present an argument. I was extremely genteel. . . . How did you know he was book hunting?"

"He told us."

"He offered me a large sum—even for these days—which was, I think, slightly gauche. Usually this is done while you sit across from someone at a large expensive desk in an office."

"You weren't even tempted?"

"Money's always a temptation to everyone. But I have managed to resist it. This isn't the first time I've been offered a platinum pen by publishers. I've always refused. Actually, there aren't too many people who'd be hurt by what any publisher would hope were lurid disclosures. Adam, of course, although he'd probably be merely entertained; his parents, naturally, and here and there, a child or grandchild of someone might exist and perhaps sue. Who knows? But it's more satisfactory and safer to remember and not to put it in writing."

"Why?"

"I've read a number of such books and have concluded that those who rush to Tell All in this era of candid, explicit confessions are often carried away by their imaginations, or deliberately blow up encounters into affairs—especially when the material can't be checked. Most of the people they write about are no longer on this earth. Sometimes I remember aloud, during a conversation; the sound of one's own voice is mesmerizing. In any case, writing or talking, one's apt, I think, to mention General So and So when it was his aide, if anyone, or the Duke of This or That when it was his younger cousin——"

"How about a deathbed confession?" Stacy asked, laughing.

"I hope I won't have time. Just see to it that no one brings in a tape recorder. . . . Your show's about over, isn't it?"

"Yes. Lee will help me bring the paintings home, and Jim Swift will send someone up to take back the ones that belong to Lovemay's."

Then, June was July, and July was a green river bordered with flowers, lazily flowing along its predestined course. It had scarcely begun when the customary star-spangled celebration of a much earlier event took place, country-wide, spending itself in noise, games, food, drink and oratory. After that the month settled for barbecues and picnics. Some people in Little Oxford went off to ski in South America; others took cruises to the Midnight Sun; youngsters and their teachers flew on junkets to England and Europe. Little Oxford residents left for summer homes, or took holidays on the Cape or in the mountains. And weekday mornings and evenings commuters toiled into the city, and back; there was a spate of sunburns, summer colds, highway accidents, political campaigns, the usual run on air conditioners and, always, the hope of peace.

In short, an average July.

Stacy was busy. She saw her friends, she shopped and she worked. Jim had assigned her a new edition of E. Nesbit; seventy illustrations; an enchanting story of flesh-and-blood children of an earlier era and their delightful fictional other-worldly friends. She went several times to the Camerons' house to sketch Veronica, with Cam's permission.

Ronnie was a challenge and in the garments of the period she would be delightful, Stacy thought, consulting her costume books.

Ronnie had flyaway fair hair, big slate-colored eyes and fine features, ending in a stubborn little chin. She could sit for the portrait of any child of any era.

"Am I really going to be in a book, Stacy?"

"I certainly hope so."

"My name and everything?"

"No . . . this is a sort of fairy story."

"I know. Mom has some of E. Nesbit's books. Of course, the kids aren't very—what's the word?"

"They're not contemporary. I expect that's what you mean."

"Couldn't you dedicate it to me? Beth and Jeremy dedicated theirs to Charity Eaton and she's been dead for centuries!"

"No, Ronnie. It's the writer's privilege to dedicate books, not the illustrator's. Charity was the original writer, so your stepmother and Jeremy dedicated it to her."

"But she can't read it!"

"That's right."

Ronnie bounced up and peered over Stacy's shoulder.

"Couldn't you make me prettier?" she complained.

"Yes, but I'm not going to. You have an interesting face, which is better than pretty. Wait a few years for the prettiness."

"I do like you," said Ronnie. "You appreciate me even though I'm short and fat. I try to diet."

"I know. Then you trip and fall into a double chocolate malted."

"Check. My doctor says I'm frustrated. He explained it, but it didn't make sense. What do you think it means?"

"Well, it's the way people feel if they've lost something they can't get back."

"You mean like a husband?"

"Sometimes."

"Mom doesn't feel that way. Least she says she doesn't. What else?"

"Wanting to be something or someone you're not, or feeling that you haven't all the things you should have, or want."

"That's screwy. I haven't lost anything, and I just want to be me—only thinner and gorgeous, like Beth or that Mrs. Harden—I don't like her really—and I get most everything I want. Actually I eat because I'm hungry or bored."

Stacy said, "Boredom's one form of frustration, I think, but I'm not a doctor."

"Three of the kids at school go to shrinks," said Ronnie. "I told my father maybe I should. He said the folks who needed shrinks were people who had to have me around —him, Beth, Mom, and Mrs. Latimer, of course. I drive her right up the wall—and the people at school too. Anyway, my doctor said I'd probably slim down when I matured. That's for the birds. I've seen thousands of mature women who didn't."

"Ronnie, do sit still!"

"It's a drag. Hey, would Mrs. Steele let me come see her and her cat?"

"I'll ask her."

"She's got a grandson. She told me so."

"He's too old for you, Ronnie."

"I'm old for my age," Ronnie informed her.

"Besides, I'm nuts about older men. Jeremy, for instance. I really had a thing for him. Katie didn't mind. I got over it. Of course, it was a long time ago, last year anyway. Oh, there's Charity...." Ronnie bounded to her feet, ran her stubby little hands through her hair and went off to fall upon the large patient animal and roll with her on the grass beyond the patio.

One weekend Rosie telephoned. "Stacy? It's too hot, but would you come to church with me tomorrow? I'll pick you up."

"I thought the Bankses were on vacation."

"They are. Gordon's assistant takes over. He's all the things you're supposed to be in the modern pulpit . . . liberal, vital, good-looking, involved with social problems. His hair's long enough to appeal to young people. . . . I've no doubt he'll make first banana when Gordon retires. My interest, however, is in tomorrow's soloist, Joyce Kally, a local girl. I think I told you about her."

Stacy remembered hearing about the girl for whom Rosie had provided voice training abroad and in New York.

"We'll have lunch here," Rosie went on. "Bring your scuba-diving gear."

On the way to church, Stacy asked, "Will your protegée be with us?"

"No, she lives in a girl's club in New York, and is still studying, of course. She had an audition recently—group of young singers who do concerts all over and are often on TV. She has, she thinks, a good chance; she'll know, Monday. She spent last night with me and she's going right back to town after church. We'll take her to the station."

Joyce Kally was a big, pretty girl with, Stacy thought, a fine voice and considerable poise. She watched Rosie listening, her small face radiant, and after church she met the girl and they drove her to the depot.

On the way back to Rosie's, Stacy said, "Nice girl; pleasant, very serious——"

"She's dedicated. I hope she makes the group. They'll loosen her up. Most of the groups have to dance too. She doesn't. This is straight singing. She has a future, I think . . . oh, not La Scala or the Met, but something good, for which she has Jessica Banks to thank."

"I thought it was you."

"Jessica got me involved. She was sorry they couldn't be here today, but Joyce will come again if she can. She grew up here; her grandparents raised her. Her grandmother died while she was abroad. I flew her home for the funeral. Her grandfather went to a nursing home. Now he's dead and she has no one here, except me, a few school friends and the Bankses. Keep your fingers crossed for her; she's a good kid."

After their swim and lunch, they stayed in their robes

by the pool, on the shady side, under umbrellas. Rosie asked, "What did you think of the sermon?"

"It didn't exactly grab me. I prefer Mr. Banks."

"Well, he was once considered pretty far out, but not now. I don't think he'll really retire; he'll do guest shots, so to speak, lecture at colleges, perhaps write. They've bought a place in South Carolina—that's where they are now—and it's far enough away to keep his former parishoners from driving down to consult him. For the last few years Gordon's turned from world problems to those of people."

"I was thinking of joining his church," Stacy said.

"Go ahead. He'll be here for a couple more years, and he'll be delighted. So will Jessica. They like you very much. I'm planning to become a church member too."

"I thought you were."

"Not Gordon's. I haven't been a member of anything since I was eighteen. My parents were Polish. My grandfather came to the States, worked in the tobacco fields, and even acquired a small farm. Where he settled, they were near a town where he could hear the Mass in Polish. After my grandfather's death my father and his brother sold the farm. He said he'd worked in the tobacco fields long enough, so he took his share of the money, came down here and opened a diner. My mother was a great cook. Eventually, he had his tavern. We went to church here, to old Father Hammon. I drifted away when I married Bill. We were married by a justice of the peace in the city, which made my parents unhappy. Later Father Hammon married us—in those days it was in the vestry. Father Hammon's been gone for many years, but I've been to see Father Richards. You know, twice after Bill died I was briefly married, and divorced? My ex-husbands were much older than I. One died before I came back to Little

Oxford to live, the other since. So, no obstacles. I've had several talks with Father Richards. I'm going to take instruction."

Stacy said hesitantly, "Do you mind if I ask why?"

"No. I've managed to achieve sobriety, I hope and pray, for good. But any AA member will tell you that you have to have more than that. I hadn't been near a Roman Catholic church since my vestry marriage. Now I want to return to it. I've talked it over with Jessica. It was she who gave me my first clear long look at religion—hers, not Gordon's; just hers . . . loving and sharing. I'll miss her so much when they retire, but I'll see them wherever they are."

"Mrs. Banks wasn't upset when you spoke of returning to the church?"

"She suggested it. Why should she be upset, Stacy? She seems to know by instinct the direction you should take. My direction is in one sense back—as well as forward."

"I wonder what mine is?"

Rosie shook her dark curly head. "I don't know. You might ask Jessica," she added, smiling.

Stacy thought: I won't ask anyone, I have to find out for myself. It certainly isn't back—it must be ahead.

"Let's get dressed," Rosie said. "Before I take you home I want to show you how the painting looks in my dressing room."

Stacy said, "It's later than I thought. I promised Van I'd stop in. Adam and his current girl were coming to spend the day with her."

But when, eventually, she reached Vanessa's, her guests had gone. Vanessa said, "Come in and sit down. . . . Shadow, don't harass her. . . . Put your feet up and have a drink. I can cope with Adam, as himself, but as a starry-eyed, obviously unsuccessful lover, he's exhausting."

"When did they get here?"

"They roared up on the motorcycle in time for lunch. Adam's off his feed, *mirabile dictu*—or maybe it's normal. The girl eats like a bird, which means constantly. Shadow hid; he hates noise. When he emerged, he spoke to Adam and growled at Toby—that's the girl. I've no idea of her real name."

"Tell me about her."

"She's a year or so older than Adam, and treats him as if he were slightly retarded. She's about his height; long, streaked blonde hair; heavily made-up eyes; weird shade of lipstick. But pretty. They both wore cut-off jeans and screaming shirts. There unisex ended. Toby's jeans were embroidered with exotic flowers, especially across her bottom. She has, by the way, very sophisticated equipment."

"She's in college?"

"She quit. She gets to walk on, among other chores, in the summer theater. In the autumn she starts studying acting in the city. When she came in, I thought her straight out of early Noel Coward, but after a while she almost reverted to type."

"Which is?"

"Middle-upper-class Westchester, with doting—according to her difficult—parents. Adam told her that in my time I'd known a number of theater personalities, after which he didn't get to open his mouth. It's the nostalgia bit. She's in love with stars she's never seen in the flesh—James Dean, Bogart, Garfield. She sits up for late, late movies; she goes to film festivals; she's hooked on silents too. She asked a lot of questions. I exaggerated my acquaintance with some of the people I'd known, so I was, of course, a smash hit."

"When did they go?"

"About three. They went off to swim in the Sound. I packed a supper basket according to her specifications— a loaf of bread, fruit, cheese and a bottle of wine. I threw in a few meat sandwiches for Adam's sake. After an early supper they're going back to Westchester dripping wet, I assume, although they may have had towels in the saddle-bag or whatever you call it."

When Stacy left, Vanessa went out with her and looked at the sky. Shadow came along sulking.

"What's wrong with him?" Stacy asked.

"Nothing. Toby hurt his feelings. She called him, 'Kitty, Kitty' and 'Here, Puss!' " She added, "We'll have a thunder storm before the night's over. It will be a good one."

"Did you hear that on the radio?"

"No. I always get a dull headache before. Barometric pressure or something. Say good night to Stacy, Shadow; she hasn't big brown paws like Adam's inamorata."

"I like storms," Stacy said.

"I do too, but Shadow makes for the nearest closet. If you're struck by lightning, crawl on over." She added, "It won't hit for hours. Adam and his charmer will be home before then."

The storm broke about two in the morning and it was a dilly.

❧ 19 ❧

At breakfast the next morning Marcia said, "The phone's out. Stacy's too, probably. I tried to get her before she left for town on the early train."

"I'll walk up to the Collinses' and report it," Lee said.

"I tried them too. The lightning probably hit a transformer. I was awake and heard the crash. Did it wake you, Elaine?"

"No. Practically nothing keeps me awake," Elaine answered, looking rested and impeturbable and Lee thought: Well, that's for sure!

He said, "I'll report it from the office."

Marcia looked at him and asked, "Do you suppose there's a leak in the studio again? The last time it rained torrents there was. Remember?"

"Yes, the skylight; it was very slight."

"I know—but with all Stacy's paintings around it worries me."

"She would have come across to tell us before she took her train," he said.

"Where was she going?" Elaine asked.

"To the city. An old friend of hers from Chicago is in town and wanted to see her. Also she had an appointment somewhere. . . . I'm really worried, Lee."

He said, "I'll walk over before I go to the village."

214

He did so after breakfast and Elaine went with him. The morning was fresh and cool after the storm and the rain.

"Remember the thunderstorms," she asked, "when we were young? The tree that was struck in the field back of the house?"

He said he remembered.

"That's nice," Elaine told him. "I thought you'd forgotten everything."

"I try," he said shortly.

At the studio door he produced a key and Elaine said smiling, "How very convenient."

"You have a nasty mind," Lee told her, "and always have had."

"Nonsense. You know what propinquity does. And you've always tended to fall in love with small, dark, intense females."

In the studio, he went about checking for leaks, found a small one over the kitchen sink and said, "I'll send a man out—What are you doing, Elaine?"

"Just looking around. Stacy's not very orderly, is she?" She turned the pages of a sketchbook, pulled some of the unframed paintings away from the wall. Talent, she decided, and imagination, but no guts.

"I wish you'd leave her things alone," Lee said.

"But I never leave things alone." She walked over to the fireplace and put her arm along the mantel. "I'd love to have this Chinese bowl," she said suddenly. "Do you suppose she'd sell it to me?"

"I'm quite sure she wouldn't."

"She dislikes me," Elaine reflected. "Most women do. I've never had a woman friend except Marcia."

"And I wish you'd leave her alone," said Lee. "Breakfast in bed!"

"Only when I don't feel like getting up. Your invaluable Cora made me nervous, steaming around drawing curtains, being talkative and cheerful. I spoke to Marcia about it . . . I said I didn't want to give trouble——"

"So she carries the trays on your less early-to-rise mornings. You treat her abominably."

"She doesn't think so; she loves me."

"And now this absurd notion she should go to California and live with you."

"Oh, only if you marry, Lee. Besides, it would be good for her. We'd travel, go where we pleased when we pleased."

"When *you* pleased." He had come to face her at the other end of the mantel. He said, "Marcia met a man she liked very much on that cruise."

"I met him too. He came ashore with her briefly. Not her type."

"What is her type?"

"Oh, someone ten or fifteen years older than she, with a lot of money. She wouldn't listen to me when I told her Douglas wasn't right for her. I was astonished. But then, she thought she was in love."

"He filled your specifications," Lee reminded her. "Older, and successful——"

"But so dull. Rather like Gerry."

"You mean, Gerry didn't perceive things."

"Of course not."

"He didn't want to," Lee said. "Living as he did under a—spell. It's broken now, Elaine."

"I broke it occasionally," she said dreamily. "It was good for him. Gerry needed shaking up. Naturally, I was always very contrite. . . . Now, you're angry!"

"No, just revolted. And I don't believe it, anyway."

She said, "Gerry always forgave me; he said it was never my fault. I don't suppose you'd believe that I told

216

him about you when we were in Jamaica? That was a little different. It could have caused his heart attack," she added thoughtfully.

Lee was white under his tan, "You were always a liar. You were born a liar. No, I don't believe it."

"However," said Elaine, "you'll never really know, will you? You'll go on living with guilt. It's changed you very much, which I find attractive. Most women would, I think. The inaccessible man is always a challenge. Your little Stacy, for instance."

"Leave her out of this."

"That touched a nerve. Whatever happened to the boy who tagged around after me and took orders? He and his sister——"

"I grew up. Marcia didn't."

She said after a moment, "Perhaps I'll try and explain you to Stacy."

He made a violent gesture and the Chinese bowl shattered on the hearth.

"Good," said Elaine, "as I have the painting. How will you explain it to Stacy? Mice?"

He went over and took her roughly by the arm. He said, "Suppose we get out of here?"

"You don't trust yourself?"

"No. And you'll tell Marcia that you've decided to go on home."

"I've no such intention—although I'm beginning to be very bored. Why do you think I went to Boston?"

"I don't know, but whoever he is, I'm sorry for him."

"You're hurting me. And you talk as if I were a nymphomaniac!"

"You don't even have that excuse."

He held her arm tightly and walked her out of the door, pressing the inside button which locked it.

Before they reached the house, he broke the silence. He asked, "Suppose I tell Marcia—not about my lapse—but all of yours?"

"You wouldn't."

"Yes, if necessary. Chapter and verse."

"But you don't know."

"I know. Gerry told me, two years ago."

"I don't believe it!"

"He was drunk," Lee said. "Also very unhappy. I advised him to leave you . . . and let you get the divorce."

"Even if you're telling the truth," she said, with the first sign of anger, "he would never have named names!"

"He did—also places. He finally had you followed, Elaine."

"He'd never do that."

"Oh, but he did."

Now they were standing by the kitchen door and she cried out at him, "Then why *didn't* he divorce me?"

He said soberly, "As you explained about Marcia, he loved you. He couldn't understand why, but he loved you."

"If you tell Marcia, it will break her heart."

"Maybe just the spell."

Marcia popped out of the kitchen door. She asked, "What's with you two standing there arguing? Over what, politics? Is the studio all right, Lee?"

"Fine. Just a small leak over the kitchen sink. I'll send a man out when I get to the office."

Elaine said sadly, "I've just told Lee I feel I must go on home. I'm sorry, Marcia . . . but I'm getting restless. I'd be poor company for the rest of the summer. How about coming along?"

Marcia shook her head. "I can't; I've promised too many people to do too many community jobs." She led the way into the house and said, "I know there's not much sense in trying to change your mind. We never could, could we, Lee?"

"No. Never."

Elaine went to the telephone. "I'll call your travel agent and check on planes," she said.

Marcia asked, dismayed, "But you don't mean right now. You can't!"

"Once I make a decision," Elaine said briskly, "I act upon it. I didn't tell you, but Saturday's letter from Gerry's lawyers was unsettling. So much to sign—and they intimated I'd get things done faster if I were in California, which reminds me, Lee, I was astonished when I saw Gerry's will. He wanted you to be co-executor with me. Now it's the bank. I wonder why he altered it."

"I told him two years ago I didn't want to," Lee said stonily. "I was here in the East. I couldn't go out when-ever my presence was required . . . and it was all a little too complicated. You'll handle things—along with his lawyers and bank."

She said after a minute, "But I'm not being driven away, Marcia, by lawyers or banks or anyone else. I just think it's time I went. It's an 'impression,' as I believe your friend Mrs. Banks sometimes says. I'm really terri-bly sorry. By the way, you forgot to leave a note for Stacy, Lee."

"What note?" asked Marcia. "Really, you two are in-credible. I don't know what you're talking about."

"There was an accident," Lee said. "I broke her Chinese bowl—the one on the table."

Marcia shook her head. She said, "Stacy will be upset. She's so fond of the bowl. How did it happen?"

"She'll get over it," Elaine said lightly, "unless she's like me. I'm a hoarder. I cling to possessions. Remember the Japanese doll, Marcia?"

"I certainly do; you clobbered me. I wasn't trying to take it away from you; just hold it for a while."

"I was a dreadful child," Elaine said.

"You were not," Marcia defended her. "Spoiled, of course. . . . Remember how she'd get us into trouble, Lee? And Mother wouldn't believe you when you told her? She'd say, 'No gentleman tattles.' But you never owned up, Elaine, just looked at her, and us, with those big eyes. So we were punished. You weren't."

"Which should have been a warning," Lee said.

"Warning?" Marcia repeated. "But we're grown up now. Elaine, please don't go——"

Lee said, "Never mind the reservations. I'll telephone the agency from the office. Dinner flight suit you? Window seat, of course."

Elaine put her arms around Marcia and offered her hand to Lee. "You're both so good to me, and I love you," she said.

She smiled, released them, went out of the kitchen and they heard her light step on the stairs.

"Whatever got into her?" Marcia asked anxiously.

"Who knows? She's always been like that."

"The times she came home suddenly from school and college? I remember hearing about them . . . but I understand her being restless after the shock of Gerry's death."

"Quite," said Lee.

"How did you happen to break the bowl? You didn't answer when I asked you."

He said truthfully, "I was standing by the mantel and made, I suppose, a rather too sweeping a gesture. . . . When is Stacy returning?"

"I think, late, probably after dinner; she didn't say exactly."

"Who's this friend she's seeing?"

220

"A girl she knew in art class in Chicago and with whom she stayed for a while—I think, after her divorce. Seems she's getting married and has come East with her fiancé to meet his parents. His mother's an invalid . . . Lee, for goodness sake, go to the office. It makes me nervous not to have a telephone."

"I think we have one. When Elaine picked it up, I heard the dial sound before she replaced it. Let me check."

He did so, called the office and said, "I'll be along presently," and turned back to his sister. "You're all set," he told her. "Someone else reported it, probably quite early."

"I'll go up and see if I can persuade Elaine——"

"Don't. She's always had her way; don't try to change that now."

Marcia said after a moment, "What's wrong with you and Elaine? I'm not so stupid that I can't feel it every time you're together."

"I've never liked her, Marcia."

"But you must have—as a little boy you followed her everywhere."

"As you said earlier, usually into trouble. I didn't like her then, dear. I was fascinated by her."

"Well, you've fooled me until now—or have you? I remember wondering now and then, especially after you came back that time Gerry had you advise on the house. You talked so little about it, I wondered if you and Gerry had had a disagreement."

"No."

After a minute Marcia said, "Elaine's always been wonderful to me. . . . Remember her at my wedding and when we went to hers? I don't really understand her, of course. But if I needed her she was there—when Douglas was killed, for instance. I was glad I could be with her in Jamaica."

"Your cruise escort—Stone—what's his first name?"

"Harry. What about him?"

"Heard from him recently?"

"Last week. . . . He said he might be coming east."

"Elaine met him," he remarked. "He went ashore with you."

"Well, everyone went ashore. I stayed with Elaine, of course. She didn't like him; she told me so afterward. I can't imagine why. He's just plain nice and good fun to be with. Gerry said so too."

Lee thought, driving to the office: Wonderful? Yes, very. Marcia being no threat, a foil, and creating a pleasant background like soothing music. I wish Harry Stone all the luck in the world, he thought frankly.

Stacy caught the nine-o'clock train home. She'd had a good day, first an appointment with Jim Swift and a group from the art department, then lunch, and the afternoon meeting with Sally Babcock at the hotel in which she was staying.

Sally looked much the same, and was, except for the solitaire on her left hand. The man she was going to marry had reserved a small suite for her. She and Stacy talked, and Stacy saw the clothes Sally had bought and said, "You won't need mine any more."

"No. I suppose you think it's funny I'm not staying with Don's parents? But as I wrote you, his mother is ill; nurses round the clock. But I saw her for a little while yesterday, and his father. Don is taking us to dinner tonight. Honestly, Stacy, I can't believe my luck, he's such a marvelous guy."

"You're being married at your parents' home?"

"Yes, from the little old cabin in Iowa. October, sometime. I think the fourth. You have to come out and be matron of honor. She added, "We're afraid Don's mother won't be able to make it. She's such a lovely person, Stacy.

I offered to be married here; my family would come. But the problem of Don's mother would be the same . . . Stacy, say you'll come and see me safely married."

"We'll see—I'd love to."

"You're a rotten correspondent. Tell me about Little Oxford."

"Perhaps you and Don will come see it? It's in a very attractive area. I am renewing my lease, I hope."

Toward dinnertime Sally said, "As you seem to be hooked on the place, there must be something beside scenery. How's your love life, Stacy?"

"Zero."

"You probably deserve it. . . . Look, haven't you met any man who interests you?"

"Oh, sure," Stacy answered. "Unfortunately, I don't interest him."

She was so astonished at hearing her own words that for a moment the room tilted as if the earth were shaking and Sally asked, "What's the matter? You look as if you'd seen a ghost."

Stacy shook her head. "I don't know," she said. "I swear that until I told you so, I wasn't consciously aware of being interested in anyone!"

"You've got to be kidding. Who is he?"

"No comment."

"Okay. You always kept things under wraps . . . like going to Nevada to get your divorce; you didn't tell me until you were practically on the train. . . . Have you seen Bob?"

"He and his wife stopped by this summer."

"And?"

"Nothing. Absolutely nothing."

"You mean that?"

"Yes."

"You must be cured," said Sally. "Well now, about Mr.

X—you've admitted to a weakness. Use it. Remember me, the independent, come-hell-or-high-water career gal who worked as a legal secretary—that's how I met Don in Chicago on business—he's a lawyer. Did I tell you that?"

"Several times."

"Anyway, little Miss Play the Field. Then I went helpless. I couldn't open a door or light a cigarette. It took me quite a while to get anywhere with Don. Happily for me, he had to show up in Chicago every so often."

"I can't picture it. You, helpless!"

"Wait and see."

Don arrived and they all went out to dinner, but Stacy didn't remember much of the evening. She was certain afterwards that she had asked sensible questions and, when spoken to, made reasonable replies. She was sure that Donald West was a pleasant man, with charm, humor and obvious intelligence and that he liked opening doors for Sally and lighting her cigarettes.

After dinner, they took her to the station, went with her to her gate, and departed, after insisting that she had to come to their wedding. Stacy rode home in a hot, dust-smelling car. The air conditioning had gone off; it was the opinion of most passengers on that line that it worked only when unnecessary, which was in winter.

She listened to the wheels and the voice of the conductor. This was a local; they stopped at several depots, and she was unmindful of people exiting or entering, even of someone who sat beside her most of the way. She was trying to assemble her thoughts; they scattered like leaves in a high wind, like snowflakes blowing in every direction, or were as flat stones skipping across a pond, changing its pattern.

It was idiotic. She had known Lee Osborne for—how long—a year? She hadn't liked him at first; then, she had.

They were friends, and as a person he interested her, as a number of other people did. But a romantic or merely sexual interest? No.

Being with the euphoric Sally had infected her, she thought, the insanity momentarily contagious—which didn't explain why, hours later, she was still shaken. But you couldn't arrive at a valid awareness of love while talking, idly, to an old friend. If you were Stacy you fell in love almost at once, fathoms deep, and you didn't start by liking someone.

It occurred to her now that she had never really liked Robert Armitage; she had simply fallen in love with him.

She took a taxi to the studio. The lights had been switched on. Someone—Marcia or perhaps Lee—her heart stumbled a little—had done this for her.

Walking in, the first thing she noticed was the absence of her Chinese bowl and an envelope propped against the mirror over the mantel.

❧ 20 ❧

Stacy took the envelope, and opened it, sitting on a love seat. It was unsealed; and in it there was a note written on a memo pad. "Stacy," it said. "I came in this morning to see if the storm had done any damage. There's a small leak over the sink. Someone will fix it presently. But I broke your Chinese bowl. I put the pieces in the kitchen. Perhaps I can have it mended. I'm so sorry. I'll call you early tomorrow from the office. Lee."

She went into the kitchen. There, on a dish towel, were the pieces, large and small. She picked them up, one by one, looking at the colors, the broken pattern. It couldn't, she thought, be mended. She felt saddened, but not angry or distressed. It was just porcelain; it was something you had had and enjoyed. So you'd always have it; it was there, whole, unaltered, in your memory.

She put away her handbag, hung up her clothes, took a shower and went to bed. She did not sleep. She thought: Perhaps I should try to think that way about people? My father—remembering the closeness, the good times, the long talks, the walks on a beach, the fishing trips, the sound of his voice reading to me. Then I'd still have him for as long as memory lasts.

Bob? There was only the beginning to remember— from the time he had turned away from Amy, and to her.

Someone had said—what was it—"A sorrow's crown of sorrow is remembering happier things."

She put on the light, found her slippers and padded into the studio. There were bookcases there. Some of her own books were stacked on the lower shelves; the other books were, as Marcia had said when she took her and Katie into the room, "Leftovers, I'm afraid, from our last tenants. Novels, paperbacks, biographies, a *Bartlett's Quotations.*" Stacy remembered Vanessa dragging that out to settle a who-wrote-that discussion in her own mind.

Now Stacy sat down in a big chair, switched on the light, and looked in the index.

Chaucer had said it, as well as a gentleman called Boethius (in Latin) and Lord Tennyson.

She thought, the heavy book crashing on the floor: But I no longer feel sorrow. If now and then I think of my deluded happiness with Bob, there'll be no sorrow—not any more.

She fell asleep curled up in her chair and woke, very late. The light was still burning and a cool wind blowing through the room. Shivering, she made her way back to bed thinking: I can't go back to sleep now. But she did, almost instantly.

She was drinking her coffee in the kitchen when the telephone rang, at a little past nine. She reached for the instrument on the counter, caught the sleeve of her light robe on her cup, and spilled the coffee. She picked up the phone and Lee said, "Stacy? Sorry to call so early, but I'm going to Deeport with a client who is building out there. I'll be gone until almost time for me to take Elaine and Marcia to the airport."

"Airport?" she asked blankly.

"Elaine's returning home. Marcia and I will stop for dinner on the way back. Then, if I may, I'll come see you."

She said, "I'll be here, Lee. . . . I'm just going to take Vanessa to Mrs. Irvington's this afternoon." She hesitated and added, "I'd be glad to give you and Marcia supper on your way back from the airport."

"Thanks, but no . . . see you later, Stacy."

She restored the instrument, mopped the counter, took off her robe and put it in cold water, and then poured a fresh cup of coffee. She thought: Why is Elaine going home? Why does Lee want to see me this time? Perhaps about the lease?

She'd spoken about that to Marcia a week or more ago, and Marcia had said, "Do you think we'd let you go? I'll tell Lee to attend to the formalities, if any—or does it go through Katie's office? I'll ask him."

The lease, certainly.

Deduct one Chinese bowl, she thought, half hysterically.

She managed to get through the morning; laundry, washing her hair, sitting out for a time in the sun looking at her mail, opening it, putting it aside. She had planned some work after the illustrations were finished, but not today. Today was new, unfamiliar and frightening.

The telephone rang and she jumped. Marcia said, "Stacy—Elaine's on her way over to say good-bye. She's leaving for home tonight. I could murder her. You're not going out, are you?"

"Only to Vanessa's, about four."

"Good. . . . Lee call you?"

"Yes."

"Then he told you he'll stop by after we get back from the airport. I spoke to him about the lease; I'd come with him, but I expect to be flat-out. Elaine made up her mind in just three minutes."

Elaine. . . .

Stacy waited in the studio. When the bell chimes spoke, she called, "Come in," and Elaine came, cool in a dark green dress and jacket.

"Sure you're not busy?"

"No . . . it's cooler in than out. . . . Please sit down."

Elaine said, "Marcia told you I'm leaving? She's very upset, poor darling. It was a spur-of-the-moment decision."

"I'm sorry," said Stacy mechanically.

"No, you're not. No one's really sorry but Marcia." Elaine shrugged her shoulders slightly and looked toward the mantelpiece. "I suppose Lee called you about the bowl."

"I found a note when I came home last night," Stacy said.

"Oh? He must have brought it over, after we were here."

"We?"

"Of course, I was with him here yesterday morning. We came in to see if there was storm damage, but the only damage was his. It was very careless of him. We were having, you might say, words—and he made one of those dramatic, sweeping gestures and that was the end of your Chinese bowl!"

"It doesn't matter."

"Of course it matters. I told Lee so. I said you were so fond of the bowl. Perhaps you'd like the painting back as a farewell gift?"

"Thank you," Stacy said, "but no. I don't want it back."

"I'm glad," Elaine told her. "I hate giving anything up. That's what Lee and I had words about. Ever since we were children . . ." She moved her shoulders again, an exasperated yet tolerant gesture. "He'll be glad to see the

last of me, for a time, anyway. He doesn't like remembering——"

"A sorrow's crown of sorrow," thought Stacy.

"He doesn't like me," Elaine said lightly, "but in a
curious sort of way, while we don't get along, we have to,
if you follow me." She rose and held out her hand. She
said, "I don't envy the woman he marries, if he ever does.
Good-bye, Stacy. I'll probably come east again someday.
Meantime, if you're in California—you said your mother
was there, didn't you?—you must look me up."

She smiled and was gone before Stacy could get to her
feet and follow her to the door.

"That was that," she told herself, getting ready to pick
up Vanessa and Shadow and take them to Letty Irvington's. . . . Nothing said, everything implied, including a
warning.

Vanessa said on the way to the Irvingtons', "You're
very quiet, young woman."

"Tired maybe; all day in town yesterday."

"You," said Vanessa firmly, "are in two minds. I don't
know what about, and I'm not the maternal type. But if
you'd care to confide in me . . ."

"There isn't anything to confide."

"Oh, so that's it," Vanessa remarked. "Did Lee tell you
about the bet I made with him?"

"No."

"Well," said Vanessa, "I can be mysterious, too. It's part
of my image. I'll bet you too."

"What?"

"I'll bet a lunch at that outrageous Saltmarsh place
against that little Hudson River school painting you admire, that Lee will tell you about his bet with me before
Thanksgiving. . . . Here we are at Letty's. There's Oscar.
For heaven's sake, grab Shadow. This is as odd a misal-
liance—using the term loosely—as I've ever seen."

230

They removed Shadow from the car and he and Oscar, the soulful beagle, immediately fell upon each other's necks.

"A miracle," Vanessa observed. "When Oscar dies, Shadow will send him a wreath: 'To the only canine I ever loved.'"

"Who says Oscar's going to die?" Letty demanded, flying down the steps. "Oscar, be careful; don't hurt that cat. On the other hand, Cat, be careful you don't hurt Oscar. Come on in, all of you. Shadow," she reminded Vanessa, "is years and years older than Oscar."

"Cats have long lives, barring accidents; also nine of them," said Vanessa as they went into the house, leaving the friends outside. It was Stacy who asked anxiously, "Shadow won't run away, will he?"

"Of course not. He knows which can his dinner comes from," Vanessa said, "and Oscar can't lead him astray. Oscar, on his own doorstep, is a gracious host. Shadow has more sense than to pussyfoot off hunting with him."

"Lets bring them both in the house and put them out on the porch," said Letty. "Then everyone will be safe. Bing's in the study; he'll join us for tea."

They stayed until nearly six and Bing emerged to inform Vanessa that she looked, as usual, like a haunted house but incredibly healthy. "I can't say the same for you," he told Stacy. "As you are my son's patient," he said sadly, accepting tea from his wife's hands, "I can't advise you."

"I'm fine, Doctor Bing," she said. "Just tired."

"It's absurd the way young people get tired. I mean, those who neither toil nor spin. Neurotic, most of them. Letty, did you ever get tired when you were Stacy's age?"

"I've been tired," said his silver-and-gold-haired wife, "since at eighteen I married you. And keeping up with

231

two doctors in the family has aged me. I'm beginning to totter."

"Anytime you totter," he said fondly, "that will be the day. And you don't have to supervise Ben. He's got a wife too, remember? Also a son; I expect your entire dedication to be to me."

Happy marriages, thought Stacy. Letty and Bing; their son and Amy; Katie and Jeremy. In a village like Little Oxford, you get to know almost everything about everyone.

She took her charges home. "Stay to supper," said Vanessa imperiously.

"No, I can't."

"A date?"

"Not really. Lee's coming over after he and Marcia take Elaine to the airport."

"Don't tell me," said Vanessa dramatically, "she's going somewhere for good—if that's the word—I hope."

"She's going home," said Stacy wearily, "and Lee's coming over to talk about my lease."

"That should be interesting. You're going to renew it, of course?"

"I'm not sure," said Stacy slowly.

"In two minds again?" Vanessa inquired. "Well, go back to your cave and brood." But her eyes were kind. It had taken Stacy some time to learn to watch Vanessa's eyes instead of listening to her words.

Lee came in before eight. He said, "Traffic. People. It's incredible. The airport was a madhouse."

"May I fix you a drink?" Stacy asked. She looked at him. His face was drawn, but his eyes were clear, dark blue. He ran his hands through his thick, extraordinary hair and said simply, "I'm beat. Stacy, I'm so sorry about this bowl. I was standing by the mantel, I made a gesture——"

"Elaine told me."

"Elaine was here—today?"

"She came to say good-bye. And explain about the bowl."

"What was there to explain?" he demanded. "I knocked it off, like a clumsy fool."

She said, "I believe she said that you were having words."

"We were," said Lee. "Lots of them." He added half to himself, "I can't stand that woman."

"She told me that too," Stacy said evenly, "although she didn't put it as strongly. She said you didn't like her."

"I never have."

Stacy said, "When you first talked to me about her I remember your saying you were all in love with her; Marcia, you, your parents."

"Oh, yes," he agreed. "I was a kid fascinated by daring. I suppose you'd call it that. There used to be a game called 'Follow the Leader.' We followed. As for our parents, no one who looked like Elaine could possibly be anything less than an angel. You've seen her now, so you've also seen her then; a younger edition, the grace, the composure, the beautiful, candid regard. Her appearance has always been an illusion. Sometimes I think she has no soul." He took Stacy's hand, folded her fingers down, folded his own over them. She tried to free herself and he said, "Don't, please. This isn't easy to say."

He was quiet for what seemed like a long time. She was aware only of his hand over hers. Someone went by on the road, and a bird woke and sang briefly, just beyond the windows, a broken, sleepy melody.

He said finally, "Long before I went to Greece for the first time, I'd seen through the illusion," and added, "I fell in love with Greece then."

"And with a girl?"

"That too," he admitted, smiling. "Did Marcia tell you?"

"No. Elaine did."

"That figures. I sometimes think of her—her name is Hermione. I hope her marriage is happy, that she has lots of children and never grows fat," he said.

"And after that?" Stacy asked.

"No one of consequence. And then when I went west to make suggestions—Gerry asked me to—when he and Elaine were building the house. I had my conferences with their architects and builders—they didn't need me," he said. "It was Gerry's way of sharing, of making me feel important. They were living then in a house they afterward sold, a few miles from the site of the new one and Gerry had to leave, to be in San Francisco for a few days."

She said sharply, "Don't tell me, Lee."

"I don't have to, do I?" he said, his hand tightening on hers. "I have no excuse, Stacy, none at all, not even that of a man who picks up a girl in a bar."

"I don't understand you," Stacy said in a small voice.

"It's not expected of you."

She said presently, "But she must have loved you——"

"Not me, not anyone, not the others. There's no normal, pardonable drive in her, no warmth, no—anything."

"But why——"

He broke in, "She has to possess—people, things—she has to subdue, to maintain a hold."

"And you never broke away——"

"I did, as far as that episode was concerned. It wasn't repeated. In another sense, no. She threatened—and that's the word—to tell Gerry. Yesterday in this room, she intimated that she had, in Jamaica, and added that perhaps it had caused his heart attack."

Stacy was cold with revulsion. "You believe her?" she asked.

"No, Stacy. I haven't believed her for many years. She is, among other things, an accomplished liar."

"Marcia?"

"She's still under the illusion; and Elaine would never destroy that; Marcia's useful to her."

"I wish you hadn't told me," said Stacy and to her horror her throat closed, and she shook her head, trying to repress the tears.

He said gently, "But we're to be friends the rest of our lives. From the moment I walked into Van's house and saw you, and felt your hostility—but you got over that."

"Only because I was sorry for you," she said, with considerable spirit. "I saw you watching Elaine; I thought you were miserably, hopelessly in love."

"So you felt a relationship? I've watched you recover from your hopelessness, so I waited, and made plans, thinking because you began to turn to me, even depend on me, a little, that you might someday love me. Could you?"

"It's too soon, Lee."

"I suppose so. We'll forget the plans—for now."

"I don't know you," she told him, "not really. You are not at all as I first thought you, of course, but——"

He said, "If we're going to be together, it seemed necessary that you share the burden of guilt. Only, I suppose by sharing, can I come to terms with it. Gerry was the best friend I had in the world. I suppose I despised Elaine for causing me to despise myself. . . . No, that's not entirely fair. I had, or so I thought, free will . . . not that any man enjoys the Joseph role. I remember your nightmares, Stacy. I had some too, for what is it—seven years. Different of course, but destructive." He broke off, remembering the dreams, always the same: the room, the wind blowing the curtains, Elaine, himself—and Gerald walking in. He said, "Your nightmares reflected no self-reproach—mine did. I'd wake up sweating as if it had all happened as in the dream. It hadn't. Gerry," he added painfully, "had an enormous capacity for forgiveness, but it wouldn't have extended to me."

"Perhaps now——" she said.

"I don't know. I'll never know."

"When it's autumn and cool, perhaps you'll burn the sketchbook for me, here in this room?" she said.

He leaned over and kissed her cheek, released her hand, and rose. He said, "Your lights were burning half the night here, and in the bedroom. I saw them. Why?"

"I couldn't sleep."

"Any special reason?"

"Yes."

"Then tell me."

"Someday," she said, and took a long breath. Her heart steadied and lifted.

"All right, Stacy. Can we mend the Chinese bowl?"

"No," she told him, "mended things aren't the same."

"Vanessa has two somewhat like it," he said. "Maybe I could get her to part with one."

"No. Someday we'll find another."

"Did Van tell you about the bet she made with me?"

"No. But she bet me you'd tell me about it. What was it? I don't mind losing."

"Someday," he said, smiling. He started to take her into his arms, but she said, "No, please, Lee." He let her go. "All right," he said. "I'll keep on saying 'Someday.'"

"I need time; we both do."

"I don't."

"Give me a chance to grow up."

"Agreed. We have all the months ahead—few or many,

I don't know—in which to talk, go places, quarrel, make up, try to see things through each other's eyes—and then, make plans. Mine's a planning profession. Greece, for instance, next summer, if I can get away. If I can, I don't intend to go alone. Meanwhile we must plot a little for Marcia."

"What sort of plot?"

"On her cruise Marcia met a man she likes very much."

"Just as she hoped she would," said Stacy.

"Did she? And told you so? Fine. Maybe we won't have to connive. The cruise ended for her in Jamaica. On the day she went ashore, he went with her briefly. Elaine disapproved of him; she didn't like Douglas, either, you know. She was not born to stand in anyone's shadow; she can't tolerate it."

"Who is he . . . or would Marcia mind your telling me?"

"Undoubtedly she'll tell you herself. His name's Harry Stone. He's about her age, a Texan, a widower with two kids. And she's heard from him. He's coming east before long. . . . What's the matter, Stacy?"

"Nothing. I'm tired. Doctor Bing would say it's neurotic. I don't think so."

"I'll go," he said, and she watched him walk to the door, turn, smile and raise his hand in salute.

Going to bed was a chore. She stumbled with fatigue, her eyes heavy with drowsiness, her muscles loosening, the tension draining out. She dropped her clothes on chairs, on the floor, went into the bathroom, looked at herself in the mirror and shook her head. And thought with astonishment just before she slept: But he fell in love with me *first*.

⚶ 21 ⚶

In early October, Stacy flew out to be at Sally Babcock's wedding. She'd gone on the condition that she needn't be matron of honor. "Just an honored guest," she told Sally on the telephone. "Get me a motel room if you can pull yourself together."

"You'll stay here, idiot."

"You'll have a full house. Motel," said Stacy firmly.

Lee took her to the airport and picked her up when she returned on a dinner flight.

"Have fun?"

"Well, it was pretty exciting. Sally didn't know which way was from here. There were half a dozen bridesmaids from the home town and Chicago. Don's father came out with him——"

"What about his mother?"

"She's conscious and lucid. Also, she knows the score—still has round-the-clock nurses. Mr. West flew home right after the reception. . . . Anything happen while I was gone?"

"You weren't gone long enough for much to occur."

"Well, thanks a lot."

"Marcia has her nightly call from Texas, and he's coming back here before Christmas, I think, to get a firm answer. Very likable guy," said Lee.

"Why in the world does she hesitate? I'm certain she's very fond of him."

"How you talk, seeing that you're setting her such a bad example!"

Stacy laughed. "I like things as they are, for the time being," she said.

"So do I. However, my grandmother once told me about a schoolteacher she knew who was, to coin a phrase, 'going steady.' He couldn't marry her; he had a wretched old mother who had a heart attack every time he mentioned the possibility. So every Wednesday night he took his patient little girl to dinner and every Saturday night she cooked for him at her place. This went on for twenty years. Then, Mama reluctantly died; the schoolteacher quietly married her guy and within six months, to the scandal of their small town, they were divorced. Twenty years is a little much. If you insist, I'll go as far as ten."

"Don't worry," said Stacy. "I'm not *that* patient."

Reaching the studio, he said, "Don't ask me in."

"I'd no such intention."

"We've a dinner date tomorrow. At Van's. I'll stop by, we'll walk over. You may not be able to resist a full moon. It's the Hunter's, isn't it?"

"I don't know. Isn't it always? Diana's a huntress."

He kissed her. He said, "I'm relieved that you're back. I kept thinking: Suppose she vanishes. Suppose she falls in love with an usher. Suppose I never see her again. . . ."

On the next day Stacy drove to the nearby town of Deeport with Katie Palmer, who was going to see an old friend and wanted company. "Now that we've a responsible baby sitter," Katie had said, "I can get out a little. I've neglected Linda Davis dreadfully."

"Why hasn't she come to see you?"

"She did in the hospital—with her husband. It upset her—the baby, I mean. She lost her first in a car accident.

239

I mean, she was pregnant and pretty badly injured. She was told she mustn't attempt to have another for some time. . . . Before we go to her house, I'll take you to see the place where they're going to build the condominiums. Lee's told you? He's the architect."

"Yes, he told me."

Katie said, "About the lease . . . of course you're staying on. Maybe," she added, "you won't be needing a lease in order to do that."

"Maybe not," Stacy said soberly.

"Everyone's wondering."

Stacy laughed. She said, "That's good."

"I give up," said Katie.

Early that evening, hearing Lee come up, Stacy emerged upon her doorstep and found him standing there counting his money and muttering, "Where did I put it?"

"Are you thinking of rewarding Van for her specialties of the house?" she asked.

"Oh, hi. . . . No. . . . Tell me, first and immediately—you don't very often—do you love me?"

"I do."

"And you're taking under consideration a legal, life-time involvement, in the not-too-distant future?"

"I am. . . . Let's burn the sketchbook some evening."

"That settles it. I owe Van a hundred bucks. . . . Ah, here it is." He unsnapped a separate small compartment in his wallet and displayed a new bill. "I've been carrying this around for weeks. She bet this against that case of old brandy she was saving for those attendants at the funeral that before Thanksgiving you'd declare yourself."

"I thought it was the male who made the declaration. So you've told me what the bet was. Now I owe her lunch at the Saltmarsh clip joint, but I can't afford it, because professionally things are a little slow."

240

"Everything's too slow."

"Don't interrupt. Anyway, I'll manage."

"Be happy to lend you a reasonable amount, at interest."

"No thanks. . . . Lee, we'll be late."

Walking along, handfast, she said, "I'm trying not to use the income from the settlement."

"You won't have to, once you accept my support."

"I want to give it all back. I don't know how."

"Leave it to me. I'm accustomed to dealing with lawyers. How about giving it to a university for scholarships for young artists? . . . Dammit, why hasn't the moon risen?"

"It won't, I think, for another couple of hours," said Stacy serenely. "Give it time."

"Sometimes I think you've broken the record."

They went, still hand in hand up the back-porch steps. Shadow, who was sitting on the railing, jumped down and greeted them with, for him, extreme extravagance.

Simultaneously, they stooped to stroke him, bumped their heads together and laughed. Lee kissed the lobe of Stacy's ear and Vanessa called, "Is that you? you're late. Come on in!"

Shadow led the way, purring like a small dynamo, and Vanessa said, "Well!"

"I come," Lee announced, "to pay a debt. One hundred beautiful devalued dollars," he said, presenting the bill.

Vanessa looked from one to the other, her white head swathed in smoke. "Thursday suit you for lunch?" she asked Stacy.

Stacy said sadly, "We both lose. If you eat a hundred dollars' worth, I'll kill you."

"I should be such a loser," said Vanessa. "Settle down. Drinks. Conversation, if possible. I'll give you a couple of bottles of the brandy," she told Lee generously. "After all, why just get my guests crocked at my funeral? I'd be happy to be at your wedding. Also," she said, "I'll dance."

"And break a leg this time?" asked Lee and Stacy said, "Van, if you don't mind, we aren't—"

"I know. You're not telling people yet. You won't have to. I mind, of course, that I can't get out the broom and fly from door to door, but I can't have everything." She regarded them with affection and added, "However, the cat's out of the bag. 'The Shadow knows.' "